BEYOND THE VEIL

S.C.Wynne

BEYOND THE VEIL

S.C. Wynne

BLIND
EYE
BOOKS

Beyond the Veil
By S.C. Wynne
Published by Blind Eye Books
315 Prospect Street #5393
Bellingham WA 98227
www.blindeyebooks.com

Edited by Nicole Kimberling
Copyedit by Hilary Hensley
Cover Art by Dawn Kimberling
Book Design by Dawn Kimberling
Ebook design by Michael DeLuca

This book is a work of fiction and as such all characters and situations are fictitious. Any resemblance to actual people, places or events is coincidental.

First Edition February 2024 Copyright © 2024 SC Wynne
print ISBN: 978-1-956422-07-8
ebook ISBN: 978-1-956422-08-5
Library of Congress Control Number: 2023951816
Printed in the United States of America

"If we could unfold the future, the present would be our greatest care."

Edward Counsel

CHAPTER ONE

"Use my body if you must, Agatha. Allow me to be your vessel." I slumped in my chair, peeking from beneath my lashes at my new client Mrs. Beckom.

Mrs. Beckom was probably late sixties with silver hair, peppered with traces of its original chestnut color. Her slender wrist was adorned with a vintage gold watch with stars and moons etched into the soft metal, and she wore a matching necklace.

The late morning sun snuck through a crack in the thick brocade curtains over the window, backlighting the particles of dust that floated in the dark room. "I'm here for you, Agatha. I can feel you hovering. I beg of you, please let me be the bridge to your sister."

Admittedly, I was laying it on a bit thick, but Mrs. Beckom seemed receptive enough. I got the feeling she was the type who enjoyed the theatre, so why not put on a show for her? Her brown eyes were wide with wonder, and it was obvious she was only too willing to believe anything I said.

However, the attractive blond guy next to her had a smirk on his full lips. He was a bit overdressed for a spiritual reading if you asked me. With his navy silk suit and red tie, he reeked of money just like his more open-minded companion. My guess was he worked as a financial advisor or some other stuffy profession. His long tanned fingers were adorned with chunky silver rings; one with a glittering green stone in particular caught my eye. The ring was nice, if a bit pretentious, but it was the guy's mocking expression that annoyed me the most. The least he could do was pretend to be impressed. Dazzling clients was no easy task these days. Especially with all the reality TV shows busting fake psychics left and right for scamming people. The con artists really made it difficult for those of us who actually had psychic abilities to make an honest living.

"Is she really here, Great Lorenzo?" Mrs. Beckom asked. We sat at a round mahogany table with tarot cards staged strategically across the polished surface. A glowing crystal ball sat atop the table, smack in the center, and beside that a red candle flickered wildly inside a vintage wax skull. Mrs. Beckom's chair creaked as she scanned the dimly lit room for airborne spirits. "She's really truly in the room?"

"Yes," I hissed, my breath almost causing the candle to snuff. Oops. "She's with us now."

"Oh, my." Mrs. Beckom clutched her vintage necklace and sniffed the air. "I smell jasmine. That was Agatha's favorite perfume."

"You know Glade makes many charming floral scents," her companion said. "Perhaps The Great Lorenzo sprayed some air freshener before we arrived."

I frowned at him. "I did no such thing."

He shrugged. "If you say so."

"Oh, Ian, you're so naughty." Mrs. Beckom sighed.

"Yeah, Ian, behave," I muttered.

"Doing my best." Ian twisted his lips.

I cleared my throat and once more tried to center myself. I forced my pulse to slow and blew out a cleansing breath. Spirits could be willful little things, and it was best if I was calm before they slipped inside. If I was agitated that could influence the spirit's behavior. The calmer I was, the calmer they were—usually. "Agatha, we need your help to find your beloved cat, Princess. Please, talk to us. We're here and listening."

"Yes, by all means, Agatha, spill the tea," Ian snorted.

"Shhh," I snapped, losing patience with his mocking attitude. Ian obviously thought I was a fake, but I wasn't. I actually was able to tap into the other side. Granted, I added plenty of embellishment for maximum client satisfaction, but the reality was I could indeed communicate with the dead.

"I can hardly breathe, I'm so excited," Mrs. Beckom whispered.

"It won't be long now," I murmured, readying myself for the spirit's impending invasion into my body. It was crunch time, and I needed complete focus.

Channeling spirits was a delicate balance, and Agatha's spirit hovered right outside of my body. While I couldn't see her, I could certainly feel her buzzing energy as it swirled around me. But she couldn't just waltz into me like a convenience store. I needed to wholly relax and allow her in. Once invited in, Agatha could have a nice little chat with Mrs. Beckom, using my body as a medium to speak from her world. But there was only a small window of time in which the magic happened. Spirits were temperamental and easily insulted. If they didn't get the attention they craved, they could throw little tantrums. If I waited too long, the summoned spirit would evaporate, and no connection could be made until another time. That would never do. I needed to get my money from Mrs. Beckom now, not later. My electric bill was past due, and it was impossible to run this business without electricity.

"This is so exhilarating," Mrs. Beckom purred.

I ignored Ian's derisive laugh and said breathlessly, "Agatha, we need your help. I invite you into my body."

Ian gave a soft whistle. "Better be careful who you say that to, Great Lorenzo."

I opened my eyes and gave him an irritable glare. "You really do need to be quiet. It's impossible to concentrate with your naysaying monologue."

He made a zipping motion near his lips.

"Are you there, sis?" Mrs. Beckom whispered, unperturbed by Ian's skepticism. "I can't see you."

"Tell her again why we've summoned her." I took Mrs. Beckom's hand in mine. "It's more personal coming from you. She'll be more inclined to help."

"Oh. Certainly." Mrs. Beckom's fingers were chilled, and her breathing was coming in fast spurts. She cleared her throat. "So sorry to bother you, Agatha, but could you possibly tell me where Princess is? It seems she's gotten herself lost."

I nodded. "That's right, just talk to her as you would have in life."

Yet another dry snort came from Ian's direction. Irritation prickled me as I studied him from under my brows. He definitely wasn't the usual type that accompanied the lonely women who visited my little yellow house on Magnolia Lane. Was he Mrs. Beckom's lover or her son? She was definitely older than him, and I couldn't quite get a read on their relationship. They weren't touchy-feely, but there was a muted affection between them.

"Did you hear your sister, Agatha?" I asked softly. "She'd desperately like to know where your beloved cat might be."

"Wouldn't it be quicker to just contact Princess directly, instead of going through Aunt Agatha?" Ian's husky voice was sardonic. "You know, cut out the middle man?"

I pinned him with my surly gaze. "You're hilarious."

Ian shrugged. "I'm not trying to be funny. I'm asking a serious question."

"Ian." Mrs. Beckom rolled her eyes. "Cats don't talk, silly."

"But they do talk to you, don't they, Great Lorenzo?" His curious gaze flicked over my face. "Cats. People. You converse with them all. It says so on the sign out front, so it must be true."

"I don't speak directly to the animals," I said snippily.

"No? My bad." As he spoke he distractedly twirled the ring on his finger.

I pressed my lips tight, wishing he'd just go outside and make a phone call or something and let me do my thing. Did this jerk actually think I enjoyed using my psychic gifts trying to track down stray animals? I didn't. Not even a little. But times were tough, and it wasn't easy to make a living during the winter in this touristy seaside town of Fox Harbor. As slow as it had been lately, I was lucky if a dog or a cat went missing. Judging by Ian's expensive suit and shiny gold watch and rings, money wasn't a concern for him.

Bully for you, Ian, some of us weren't born with a silver spoon in our mouth.

While Ian clearly considered me a fraud, the truth was I was more of an opportunist than a phony. The most I was guilty of was stretching out some sessions. If I was particularly hard up for money, I'd occasionally milk three sessions out of someone when I could have finished the job in one. I made a few more bucks doing things that way, so where was the harm really? My prices were reasonable. Nobody was going to go broke paying for a few extra sessions with me. My clients always got the performance they paid for, and I got to eat.

There were far worse predators out there than me. Some were even in Fox Harbor, in fact.

For example, my nemesis Weston Bartholomew was one of those charlatans. Weston didn't have a scrap of authentic psychic ability in him, but all the same he'd opened a shop across town. Weston gave psychic readings, and was prone to promising winning lottery numbers. He also had a bad habit of borrowing people's priceless family heirlooms to rid them of evil spirits.

Spoiler alert: they never got them back.

I wasn't like that. I didn't steal people's property or keep them talking to dead relatives for the next decade. I gave people comfort. Closure. I talked to the spirits of the dead, and people paid me a fee to be the bridge between the world of the living and those who had passed on. In my opinion, I was no better or worse than a telephone operator.

"Look," I snapped. "I need to move things along. Agatha will leave if you keep interrupting me."

"Will she?" He arched one brow.

"Yes." I met Ian's smug, honey-brown eyes, doing my best not to show how much I disliked him. "You're welcome to not believe. I don't care either way. Mrs. Beckom believes, and that's enough for me. But you must stop talking."

He leaned back in the chair, his gaze assessing. "Is that right?"

"Yes," I grumbled.

Ian gave a slow smile. "Please proceed. Don't let me interrupt the show."

"It's not a show," I said through gritted teeth, "It's a reading."

"Potato. Potahto."

Mrs. Beckom scowled. "Ian, if you're going to be such a party pooper, why did you insist on coming along?"

He lifted one smooth brow. "Because, dearest, I don't want you to lose your shirt trying to find a dead cat."

She hissed in a breath. "Don't say that. You know there's a chance Princess is still alive." She gripped my fingers tighter. "Isn't there, Great Lorenzo?"

"Most definitely." I cleared my throat. "And please, just call me Lorenzo." I didn't usually care what people called me, but something about the way Ian's mouth twitched every time she added the "Great" to my name made me uncomfortable.

She nodded. "Of course." She gave Ian a chiding look. "Please ignore him, Lorenzo, and continue."

Pulling my gaze from Ian's, I closed my eyes and concentrated on establishing a connection with Agatha. The sooner I found the damn cat, the sooner I could collect payment and send them on their way. I found Ian and his suspicious glances tiring. I didn't have to prove myself to him. Maybe I'd have to cut Mrs. Beckom loose. If he was a permanent fixture in her life, I certainly didn't want to put up with Ian if she came back again and again.

"Once more, Agatha, I'm here should you choose to use me." My head prickled as brightly colored visions flashed at me like a flickering movie screen. My limbs tingled and burned, heat shifting through my chest. I felt the spirit creep slowly into me like chilly fingers winding around my rib cage.

"Talk to me, Agatha," Mrs. Beckom whispered. "I'm listening."

I opened my eyes, throat muscles squeezing as the spirit oozed into my body. My vision blurred, and the sensation of Agatha's spirit slipping into my core was uncomfortable. I felt flushed and overheated, and the center of my chest ached as the spirit made herself at home. I was no longer able to speak freely now that Agatha was in charge of my body. I shuddered as Agatha's throbbing presence compelled me to ask, "Is that you, Sylvia?"

Leaning forward eagerly, Mrs. Beckom nodded. "Yes. Yes, it's me."

I studied Mrs. Beckom, feeling disconnected from her. I had a sense that Agatha hadn't been fond of her sister. There was a lot of sudden resentment simmering inside of me. It seemed in life Agatha had been jealous of her younger sister, and she felt their parents had spoiled her rotten.

"It has been a while," I heard myself murmur.

"Yes." Mrs. Beckom grimaced. "How are things on . . . the other . . . side?"

It seemed Agatha wasn't in the mood for small talk because a swirl of irritation shifted through me as Agatha snapped, "Never mind that. I have a question for you, dear sister."

"What is it?" Mrs. Beckom swallowed loudly.

"Why are you squandering Daddy's fortune?" My voice sounded low and gravelly. I wondered if Aunt Agatha had perhaps been a smoker.

"But I'm not." Mrs. Beckom wrinkled her brow. "Why would you say that?"

"What about the sailing yacht?" Agatha asked, her tone accusing.

With a gasp, Mrs. Beckom straightened. "Agatha knows about the yacht." She turned to Ian. "How would she know about the boat when I bought it after she passed?"

"Well . . . it's not exactly a huge leap that a wealthy person who lives near the sea might have a yacht." Ian's voice was dry, and his eyes never left mine. "Could be a lucky guess."

Unable to address him directly, I continued to channel Aunt Agatha. "Of all the things to buy."

Mrs. Beckom grimaced. "I've always loved the sea. Why shouldn't I buy a boat?"

"So frivolous. But then you always were the impractical one, Sylvia." Agatha spoke slowly and sluggishly. Her energy seemed to ebb and flow through me, washing in and out like the tide.

"Me? Frivolous?" squeaked Mrs. Beckom. "I'm nothing of the kind."

"You're far too old for a yacht," Agatha grumbled. "And since when do you date younger men? Ian is young enough to be your son. You should be ashamed of yourself, robbing the cradle like that."

"But . . . we're not . . . that—" Clamping her mouth tight, Mrs. Beckom seemed to gather herself. "Agatha, that isn't why I'm here. I'm not dating Ian, for goodness' sake. You're getting me all flustered. None of that has anything to do with what I need to ask you."

"What is it that you want from me?" Agatha asked.

"As I said earlier, Princess is missing. That's what I want your help with." Mrs. Beckom shifted nervously.

"Ahhh, yes. Princess has been missing for days," Agatha said. Her voice was almost slurred now. The spirit's energy was strange and shifting. It worried me she'd leave before we got our answers.

"You knew?" Mrs. Beckom looked startled.

"Of course."

Hanging her head, Mrs. Beckom sighed. "I've searched everywhere." She looked up, lines of worry around her eyes. "Is . . . is she with you?"

"No."

Mrs. Beckom looked relieved. "Can you help me find her?"

"Yesssss."

Ian gave a gruff laugh but didn't speak.

"Princess is quite terrified." Agatha leaned toward her sister, and I resisted the movement. I wasn't sure of Agatha's intentions and didn't want to play any part in her physically harming her sister by using my hands.

Mrs. Beckom let go of my hand, looking hopeful. "But she's alive?"

"She izzzzz." Again Agatha's energy dropped. My vision blurred, and my body ached. Agatha's energy was unstable. Unpredictable. She made me uneasy because one minute she throbbed through me like lightening, and the next she faded and swirled as if disinterested.

Ian pushed his tongue into his cheek. "I'll believe it when I see Princess in the flesh."

Mrs. Beckom chewed her lip. "Where is she, Agatha? I'm losing my mind with worry."

"Perhaps you shouldn't have lost her in the first place," Agatha responded.

"Don't be that way, Agatha. We all make mistakes. Please, tell me where she is."

My head dropped to my chest as the spirit seemed to fade. But then she was back, stronger than before. "The tool shed behind the house."

"What? The tool shed?"

I felt my head nodding. "Yesssss."

Covering her mouth, Mrs. Beckom cheeks paled. "The poor little dear must be terrified."

Drumming his fingers on the table, Ian said, "I'll bet."

"Thank you so much, Agatha. I'd never have thought to look there." Mrs. Beckom sounded breathless.

I expected Agatha to withdraw from me as spirits usually did once they'd spoken to their loved ones. But instead, her energy surged again, and I winced at the swell of angry emotions that rolled through me. "Perhaps I should return home and keep watch over things, dear sister."

Mrs. Beckom's eyes widened. "Oh, well . . . but you're . . . dead."

Agatha's wrath boiled inside of me, and before I could stop her, Agatha slammed my palm on the table top. "You lost my favorite cat, dear sister. I can't allow that sort of thing." Witnessing the anxiety on Mrs. Beckom's face, I struggled to control the spirit inside of me. But Agatha resisted my efforts, clinging to me like a piece of food stuck between my teeth. I once more pushed against her spirit, trying to expel her from my body, but she clawed at me and slithered deeper inside my chest.

Mrs. Beckom stood abruptly, bumping into the table. "Well, try and understand, Agatha. I was ill and in the hospital for several days. Alfred left the kitchen door open and she just slipped out."

"Inexcusable," Agatha grumbled, sending angry heat coursing through me. My limbs throbbed as her energy spread, trying to take charge of my body.

I clenched my fists, struggling to control the willful spirit within. I didn't want this entity inside of me getting too angry. Spirits were harder to get rid of when they were mad. The anger seemed to bind them to their host, and extricating them became a huge chore. I'd never expected Agatha to be an angry spirit, so I'd been caught off guard. I'd assumed this would be a simple conversation between sisters.

Apparently Old Agatha has other ideas.

"I had surgery, Agatha. Don't you even care?" Mrs. Beckom sounded hurt.

"You lost my favorite cat." Agatha's angry words came from my unwilling lips. "You're as irresponsible as ever."

"This is so like you, Agatha, to put a cat above me." Mrs. Beckom sniffed, and dabbed at her eyes with a tissue she'd pulled from her pocket.

"Sylvia, are you seriously arguing with a supposed spirit?" Ian asked, looking skeptical.

"I raised her from a kitten." Aunt Agatha spoke through me again.

Mrs. Beckom lifted her chin. "Stop lecturing me, Agatha. I'd forgotten how judgmental you could be."

"I still think I should come home and keep an eye on you." Agatha's voice was determined now.

"No. That . . . that isn't necessary. I thank you for your help, but you can go now, Agatha." Mrs. Beckom crossed her arms stubbornly.

A bitter laugh erupted from me, courtesy of Aunt Agatha. I struggled against her willful hijacking of my body.

I pressed my hand to my throbbing chest as the frustrated spirit wrestled with me for dominance.

You need to go, Agatha.

Her spirit ignored me and clung tighter, clawing and attempting to stay put. I gritted my teeth and tried again.

I take back my permission. You are not welcome and you need to go.

"Are you all right?" Ian peered at me warily. "You look a little blue around the gills, Great Lorenzo."

I had trouble pulling in a full breath, and I felt sweaty and chilled all at the same time. My stomach churned as I struggled to force the obstinate spirit from my body. But no matter how hard I tried, she dug deeper.

My lungs burned as I struggled to breathe and a hot squeezing sensation surrounded my heart. It was as if Agatha was trying to kill me so that she could then take my place. I'd never experienced anything quite like what was happening, and I began to panic. Could I die if she flat out refused to leave? It certainly felt like things were heading that way.

Leave me now. Do you hear me Aunt Agatha? I command you to get out.

"Seriously, Lorenzo, you don't look so good." Ian leaned forward and touched my wrist.

The heat of his firm living skin sparked over mine, anchoring me to the real world. His energy was pure and powerful, and feeling desperate, I drank some in. Agatha's grip broke instantly, and her spirit shuddered and recoiled. Guilt nudged me as I absorbed a tiny bit more of Ian's life force, but my fear of dying outweighed the shame.

With a shuddering exhale, I slumped in my chair as Agatha slowly withdrew, leaving me weak, breathless, and embarrassed. I hadn't had a spirit stubbornly refuse to leave my body since I was a teenager, and I'd never had any spirit that aggressive. Who'd have thought a stupid cat could get anybody so worked up? I opened my heavy lids and found Ian studying me with a deep line between his eyes. Whether it was anger or concern I couldn't tell.

I averted my gaze so he wouldn't see how rattled I felt. I was still guilty I'd swiped some of his energy. "Aunt Agatha's a bit of a bitch," I said hoarsely.

Mrs. Beckom nodded, her lips in a pout. "She didn't even care that I was in the hospital."

"If I wasn't a rational man of science, I'd be inclined to believe your little act." Ian stood and crossed the room to the curtains, yanking them open with unnecessary force. He gave a little cough when dust particles wafted into the air. I winced as light flooded the room, revealing my shabby garage sale furniture. When clients were here, I kept the room dark for a reason.

Ian returned to the table immediately and then took my wrist and pressed his fingers to my pulse. "Are you light headed? You're still very pale."

I took a deep breath and pulled my arm away. Rubbing my tingling flesh, I tried to ignore his effect on me. "I'm fine."

"If you say so." He narrowed his gaze.

I straightened my spine, forcing myself to sit up. I felt drained from my struggle with Agatha, but didn't want Ian's pity. "She's gone now."

"She was so mean," complained Mrs. Beckom.

"Yes," I murmured. "She was strong-willed too."

Ian met my gaze, his expression a mixture of concern and skepticism. "You seriously want me to swallow that Aunt Agatha's spirit was talking to us through you?"

"You can believe what you want." I rubbed my woozy head. "I've done my part. I'm not concerned with what you do or don't choose to . . . swallow."

"It's difficult to accept." Ian frowned. "It defies logic."

"Spiritual things have nothing to do with logic, silly." Mrs. Beckom laughed, patting his arm.

I said, "It's always funny to me how some people struggle with this stuff, yet blindly believe in God. If you believe in God, you already accept a spiritual world exists."

"Who said I believe in God?" he murmured.

I met his gaze but said nothing.

"The Great Lorenzo comes highly recommended, Ian." Mrs. Beckom shrugged. "Why else would I be here?" She pouted. "I always thought you were more open-minded than you apparently are."

"I'm open-minded about things that make sense. Talking to dead people is one way con artists swindle trusting women like you out of their life savings."

I bristled. "Mrs. Beckom came to me. I didn't seek her out."

"I guess that's true." He looked around the small cluttered room, taking in the beaded curtain that separated my bedroom from my work area. "I will admit, your décor doesn't suggest you've ripped off anyone's millions."

My face warmed at his judgmental tone and expression as he examined the cheap pine furniture, worn throw rugs, and archaic VCR.

"Ian," Mrs. Beckom gasped, "you can't say that."

He grimaced. "I don't mean to be rude."

I squinted at him. "Right."

He gave the shabby room another once-over. "But . . . is this really a viable business idea? Surely you could make more money doing something else?"

"A man does what he must to survive." Did he seriously think I wanted to have this discussion with him? "Besides, money isn't everything."

"I guess." He sniffed. "There's another psychic in town, right? Are you two rivals? Mortal enemies? Secret lovers?"

"I'm more likely to strangle Weston Bartholomew than to date him." I scowled. "But obviously we're in competition with each other. After all, there are only so many missing pets to go around."

"If things are so dire, how is it you've stayed in business this long?" His tone implied he knew exactly how—by ripping people off.

"Clean living and a solid work ethic?" I smirked.

"Sure. That must be it."

"You could move to a bigger city." As she spoke, Mrs. Beckom reached in her purse for her wallet. "You're excellent at what you do. I'll bet you could make a bundle where there are more people."

"While that may be true . . . I have . . . things . . . that keep me here." I averted my gaze.

She handed me my sixty dollars. "Do you have family in the area?"

I swallowed against the lump in my throat and turned my back to them. "Not really." I tucked the money into my jeans and moved toward the door to give them the idea it was time to leave.

"Not really?" Ian murmured watching me with a curious expression. "You either do or you don't."

I ignored him.

"Are your parents living?" Mrs. Beckom asked, peering at me closely.

I wasn't sure why they seemed so interested in my personal life suddenly. Ian especially seemed focused on me now, which was disconcerting. "Yes. They live in Texas. But we're not close."

"That's too bad." Ian's tone was sincere.

I shrugged. "It's no biggie." There had been a time when I'd cared. A time when I'd craved their acceptance. Love. But too many things had happened, and I was numb to my parent's cold shoulder these days.

"Sometimes not talking to family is a good thing." Mrs. Beckom sighed. "Look at me and Agatha. We fought when she was alive, and we fight now that she's dead. I guess it's best to just not speak to each other."

I shivered as I remembered Agatha's tenacity at trying to stay in control of my body. "You don't pick your family."

"True enough," she agreed.

I cleared my throat and addressed Mrs. Beckom. "Did you want to schedule another session? I believe you expressed an interest in reaching out to your late mother?"

Ian grunted his disapproval.

"Oh, yes. That would be lovely." She sighed. "I do so miss her. She was warm and cheerful. Everything Agatha wasn't."

"How about next week at the same time?" I smiled politely.

"Yes, please." She nodded eagerly.

"I'll text you a reminder the day before." I opened the front door. "Well, it was nice meeting you."

Mrs. Beckom chuckled. "Ian, you were so rude Great Lorenzo can't wait for us to vamoose." She made her way down the stairs, but Ian hung back on the top step.

"Can I ask you something?" He shifted uneasily, and the sunlight made his golden hair look like a halo around his head. The light also caught the green jewel in his ring, casting a kaleidoscope effect across the lower half of his strong jaw.

"Sure." I lifted my chin because his intense stare put me on edge.

"If we go to that tool shed, will we actually find the damn cat there, or are you sending us on a wild goose chase? I'd rather not waste my time if I don't have to."

"Well, I'm not Aunt Agatha, but she seemed pretty sure her beloved pet was in that shed."

His piercing gaze seemed to look right through me, and under his breath he said, "It would be cruel to get her hopes up if we're just going to find a dead cat."

My gaze flicked to the older woman hovering near the car. "Princess will be where Aunt Agatha said she was. Alive."

He watched me in silence for a moment, then said, "I don't believe in psychics."

"Really? You hide it so well I had no idea."

He smiled, but then it faded. "I can't deny you seemed genuinely shaken earlier."

I made sure my expression remained blank. "I have no interest in converting you. You can believe what you want to believe. I did my thing, and I got my money. Our transaction is complete."

His mouth hardened and he leaned in toward me. "If you lied, I'm going to be upset."

I laughed, even though his intimidating expression did make my stomach tighten. "What are you to Mrs. Beckom?"

"Pardon?"

"Are you her lover? Her son? What?" It was obvious they were close, but I couldn't quite get a read on the actual nature of their relationship.

"Her lover?" He recoiled and his cheeks tinged pink. "I'm her doctor."

"You are?" I raised my brows. "Huh. My doctor doesn't follow me around like a puppy."

His gaze had an edge to it. "She needs looking after. She's way too trusting."

I was getting tired of his digs. "And by that I assume you're implying trusting me is a mistake."

"Probably."

I sighed. "Look, I made sixty dollars on the deal. I'm not exactly skinning her alive. If she has a fortune, it's still intact."

He gave a tight smile, and my pulse quickened in response. "Maybe I'm being too overly protective. My dad was her doctor for thirty years, and when he died last year I took over."

"Is that right?" Did he think I cared?

"She's like family."

"Yeah?" I wanted him to leave. Now that my curiosity had been satisfied about the nature of their relationship, I didn't need to hear more. I wasn't even sure why I'd asked what their relationship was. But I definitely didn't like the strange effect he seemed to have on me. I kept to myself for a reason, and I didn't need some guy I barely knew making me feel things I hadn't felt in years. "That's nice."

He narrowed his gaze. "You don't really give a shit, do you?"

"Ian, are you coming?" Mrs. Beckom called from near the car. "We shouldn't keep Princess waiting."

"Yeah, Ian. You'd better run along. Your master is calling."

He gave a hard laugh. "My master. That's funny. She's my friend and I'm just concerned about her. That's all. It's good to care about others."

"I'll take your word for it."

He hesitated. "Did you lose someone? Is that what the icy act is all about?"

I stepped back, startled by his observation. But I quickly gathered myself and hung my I-don't-give-a-fuck expression. "If you want to fork over sixty bucks, we can talk about your life. But no one comes here to talk about mine. That's not how this works."

"Is that right?"

"Yep. What do you say, want to book an appointment?" I asked sardonically. "How about you drop by and tell me all your deepest, darkest secrets, Ian?"

He narrowed his eyes. "Frankly, I think you should book an appointment with me to run down your symptoms. You seem to be having some kind of seizures."

"Wow. Way to Uno reverse. Maybe you should set up shop as a con man. I think you're a natural."

He smirked. "You're deflecting. That's classic. Seriously, though, you should see a doctor. Maybe not me, but someone. A therapist wouldn't hurt either."

Heat touched my face. "Thanks for the advice, but you don't know anything about me."

"Sure I do." He leaned in close enough that I could see the dark ring around his iris. "You're more at home with the dead than the living. Why is that, Lorenzo?"

I took a step back, stomach churning. "I have other clients to tend to, but you have a nice day, now, okay?" I shut the door before he could say another word.

CHAPTER TWO

A few days later, thanks to Mrs. Beckom and some extra online clients, I was able to not only pay my electric bill but also do a little grocery shopping. Walking up the cobblestone path that led to my combination shop and home, I admired the little butter yellow flowers of winter jasmine that twisted and tangled through a worn white trellis beside the steps. Winter jasmine didn't share its fragrant summer-blooming kin's lovely scent. Unfortunate because the damp air was deathly still and fishier smelling than usual.

Holding one plastic grocery bag in my teeth and the other slung over my arm, I clumsily unlocked the back door to my little shop. I entered, wincing at the scent of rotting fruit in the kitchen. I'd been lazy about housekeeping of late. Partly because I hadn't had any in person clients the last few days. It had been alarmingly slow since my session a few days ago with Mrs. Beckom.

It was my hope she'd tell her rich friends how thrilled she was with my amazing cat-finding skills. With our second meeting next week, my fingers were crossed that she'd still be pleased with me. Word of mouth was a wonderful way to get more clients. I couldn't afford to advertise in the local free newspaper, the Foxtrot Gazette, but if I didn't do something I'd never survive until the more lucrative summer tourist season. Most of the small businesses in Fox Harbor held on by our nails until the warm weather hit. Some made it, some didn't. I sincerely hoped I wouldn't be a casualty this time, but it was gonna be close.

There was nothing like money problems to make one feel hopeless. Maybe I needed to be more like Weston

Bartholomew. He was thriving, while I was dying on the vine, clutching tight to my morals.

I dropped the groceries on the kitchen table, and as I began to put them away, the hairs on the back of my neck prickled. I glanced around uneasily, unable to shake the feeling someone had been in my home while I was out. I stopped unpacking the groceries and listened. I didn't hear any creaking floorboards or see anyone lurking around the corner of the kitchen door. However, all my senses told me I wasn't wrong. I'd bet my left nut someone had been in my home.

I slowly moved into the front room, muscles tensed just in case I was wrong and the person was still in the house. Flaring my nostrils, I detected the scent of tobacco lingering. Not regular tobacco though. The odor was spicy like nutmeg or star anise. It was vaguely familiar to me, but I couldn't quite place where I'd smelled it before. The scent coaxed uneasiness in me, making me certain something unpleasant was connected to the scent. Was that unpleasantness derived from a person or a place? I wasn't sure.

I scanned the room, searching for anything missing or out of place. The archaic tube TV was untouched, no surprise there. My precious books, though dusty, seemed intact. I narrowed my eyes at a spot on the mantel over the small fireplace. There was a bare circle of wood surrounded by dust. My heart sank as I realized what was missing. There had been a small green aventurine stone shaped like a flame there. Anger shifted through me as I moved to the spot. The stone had been a gift from my late younger brother. Why the hell would anyone have taken it? Its only real value had been sentimental. I had a worn first edition of Agatha Christie's *Sad Cypress* on my bookshelf. Why would any burglar worth their weight in salt take a cheap ornamental stone over that?

Infuriated anyone would have invaded my sanctuary, I headed to the front door, but the lock seemed untouched. I next examined all the windows in the small house and didn't notice anything amiss. I knew without a doubt that someone had been inside my home, but how had they entered? A chill went through me at the thought someone might have had a key to my place. I wasn't the type who handed out my key easily. My closest friend Claire didn't even have a key to my home.

Perhaps I simply hadn't closed my door all the way? Maybe no one had broken in. Maybe whoever had taken the stone from my mantle was simply an opportunist. Occasionally, local kids cut through the deserted field behind my shop to get into the heart of town quicker. It was possible one of them had noticed my back door wasn't closed all the way and had snuck in. The colorful green stone was something that might catch the eye of a kid.

I wanted to believe that theory, but my gut said I was rationalizing. My intuition screamed I'd had a prowler. But why me? It didn't take a genius to see my shop wasn't exactly thriving at the moment. Pierson's candy store down the street would have been a far more lucrative target. They made money no matter what the weather. And Linda Coleridge's nail salon, The Lacquered Labyrinth, on the other side of me did okay. The locals and their fungus-laden toenails kept her in business year-round.

If I suspected someone had a key to my place, the obvious next step was to have the locks changed. Hiring a locksmith meant spending money I didn't have or want to spend. Of course, there was always the DIY route. I could probably fumble my way through changing a door lock if I had to.

Feeling agitated, I went back into the kitchen and finished putting away the groceries. I saw no point in calling the cops since no one had broken in, and the only thing taken that I knew of was the stone. I felt sick that the stone was gone, but knew the cops weren't exactly going to put out an APB for my lost treasure.

Once I had everything put away, I went to check the small attached garage on the side of my shop to see if that lock had been tampered with. It was called a garage, but technically it was just a little shed. The lock seemed untouched, so I decided to go next door to the nail salon. I was curious if perhaps my immediate neighbor Linda had seen or heard anything suspicious. As I entered the shop, a little bell jingled over the door and all the women sitting at the little tables turned their heads in unison. I winced at the pungent scent of acetone. Feeling conspicuous, I acknowledged the young man, Julian, who worked as a receptionist at the salon with a nod.

"Hey, Lorenzo," Julian said, his gaze sharpening. He was an attractive blond with light green eyes, a lip piercing, and a perpetual smirk. "I just got here. My calculus class ran late. I'm glad I didn't miss you."

"Is that right?" I gave a stilted laugh.

"Damn straight." Julian winked. "Seeing you is always the highlight of my day."

"Is that so?" I was still painfully aware of the women staring at me.

"You betcha."

I grimaced. "Okay, rein it in, Casanova."

Julian's flirtatious interest in me made me uncomfortable. First of all, he was only nineteen. While he was a good-looking kid, he was way too young. I suspected his interest in me stemmed from his fascination with all things psychic. He'd begged me many times to help him develop his psychic abilities. I'd tried to explain that wasn't what I did, but he persisted.

"Haven't seen you around lately." He rested his chin on his knuckles, running his eyes over me. "You're a sight for sore eyes."

I sighed. "Julian, stop."

He grinned. "Why?"

"Because," I spluttered. "You're too much."

"Or, am I just enough?" He batted his lashes.

"God," I groaned. "You're going to start rumors." One of the women nearby giggled, and I hoped it wasn't because of my conversation with Julian.

"I don't mind if you don't."

I widened my eyes. "I think I've made it clear that I definitely mind." I glanced around noticing two women watching me as they soaked their feet in bubbly water.

He laughed and straightened. "Okay, fine. I can see you're shy."

"I'm not shy. I'm too old for you."

"I disagree. But if you won't let me seduce you, will you at least change your mind about taking me on as a student?"

I grimaced. "No."

He frowned. "Why not?"

"I don't really have time to do that, Julian." Obviously, he knew that was a lie. From the reception desk, he had a clear view of the front of my shop. He knew perfectly well I had plenty of time on my hands.

"You're so stubborn." His face fell and he tugged at the piercing in his lip. Then he brightened. "Hey, maybe if you don't have time to teach me stuff, I could just learn from watching you. I could be your assistant."

I found Julian's persistence bewildering. I'd made it more than clear I wasn't interested in anything sexual, but he still kept flirting. Was he simply someone who couldn't take no for an answer? Or was there something more going on? He said he wanted my help to grow his psychic abilities, but I'd never found him to be particularly intuitive or psychically inclined. Whatever his reasons for being so pushy, I still didn't want to become involved with him on any level. I simply didn't have the energy to feed whatever need he had. "I'm sorry, Julian. At the moment, I don't need an assistant."

He sighed, his glum expression returning. "You sure?"

"I'm sure."

His eyes darkened. "You're making a mistake. I could be a valuable ally—er . . . asset, Lorenzo."

"This isn't even about you, Julian. I promise you that. I'm sure you'd be a great help to me," I said, hoping to pacify him. "But I like working alone. It's just how I'm built."

Julian narrowed his eyes but didn't respond.

I shifted uneasily. "Is Linda here today?"

"Yeah." Still looking crestfallen, he pointed toward the long row of work stations. "She's at the end doing Mrs. Tully's nails."

I scanned the room and pinpointed Linda at the end of the work stations working on an older woman's nails. She was a short full-figured redhead with a ready smile. She was the sort of person who, even if you'd just met her, made you feel like you were her best friend. She had hundreds of customers, but she managed to make each one feel special. "I see her. Do you think it's okay if I interrupt her while she's working?"

"Sure." His eyes were alert and fixed on me. "Is something wrong? Is that why you need to talk to Linda?"

"Nothing's really wrong." I hesitated, wondering if maybe I should ask Julian if he'd seen anything. But he'd just arrived to work, so he wouldn't have been at the salon when I had my unwelcome visitor. "I just need to ask her a question."

"In that case, you can go talk to her. I'm sure she won't mind."

"Thanks, Julian." I ignored the stab of guilt I felt at his morose expression and headed toward Linda's workstation.

"Hello, Lorenzo," Linda said brightly as I approached. "Finally decided to get a manicure?"

I laughed. "Not today."

She pouted. "One of these days I'm going to get my hands on those ragged cuticles of yours."

I winced. "I know. They're pretty bad."

"Yes, they are and they aren't going to get any better on their own."

"I promise to make an appointment soon."

"You've been saying that for years." She smiled good naturedly. "So, if you aren't here to have your nails done, what can I do for you?"

I glanced hesitantly at the older woman whose nails she was doing. "I'm sorry to interrupt."

"That's okay," the woman said, giving me a curious glance. She had a grandmotherly vibe, with permed white hair and rosy cheeks.

Linda smiled. "Lorenzo, this is Helen Tully. Helen, this is Lorenzo Winston, psychic extraordinaire."

I laughed at her description of me.

Helen studied me with curious gray eyes. "You're the Great Lorenzo?"

I winced inwardly at the "Great."

"That's me."

"You're so much younger than I pictured."

"Oh, I'm old enough. Psychic powers aren't attached to age. I've been psychic my whole life."

"Goodness," she murmured. "I . . . I was toying with the idea of having a reading with you."

"Were you?" I tried not to sound too excited.

"Yes. So, you actually talk to . . . dead people?" Helen's voice wobbled.

"I connect to their spirits, yes." I gave her a reassuring smile. "I know it sounds strange, but it's not scary at all. It's actually very comforting. Most of my clients come away feeling so happy they gave it a chance."

She sighed. "My sister passed last weekend, and I was hoping maybe you could help me say goodbye. She died so suddenly, I didn't get the chance. Now there are so many things left unsaid."

I frowned. "I'm sorry. Closure is important. I could definitely help you talk to her. Then you could say all the things you didn't have time for before she died."

Helen nodded hesitantly.

I tugged a card from my shirt pocket. "Give me a call when you're ready."

Helen looked at the card and then at her nails. "I don't want to smudge the polish."

I smiled and set my business card on the table next to her. "No problem. My number's on the card. Feel free to give me a call anytime. My schedule is very flexible."

Understatement of the century.

Maybe Linda took pity on me because she gushed, "He's really good. You should definitely book an appointment with him, Helen." Then, to me, "Now, what was it you wanted to ask me, Lorenzo?" Linda smiled politely, going back to painting Helen's nails.

I cleared my throat. "I was wondering, did you notice anyone hanging around my shop earlier?"

She frowned and stopped painting Helen's nails. "No. Not that I recall. To be honest, though, I've been busy today. Haven't gone outside at all."

"I see." I tried to stuff down my envy that she had so many customers.

"Why do you ask if I saw anyone around your shop?" Linda blinked up at me.

Grimacing, I said, "I think someone might have broken—gotten into my shop while I was at the market."

"Goodness." She bugged her eyes. "In broad daylight?"

Helen looked startled. "Someone was inside your shop when you weren't there? Good Lord. I had no idea this neighborhood had gone downhill like that." Helen shuddered, glancing warily around as if criminals lurked beneath the little work stations.

Linda grimaced. "Oh, the neighborhood is fine. I'm sure that was just an isolated incident."

Feeling guilty that I'd possibly scared off one of Linda's customers, I said quickly, "I'm sure Linda's right. The area is fine. Just fine. Nothing was really taken, so it was probably just kids."

Child burglars who apparently could teach John "The Cat" Robie a thing or two.

Helen appeared unconvinced. Lowering her voice, she said, "Did you hear about the body they found near the library?"

Linda shivered. "Yes. Ghastly."

Recoiling, I asked, "What?"

"They found a body." Looking around shiftily, Helen hissed, "They say he was missing his head."

Gasping, Linda said, "I know. It's too horrible."

"When was this?" I asked, rattled.

"Yesterday evening." Helen gritted her teeth. "I know the woman who found the body. She was traumatized. Probably going to need therapy now."

"Of course," I murmured as a chill zipped up my spine. "Do they know who the killer was?"

"No. That's the scary part. So far the police have absolutely no clues. None at all." Helen shook her head. "Fox Harbor PD had better get their act together."

"I haven't been getting the paper lately," I murmured. "I hadn't heard anything about any of that."

"Grisly business." Linda shuddered and then tsk-tsked, frowning at Helen's nails. "Boo. I messed up."

"Oh, dear." Helen lifted her brows.

Linda smiled. "Not to worry. I know how to fix it." She hesitated and glanced up at me. "I'm sorry I didn't see anyone around your shop, Lorenzo, but I'll definitely keep my eyes peeled from now on."

"Uh, great." I was still reeling from the news about the headless body.

"Maybe you should buy a burglar alarm while you're at the hardware store, Lorenzo." Linda's gaze was very serious. "Locks can be picked."

"She's right." Helen nodded eagerly. "That headless corpse might just be the first of many. Who knows?"

I winced. "I hope you're wrong."

"Of course. I hope I'm wrong too." Helen sighed. "But I've always heard that once someone kills, they can't always stop. They get a taste for it."

"Dreadful." Linda shivered.

"I might buy one of those do-it-yourself alarms." I rubbed the back of my neck. "You ladies have me a little freaked out."

"Everyone is freaked out. Mayor Spears even held a press conference telling everyone to keep their eyes and ears open. She also said we all needed to stay calm." Helen grimaced. "Easy for her to say. She lives in a gated community with private security."

"I probably should have installed a burglar alarm ages ago," I said, moving toward the door. "Well, you ladies have a nice day."

"You too," Linda said cheerfully.

Once more all the heads of the customers turned in unison, following me as I made my way to the exit.

Julian gave me a flirty smile as I passed, and he leaned over the counter. "Don't be a stranger, Lorenzo."

Once outside, I sucked in a breath of fresh sea air. The atmosphere inside the nail salon had been saturated with chemicals. I had a bit of a headache from simply being in there a short time. I couldn't imagine how Linda handled that smell day in, day out.

I decided to walk to the hardware store because, while I had a car, it was a piece of junk. Plus, it was a nice enough day. Brisk but not too cold. I wanted to stretch my legs to work off some of the stress that had been building inside of me for a while now.

Magnolia Lane was a charming little street with scattered shops mingled in with residential homes. The zoning had changed from residential to business-residential decades ago. The city wanted to buy out the homeowners and revitalize the street with new stores, but there were several older homeowners who refused to budge. Because of that the street remained an eclectic mix of venues.

Purple lobelia grew in thick clumps at the foot of the trees along the lane. Despite the name, Magnolia Lane had more oak trees than magnolias. I ran my fingers lightly along the top of one white picket fence, enjoying the sun on my face. I needed to focus on what was good in my life. Yes, I was having money issues. But to be honest, if your problems could be solved by throwing money at them, you were pretty lucky. I had to believe things would turn around for me. For now, I had a roof over my head. Just the fact that I still had a head was apparently something to be grateful for these days. Just ask that poor decapitated soul who'd been found down by the library.

I was jolted from my thoughts by a strange growling noise across the street. I was passing Harold's Smoke Shop and the sound seemed to come from the dumpster area to the side of the store. Frowning, I continued walking, wondering if what I'd heard was a cat fight about to begin. There were a lot of stray cats on this street and they were forever squaring off.

My head tingled, and I realized I was inadvertently tapping into someone—or—something unpleasant and inhuman. Uneasiness shifted through me as a dark presence seemed to surround me. Despite the warmth of the sun, I shivered as a chill spread throughout my body. My legs felt heavy, and my breathing became labored. Sweat broke out on my face as I continued to move along the lane. I caught a scent of the same sweet tobacco I'd smelled in my home. The hairs on the back of my neck stiffened when I thought I heard a snide laugh.

A dull ache began to spread along my lower abdomen, and I pressed my hand to my stomach.

"Shit," I hissed, feet stumbling.

I was stunned by the force of negative energy swirling around me. I'd rarely encountered truly malevolent otherworldly forces either living or dead. Yes, there was the occasional ill-tempered ghost like Agatha, but they rarely had much power. Certainly not from a distance. This force was hostile and unlike anything I'd ever encountered.

As the aggressive energy buzzed through me, it was impossible not to think of the headless corpse near the library. But surely that couldn't have been the work of a spirit? It was far more likely a mentally sick human had committed a murder.

The cloying scent of that tobacco grew stronger as did the pain in my gut. I stopped walking and pinned my gaze on the area where the growl had originated. I could still definitely sense some sort of energy over there. Sometimes angry spirits could affect humans physically when they fixated their wrath on them. It was rare that they had much range, but it did happen. Was that what was going on here? Most bitter, angry spirits were cowards when challenged. Perhaps confronting the spirit would break the connection.

Heart racing, I stepped off the curb. I headed toward the garbage area, intent on facing down the wayward energy. I was about three feet away when all at once the pain stopped and the scent evaporated. Gasping a deep breath, relief flooded me. I probably should have simply walked away, but I was pissed off that whatever it was had been brazen enough to reach out to me.

I yanked open the big metal door that hid the dumpster from the public. The rancid smell of garbage made me gag, and I waved away the buzzing flies. There didn't seem to be any lingering spirits though. Just garbage—until something glittering near the rusty wheel of the dumpster caught my eye. Frowning, I bent down and found the green stone that had been stolen from my home.

"What the hell?" I scowled and picked it up. Standing, I wiped it off on my jeans, glancing around uneasily. Why would someone go to the trouble of stealing the stone, only to discard it so close by?

I moved from the trash area, slamming the big door closed with a loud clang. I felt like I was being watched, but there wasn't anyone around. My heart raced as I stared at the green stone. I was relieved to have it back—but completely baffled as to what was going on.

Positive I still felt a lingering presence, I shivered. The entity was so intangible now, it was easy to doubt myself. I'd never experienced a spirit who could be near me but completely separate as well. Generally speaking, the spirits I'd dealt with had always either been firmly in their world, or mine, but not in between.

Crossing the street, I continued on my way to the hardware store. Whether I could figure out what was happening or not, someone had definitely been inside my home, and they'd definitely stolen something from me. Odds were that someone had been human, not other worldly. Strapped for money or not, I needed to change the locks ASAP.

CHAPTER THREE

A few days later the abdominal pain returned with a vengeance.

The pain was so excruciating I was forced to call 911. By the time the paramedics wheeled me through the emergency room doors of Johnson Memorial Hospital, I was beyond caring if I lived or died. I just wanted the pain to stop. Sweat slicked my face, and my abdomen felt like someone was stabbing me with an ethereal firebrand.

"Stay with us, buddy," one of the paramedics addressed me.

"I'm gonna be sick," I mumbled, trying to sit up and use the bag one of them had given me in the back of the ambulance. I hadn't eaten in days because the pain had been debilitating, so nothing came up.

I flopped down and writhed on the stretcher as a nurse and doctor in a white coat approached. His voice was distracted as he pressed his cool hand to my hot forehead. "Can you tell me your name?"

"Lorenzo," I whimpered, clutching my searing gut. "Lorenzo Winston." While I was burning up, the air around me was chilled and smelled of body fluids mixed with antiseptic.

"Loren—" Something about the voice seemed vaguely familiar. "I'll be damned."

"Something's wrong," I whispered, biting my lip so hard I tasted blood. "Help me."

"I will." The doctor pushed my shirt up and pressed gently on my lower abdomen. "Does it hurt when I press right there?"

I nodded, humiliated when a hot tear slipped from my eye. I didn't usually cry. I wasn't emotional like that. But the pain was so intense I had no control over my reactions. "Please make it stop," I begged. "Please."

The doctor barked out orders to the nearby nurses, and then he was beside me again. "You're going into surgery immediately, Lorenzo." His voice was tense, and I tried to focus on his angular features.

"Okay." I grunted as another jolt of pain slammed through my abdomen. "What's wrong with me?"

"I suspect it's your appendix."

"Oh, God. That's bad, right?"

"We have the best trauma surgeon in the county on tonight. You're in good hands." His voice was soothing as he leaned over me.

The edge of my vison was dark and blurry, and I could feel myself losing consciousness. "Do you think he's forgiven me?" I was caught somewhere between the real world and a dream as my younger brother's face swam before my eyes. I panted against the pain, guilt eating at me.

"Who?"

I clenched my jaw against the agonizing pressure in my lower stomach. "I don't want to die. Not yet. Not until he's forgiven me."

"You're not going to die." The doctor sounded firm. "We're going to take care of you, Lorenzo."

Struggling, I focused my gaze on his face, taking in his strong jaw and angular cheekbones. But it was the honey-brown eyes that sent a shock wave of recognition through me. "You?" I frowned.

Ian gave an awkward laugh. "We meet again."

"How's Princess?" I slurred, wincing as sharp pains stabbed me again.

"Alive." He looked a bit sheepish as he pressed his cool hand to my hot forehead.

"Told ya so," I mumbled, wishing it was anyone but Ian

witnessing my pathetic state.

"Yeah. You did."

Two nurses grabbed either side of my gurney and pushed me down a brightly lit hallway. Somewhere nearby a baby screeched and a recorded voice crackled over the intercom system. The last glimpse I had of Ian was of him standing at the end of the hall looking perplexed.

"Morning, Sleeping Beauty." A nurse beside the bed was hanging an IV bag. She was thin with short gray hair and wearing a smock with teddy bears on it. She finished what she was doing and faced me. "You're one lucky guy."

I cleared my throat, attempting to speak, but all that came out was a croak. My brain was foggy, and I half-wondered if I hadn't imagined running into Ian in the emergency room.

"Against all odds, you should make a full recovery. Your appendix was on the verge of rupturing." She poured me a glass of water from a plastic pitcher next to my bed and handed it to me.

I took it with shaking hands and sipped the cool liquid gratefully. Once I'd drained my cup, I met her gaze. "I thought I was going to die."

"From what I heard, if you'd stalled even a couple of hours, you probably would have." She shook her head. "You must have been in excruciating pain. Why didn't you come in sooner?"

I set the cup down on the tray to the side of my bed. "I don't know. I kept hoping it would go away." I avoided her prying gaze.

She laughed. "Classic denial."

Her words made me once more think of Ian. I really didn't want to run into him again. "When can I get out of here?"

She frowned. "Uh, you just had surgery. You're not leaving today."

"Okay, but when?" A loud snore caught my attention. I hadn't noticed immediately, but there was another patient sleeping in a bed across the room. He was an older man, mostly bald but with patches of unnaturally black hair still clinging to his white scalp.

"That's up to your doctor and your insurance." As she spoke, she carefully wedged another pillow behind my shoulders. "These darn pillows are like pancakes. One is never enough." She smiled down at me. "Is that better?"

"Um, sure. Thanks."

"My pleasure." She headed toward the door. "If you need more pain meds just push the green button on the side of your bed. But it's a set amount, so don't blow it all in one go. Pace yourself." She disappeared out of the room.

I adjusted my position, wincing as the skin tugged around my abdomen. I lifted one edge of the flimsy hospital gown, taking in the two small puckered incisions on my lower abdomen. I'd been expecting a huge incision, and was relieved that wasn't the case. Hopefully the healing time would be less with smaller cuts in the body.

With a tired grunt, I lay back against the pillows. I felt rattled at how close I'd come to dying. I'd already suspected I was pushing my luck by not coming in sooner, but the nurse had confirmed my stupidity. The pains had been incapacitating. I hadn't even been able to work. Of course I should have come to the hospital sooner.

But I hated hospitals with a passion.

Hospitals were a nightmare for me. They were a cesspool of whiny, bitter spirits who often wanted to settle a score. They'd see me and latch on en masse, and that was when the real fun began: migraines, vomiting, the shakes.

It wasn't pretty.

So far during my hospital stay, I'd been lucky. No spirits had come calling as of yet. The drugs were most likely numbing me to their presence. I had little doubt they were there, hovering. Nagging. Hopefully I'd stay drugged long enough to escape the hospital without being bombarded by spirits. I wasn't in the habit of taking messages from beyond the grave for free.

There was a knock on the doorjamb, and when I looked up, I found Ian standing there. My gut churned at the sight of him. He still wore his white doctor's coat, and while he looked tired, he had a sort of disheveled sexy vibe. I wasn't a vain man, but I immediately felt self-conscious about what I must look like. I probably looked like I'd been run over by a truck. I ran a shaky hand over my hair, trying to smooth down my stubborn cowlick.

"You're awake," he said.

"Yes." I felt tongue-tied, which just annoyed me even more. I didn't even like the guy. What did I care what he thought of me?

"You gave me quite a scare last night." When he was near enough, he took my wrist. The touch of his firm fingers on my flesh had my arm tingling. I noticed the only ring he wore today was the silver one with the green stone. He looked at his watch distractedly, and after a few seconds he said, "Your pulse is good."

I carefully pulled my arm away but still felt the warm imprint of his hand on my skin. "I've never been in that much pain in my life."

"How are you feeling now?"

"Drugged." I touched my tender abdomen. "Maybe that's why I feel surprisingly good."

"Yeah, when they wear off, you'll be uncomfortable. But it won't be anything compared to the pain you were in when you got here."

"Thankfully."

He studied me. "I was shocked to see you in the ER."

"It was mutual." I avoided his gaze and tugged at a string on the thin hospital blanket. "If I'd known you were on duty, I'd probably have tried to wait out your shift."

He scowled. "I hope you're kidding."

I laughed weakly. "Not entirely."

"Oh, really?"

"You were kind of an ass when we first met." I suspected the drugs were loosening my tongue. But it felt nice to tell him what I thought of him. He truly had been a colossal ass when we'd first met.

He shrugged. "I didn't mean to be an ass. I was just protecting my friend."

"Pfft. I'm sure you'd prefer to see it that way." I frowned at him. "You were out of line. You were mocking. It was rude. I'd never come to your place of work and mock you."

A muscle jerked in his cheek. "Okay, fair enough. I should have been nicer." My roomie gave a loud snort, and Ian glanced over with a concerned expression. "I was simply worried about Sylvia," he murmured. "She's very gullible."

"I'm not the one you need to worry about. Just keep her away from my competitor, Weston Bartholomew. He really will make a ding in her check book."

"Good to know." Curiosity glittered in his eyes as he murmured, "Perhaps the spirits led you here last night, knowing I'd be here to save the day."

I narrowed my eyes. "There you go mocking me again."

"No. I'm not mocking you."

I wasn't sure I believed him. "Technically, isn't it the surgeon who saved me?" He was so close, I couldn't help noticing the silky blond hairs on his wrist and the glossy sheen of his manicured nails. I slipped my hands under the thin sheet to hide my ragged cuticles. "You were simply there when they wheeled me in."

"Hey, I'm the one who diagnosed you and sent you to surgery. Give me some credit." He gave an exaggerated sigh. "I get no kudos at all."

Last night was hazy, but he had moved quickly to diagnose my problem. I suppose I owed him some thanks. "Fine. Thank you. You're my hero. There, you've gotten your accolades. Now you can go."

He pursed his lips. "Maybe I don't want to go just yet. Maybe I also want to thank you."

I frowned. "For what?"

He hesitated. "You were right about where Princess was."

I held his gaze and slowly nodded. "Yeah, I know. I knew I'd be right. But to give credit where credit is due, it was Aunt Agatha who knew where Princess was. I simply relayed the message." While I was brushing off his thanks, it actually was nice to have him acknowledge I'd been right. I liked that he was bothering to give me some sort of mea culpa.

"Yes. That's right. Aunt Agatha told you where the cat was."

"She did." I squinted at him. "Now you're a believer?"

"More than I was." Ian smirked. "Which is why I'm willing to believe you were psychically drawn to me last night. So that I could save you."

I laughed gruffly. "You don't seem to understand what I do." I relaxed against my pillows. Why was I enjoying talking to him? Was it the drugs that made him seem less annoying? I glanced at my comatose roommate. Maybe it truly was the drugs. "I talk to dead people's spirits. That's it."

"Right. And they brought you here. To me." Ian's lips twitched.

"My gift doesn't pull me to people like a magnet. I had no idea you were here. I can't see through walls. My gift doesn't give me x-ray vision."

"Thank heavens. I wouldn't want you to see my whitey-tighties." He hugged his body as if trying to hide himself and batted his lashes.

I couldn't help smiling at his fake modesty. I hadn't expected him to have a sense of humor. He'd been too judgmental and uptight when we first met. Now I could see that he had another side to his personality. I wasn't sure why he was bothering to show it to me though. "You're safe. I have no interest in seeing your whitey-tighties."

He didn't react to my comment, and instead he changed the subject. "Can you read living people's minds?"

"Sometimes." Outside the room an orderly pushed a big rattling food cart past. "I occasionally get snippets."

"Oh, dear." He lifted his brows. "That could be awkward."

"Don't worry. I'm not interested in what you're thinking." My roomie made a bear-like growl and he rolled over, facing away from us. Unfortunately the back of his hospital gown fell open, showing his naked buttocks. I quickly averted my gaze.

Ian winced at my tone. "Ouch. You're not good for my ego, Great Lorenzo."

I studiously avoided looking in the direction of my bare-assed roommate. "Sure. Because that's what we're all here on earth for, right? To flatter your ego?"

"Damn. You're really not pulling your punches."

I gave a sheepish laugh. "Sorry."

He sighed. "No. It's okay. I probably deserve it after how I was when we first met."

"Does it really matter what I think of you? It's not like we run in the same circles." I was right about that too. While he was attractive, I had nothing in common with a man like him. He was a doctor. His social life probably consisted of fancy cocktail parties where people sipped champagne while discussing the health of their stock portfolios. I spent most my nights at home microwaving Lean Cuisine mac and cheese and answering messages from depressed people online.

"We should be friends. I mean, after all, fate has thrown us together," he said.

I laughed. "Why are you trying to charm me?"

He lifted one shoulder. "Well, it's obvious you don't like me. People usually do."

"That's probably because you're a doctor. If you worked at Jack in the Box, no one would put up with your 'charm.'" I used air quotes.

"There you go again." He shook his head, but he didn't really look put out by my sarcasm. "Maybe I'll come see you when my shift is over in an hour."

"What? No. That's not necessary." Why in the world would he want to come see me? That was the last thing I wanted. He made me nervous and I didn't have the energy to deal with the weird feelings he brought up in me.

"But I want to come check on you." He appeared shocked that I wouldn't want him to come back again. "I need to make sure you're healing nicely."

"Please, you really don't have to do that," I insisted. "I don't want to put you out."

"It's no trouble. I'm a doctor." He looked like he was having trouble keeping a straight face. "I live to serve."

"Oh, brother." I smiled in spite of myself. It absolutely had to be the drugs that made him seem almost charming. "Aren't there any other patients you can go bother?"

"You're the only one that hasn't succumbed to my charm."

"I doubt that," I said.

He glanced at his watch and sighed. "Damn. I have to go back to work now."

"Okay."

He didn't move.

I said, "Don't let me keep you."

Ian narrowed his gaze and his expression became serious. "You know, I'm sorry that I didn't believe you the other day. I thought you were a huge fake and . . . a crook."

His heartfelt apology caught me off guard. "Uh . . . don't worry about it. I'm used to people doubting what I do or thinking I'm a shyster."

"It's just that Sylvia has been taken advantage of many a time. She's got a soft heart and she's easily suckered. I wanted to prevent that happening to her again. But it turns out you weren't doing anything wrong." He grimaced. "You really were just helping her."

I felt a little twinge of guilt, seeing as I planned on getting more sessions out of Mrs. Beckom. "It's fine. I know plenty of fake psychics."

"You mean your competition across town?"

"He's not the only one, but yes, as I said earlier, Weston is a fraud. He has zero actual psychic ability. Make sure Mrs. Beckom doesn't go to him while I'm out of commission. He'll do his best to clean her out."

"I'll make sure she steers clear of him." He looked at his watch and frowned. "I really do have to go. I'm glad you're feeling better."

"Me too. Do you by any chance know when I can get out of here?" The sooner the better. I was beginning to sense spirits in the room. I'd known it was only a matter of time before they sought me out. There was one particularly curious spirit hovering near my roomie. While I couldn't see her clearly, her shimmering form seemed to be that of an older woman dressed in a 1940s era nurse's uniform. She swirled around my roomies bed, apparently fascinated with the gurgling snores emanating from his open mouth. "I really would like to get out of here," I said.

"Chomping at the bit to escape?" Ian asked.

"It's a lovely hospital and all, but I don't like hospitals."

"Few people do." He grabbed my chart off the end of the bed. "You had a laparoscopic appendectomy, so your hospital stay should be about two days, I believe." His expression brightened. "Hey, that means I get to see you again tomorrow."

I didn't really want to get to know him better. He was charming, but I wasn't interested. I didn't have the energy to invest in the living. "As I said before, you don't have to come see me. I'm fine."

"Lorenzo, Lorenzo, Lorenzo." He rehung the clipboard on the bed. "You won't be able to fight my charm forever."

"I can try though," I murmured.

"It's probably futile, but you do what you need to do." He headed toward the door. "I'm pretty irresistible."

"Should we be fraternizing? Isn't there some sort of doctor-patient rule-thing against that?"

He stopped, and his shoes squeaked on the vinyl floor as he turned to face me. "There might be. But we're safe."

"Why's that?"

"Because, while I'm an amazing doctor, I'm not officially your doctor." He grinned. "So I can annoy you all I want."

"Awesome?"

He pointed at me. "See ya tomorrow, Lorenzo."

Shaking my head, I watched him leave. I was confused about what he hoped to get out of this acquaintanceship. Was he like this with all of his patients? Maybe I was taking him too seriously. Odds were, he wouldn't come see me again. A guy like him had more important fish to fry.

My cell buzzed on the table next to my bed, and I groaned. I didn't want to talk to anyone, but my business calls were routed to my cell. If it was a customer calling, I couldn't afford to miss the call. I was already broke, and now I'd also have medical co-payments to pay. Gritting my teeth, I stretched my arm to grab the phone, wincing when the movement pulled my stitches. "Hello?"

There was some labored breathing, and then an agitated male voice said, "I need help. I don't know who to trust."

"Who is this?"

The person sighed. "It's been so long. I suppose it's only natural that you don't remember me."

I wrinkled my brow, and the hospital bed squeaked as I struggled to sit up. "We know each other?" I didn't recognize the voice but that didn't mean we'd never met.

"Yes. From before."

I hesitated, gripping the cool metal of the bed railing. "If you feel you're in danger, you should go to the police." I wasn't sure why this person was calling me. What help could I be on the phone? I was picking up waves of fear, although it didn't take a psychic to know he was scared. There was obvious panic in his tone.

"I'm not sure how far he'll go to stop me." His voice was hushed.

"Stop you from what?" I had to strain to hear his voice as an announcement about the hospital's vegetarian meal offerings came over the speaker system.

He exhaled tiredly. "Maybe I should have kept you in the dark longer. I just know he's coming soon. Be very careful, Lorenzo. He's well aware of the prophesy."

"The prophesy?" I scowled. "Look, why won't you tell me who you are?"

The line went dead.

"Hello? Hello?" Blinking at my phone, I tried hitting redial but the phone just rang and rang. I set the phone back on the side table, feeling uneasy. If I called the police, there probably wasn't much they could do. I didn't know anything about the caller. The cops might assume it was a prank. Perhaps it had been a prank. People often felt threatened by my psychic abilities. They didn't understand them, so they mocked them.

I sat back against the pillows, trying to still the disquiet I felt. The caller had implied we knew each other. I definitely hadn't recognized his voice. Was he a past client? I closed my eyes, feeling drained. The pain meds were kicking in and I was drowsy. If the man called again, I'd do my best to get more information out of him. For now, healing was what I needed to concentrate on.

CHAPTER FOUR

Two days later, things had gone downhill rapidly. Not with my health, but with the hospital environment. The nurses were giving me less pain killers now, and the spirits had tracked me down. Unfortunately, my sleepy roomie had been discharged but not yet replaced. That meant the old lady nurse spirit now hovered near me day and night.

She lamented the death of her lover, killed in the war while flying a P-51 Mustang. She begged me relentlessly to reunite them in the spirit realm, which wasn't something I knew how to do. But she was like most willful spirits and wouldn't take no for an answer.

However, it wasn't just the old lady ghost who wanted my attention. There were droves of spirits visiting daily, screeching and complaining they'd been wronged when alive. They all wanted me to seek vengeance for them, which was obviously impossible.

At present, though, the immediate challenge was my flesh and blood tormentor, Nurse Brown. While she was more drill sergeant than life coach, she was entertaining. She often shared gossip about Johnson Memorial's hottest, most eligible bachelor, Dr. Ian.

Nurse Brown was a no-nonsense fifty-something woman with short white hair and piercing blue eyes. I suspected she'd been a prison warden earlier in life because she had no sympathy for me and my stitches at all.

Twice a day Nurse Brown would drag me from my hospital bed and insist I walk around the room. She insisted it was imperative that I do that in preparation for me going home. To be honest, she scared me a little, so I didn't argue. I just obeyed.

Trying to ignore the spirits yammering at me for attention, I shuffled slowly across the room. I met Nurse Brown's steely gaze and asked, "How much longer?" Feeling lightheaded, I bit my lip and grabbed the nearest wall to steady myself. "Is that enough? Can I sit down now?"

"Nope," she said, frowning.

"Really?" My incisions ached and my legs were shaky. "But I feel dizzy."

"That's because you're in bed all day. Your muscles are wasting away."

"Come on," I whimpered. "Surely I've walked enough for now. I'll do more later. I promise."

"No. Keep going." She clapped her hands. "Just a bit more. Walking will do you wonders."

I shuddered as the spirit of a middle-aged man fluttered closer. Nausea hit me and bile rose in my throat. His energy sent a chill through me as he hissed, "You need to tell the doctors that I was poisoned. My wife murdered me. She can't get away with it. You need to *do* something."

I waved him off, scowling. "Not *now*."

"Pardon?" Nurse Brown asked, looking annoyed.

I grimaced. I couldn't very well tell her I was talking to a ghost, so instead I said, "Please just let me walk some more later. I really am tired."

And nauseated. So very, very nauseated.

Nurse Brown sighed. "Don't be a wimp. You need to move around so the gas that's trapped in your abdomen can work its way out."

"I keep telling you—I don't have any issues like that." It would probably serve her right if I hurled on her.

"Like what?" Ian asked as he suddenly walked into the room.

Flushing, I grabbed the back of my hospital smock where my ass was hanging out and sent the nurse a warning glance. "Nothing."

Nurse Brown smiled slyly. "Just the usual, doctor."

His eyes widened. "Ohhh. Should we keep all open flames away from this patient?"

My cheeks warmed. "God. Shut up."

"Is that any way to talk to the man who saved your life?" He squinted at me as he approached.

"You didn't save my life. Doctor Smithfield did." I hobbled to the bed and sat slowly with a groan. My lower stomach area was tender, and I took care as I dragged myself onto the squeaky bed.

"I thought that we'd already established I diagnosed you in the nick of time." He put his hands under my legs and lifted gently. "I knew you were in the danger zone."

I hated how my body reacted to his touch. He'd visited me at least once a day for the last two days. I kept waiting for my attraction to him to fade, but each time he touched me, the feel of his fingers on my bare skin had my heart bumping in my chest annoyingly. Why did he keep touching me? Was it because he was a doctor that he thought nothing of putting his hands on strangers? I clenched my jaw, hoping to squash whatever misguided attraction I might have for Ian.

"So, the scuttlebutt is you get released tomorrow morning," Nurse Brown said as she came over to fluff my pillows.

"What time?" Ian asked. He perched on the edge of my bed, toying with his stethoscope. "Do you have anyone to give you a ride home?"

I didn't. But I felt pathetic having to admit that. "I'll find someone." I had no idea who. I had one real friend in town, Claire, and she happened to be on vacation in Hawaii with her latest boy-toy.

"I have tomorrow off," Ian said.

"Good for you?"

He sighed. "What I'm saying is I could give you a ride home."

"You running a taxi service now, doc?" Nurse Brown sniggered as she headed toward the door. "I'll let all the other patients know."

"Don't you dare, Deloris." He returned his gaze to me once she was gone. "What do you say? Can I drive you home?"

"No. That's okay."

"Why not?" He frowned.

Considering how he'd first been when we met, I was baffled as to why he was suddenly being so friendly. "Why are you offering me a ride?"

"Why wouldn't I offer you a ride?"

"Because you don't know me." I cringed as a little girl's spirit joined me on the bed. She was crying and clutching at me, and I didn't have the heart to push her away. Instead, I allowed her to sit on my lap, trying to focus on my conversation with Ian. She was young enough that her energy didn't drain me as much as older spirits.

"I kind of know you," Ian said.

"Not really."

He shrugged. "Perhaps I'm offering because I'm a nice guy."

I studied him. "Maybe you are, maybe you aren't. Either way, I'll just take a taxi home."

He hesitated and then said, "Lorenzo, correct me if I'm wrong, but you don't have a lot of money, right? I'm not saying that to be a jerk, but it was obvious from your shop you aren't rolling in the dough. Now you also have hospital bills to contend with."

"Thanks for reminding me." My medical insurance would pay most of my hospital bill, but not all of it. There would be a nice little chunk left for me.

"I'm simply trying to make a point. Taxis are expensive. Why turn down a free ride home?" He wrinkled his forehead. "It makes no sense."

I hesitated. He was right about my finances. I didn't have a lot of discretionary income. Hell, I barely had regular income. I might need to swallow my pride and seek out some sort of debt forgiveness program. But regardless of that, I still wasn't sure what Ian's motives were. If he gave me a ride, would he expect something from me? Few people did things out of the goodness of their heart. "Look, you must have more important things to do than drive me around."

"Not tomorrow."

"It's kind of you to offer, but I'd rather find my own way home." I smiled, hoping that would make my rejection seem less personal. It really wasn't personal. I just didn't accept rides from people I didn't know well. I had my reasons, but wasn't going to share them with Ian.

"Come on, Lorenzo." His voice was coaxing. "Let me drive you home."

My stomach responded to his husky tone with warm flutters, but I clenched my jaw. "If you drive me home, will you expect something in return?"

"Like what?"

"I have no idea. People want things . . . sometimes." I glanced down at the little girl spirit on my lap. The way she clung to me showed she definitely needed a whole lot of things from me. Things I couldn't give her.

"What could I possibly want?" He wrinkled his brow, looking bewildered.

Was I being too suspicious? His desire to help seemed earnest. Plus, he'd offered the ride in front of that nurse. He wasn't trying to hide his offer of a ride. Was I being paranoid? I watched him, uneasiness swirling inside of me. But how could I not be paranoid with at least five spirits hanging around me at all times. Not to mention the scary prophesy phone call guy? He'd obviously wanted something from me. It wasn't inconceivable Ian would want things too.

When I didn't respond to his question, his expression gentled. "I gather you have reasons for being careful. I can respect that. But I have no ulterior motives. I simply know you probably could use a ride, and I have a free day tomorrow."

I stopped trying to read his expression and instead searched his mind. Happily, his thoughts were easily accessible. Not everyone's were, but I was able to tap into his. His sincerity washed over me, reassuring me where words couldn't. I let out a shaky breath. "Okay."

"Yeah?" He smiled. "You'll let me give you a ride?"

"Are you sure it's not any trouble?"

"It's not. I promise." He shrugged. "I wouldn't offer if it was."

I frowned. "I don't know what time I'm being released."

"No worries. I'll figure it out." He glanced at his watch. "I should get back to work. I just wanted to see how you were doing."

I held his gaze, uncertain of how to respond. I was mystified by why he seemed to care one way or the other about me.

He cleared his throat. "Anyway, I'll see you tomorrow, Lorenzo."

"Okay."

Once he'd left I struggled with nausea as the spirits circled. My head pounded and my muscles trembled as they each took turns badgering me. All the while the little girl spirit cried quietly on the bed next to me. I could have kissed Nurse Brown when she finally arrived to give me some pain medication.

Once the voices quieted, I managed to doze off. My dreams were filled with my younger brother and faceless people stalking me. It was late afternoon when I was awakened by a young nurse rolling a food cart into my room.

"I'm sorry. Did I wake you? It's snack time," she said brightly.

"Oh." I sat up, blinking groggily. The little girl ghost was gone, as was the old woman. The angry man who suspected his wife had poisoned him still lingered, sitting in the corner glowering at me.

She set a saran-covered dish on my tray and also plunked down a small carton of milk. "It's a gluten-free brownie. It's actually delicious. You'd never know it wasn't a regular brownie."

"Thanks." Her voice was vaguely familiar, and I peered at her more closely. My heart stuttered as I recognized her. "Carli?"

She gave a soft gasp, and her dark eyes widened. "L— Lorenzo?" Her long, curly black hair was pulled tight in a thick ponytail, and she looked taller and thinner than I remembered.

"You're a nurse?" It was the only thing I could think of to say.

Her lips moved, but it took a second for her to find her voice. "I'm getting there."

Carli had been my younger brother's girlfriend in high school. Running into her like this was a huge shock. The last time I'd seen her had been the worst day of my life. The day Nico had died. Seeing her brought back so many emotions, normal conversation seemed impossible.

"I had no idea you wanted to be a nurse," I finally mumbled.

She grimaced, running a hand over her uniform. "I like helping people."

"That's . . . honorable." I dropped my gaze, still struggling to keep my emotions in check. I searched my brain for something to say, but I drew a blank. All I could think about was Nico and how he'd died.

"What happened to you? Why are you in the hospital?" she asked softly.

I frowned. "I had an emergency appendectomy."

"Oh, my God." She winced. "Are you serious? That's awful."

"Yeah."

Her gaze softened. "I'm so glad you're okay."

I nodded, and the awkward silence returned.

She sighed. "It's probably weird seeing me out of the blue like this." Her voice trembled. "I wanted to call you so many times, but—"

"You were just a kid," I interrupted. "I didn't expect you to call."

"You were basically a kid too, and you were all alone, at least I had my family—"

"It's fine," I said curtly. "I was fine."

We stared at each other uncomfortably for a few moments.

She cleared her throat and began straightening items on her cart. "Are you still doing the psychic thing?"

"Yeah, it's not really a choice." I sounded harsher than I wanted. I didn't want to take out my pain on her. She was a sweet girl. She'd loved Nico, and he'd loved her. I needed to be nice to her. I needed to at least be polite.

"I . . . uh . . . I didn't mean that question in a bad way," she said.

"It's okay. I know most people think what I do is weird." Most people either didn't believe in my abilities, or they thought I was a freak. Sometimes both.

"I don't think it's weird. I think it's wonderful. You help people."

I frowned. "I don't know. Maybe." I was just trying to survive. I wasn't really doing it to help people. I liked helping them, but it wasn't my motivation.

She gnawed on her bottom lip, watching me. "It's weird to see you like this. I actually was thinking about you the other day."

"Were you?"

"Yeah, I still miss him, you know? It's been five years, but I think about him all the time."

"Me too," I said against the lump in my throat.

She gave a nervous laugh. "I was thinking maybe I'd hire you to see if you could contact Nico for me."

Oh, God.

I gritted my teeth. "I couldn't help you there."

"No?" Disappointment clouded her expression. "But I thought that was what you do?"

"It is, but I . . . I can't hear Nico. I can't connect to him."

She winced. "You mean you don't want to because it's painful?"

I swallowed hard. "No, I mean I can't hear him. He won't talk to me."

She pulled her dark brows together. "Why not?"

"I don't know. I just can't reach him." I could often feel his energy around me in the early hours of dawn, like a warm breath of air hovering just out of reach. But when I tried to connect with him, he'd disappear.

"Oh, God, Lorenzo. I'm so sorry. That must be torture."

"It is." I was embarrassed when my eyes stung. I really, really didn't want to cry in front of her. I gave a hard laugh, willing the tears to dry up. "Isn't that just my luck? I can hear every asshole in the world except the one person I'd give anything to talk to." I sniffed and used the napkin on the tray to wipe my nose. "Anyway, that's just the way it is."

"That's so unfair. You were so close." She moved next to me and touched my shoulder in a comforting gesture. Carli had always been like that—warm and very touchy-feely. Nico had loved that about her because our parents had always been stingy with affection. Cold even.

"Maybe he's mad at me."

"What? No, Lorenzo. There's no way."

"You know what? I don't want to talk about Nico," I whispered, clenching my fists. It was way too painful to even begin to remember. Too many mistakes had been made. Signs I'd missed along the way.

"Okay." She nodded. "I understand."

"Sorry."

"You have nothing to apologize for." She pressed her lips together and her expression gentled. "Sometimes I hate talking about him too."

"It's the past. We should try and put it behind us." I'd probably forever be trapped in my torturous memories, but she deserved to move forward. She was so young.

"That's easier said than done. I miss him every day."

"I know. Me too." Hanging onto my control by a thread, I grated out, "I thought you were going for a business degree. How did it turn into nursing?"

She hesitated but then responded. "After Nico died . . . I graduated high school and planned on going to UCLA to get my business degree. But the plan had been to go with Nico."

"Yeah, that's right."

She winced. "Being on that campus without him just made me miss him more."

"I get it." Nico had lived with me in a two-bedroom apartment in town. After his death, the silence had made the place feel like a tomb.

"I transferred to a different private university and started with a nursing program there." She glanced over as a male nurse pushed an elderly woman into the room in a wheelchair.

I was relieved to see I'd have another roommate. Hopefully that would keep some of the spirits busy. They were drawn to humans, even though most humans had no idea they were even there. I returned my attention to Carli. "You got your degree that fast?"

She smiled. "No. I still have another year. But I volunteer here three days a week. It helps to be around people."

I grunted. I was the complete opposite.

"Do you still live at the Oakwood Apartments?" she asked.

I shook my head. "No. I live at the shop now."

"Oh." She grimaced.

"I couldn't work for a while after—" I cleared my throat roughly. "The landlord didn't feel like giving me free rent for life, so I moved."

"I'm sorry."

"Nah. It's convenient living at the shop. No commute to work." I was doing my best not to sound pathetic. I wasn't sure if she was buying it or not.

"I'm still at home." She laughed self-consciously. "Mom and dad are cool with it, so I guess I shouldn't complain. They have me pay like twenty dollars a month just so I feel like I'm contributing."

"At least you speak to your parents," I said.

She winced. "Yeah. Well, yours are dicks, and you can get mad at me for saying that if you want, but it's true."

"Like I'd argue?" I loathed my parents. Surely she knew that.

"Nico hated them so much." Her voice shook.

I clenched my fist. "We both did."

I still do.

"After they didn't even bother to come to the funeral. I knew then for sure that everything you and Nico had ever said about them was true." Her jaw was tight, and her eyes glittered with anger. "What kind of parent doesn't even come to their own child's funeral?"

"They're raging alcoholics. I doubt they even remember Nico is dead." I curled my lips with disgust. "The only reason they might have come was if they thought there was money involved. Then they'd have been here in a flash with their hands out."

"You and Nico turned out so well, especially considering what they were like." She winced.

"Nico was great," I said hoarsely.

She frowned. "You are too, Lorenzo."

I grimaced. "I wasn't fishing for compliments."

"I know."

I shifted, biting my lip when my incisions pulled. I grabbed the brownie off the tray just so I'd have something to do. She was watching me so intently, it was making me uncomfortable.

"Are you seeing anyone?" I asked. I already sensed she was and figured talking about that might make her stop staring at me so closely.

Her cheeks flushed. "Oh, um—"

When her shame washed over me, I felt guilty about asking her that. "It's okay if you are, Carli."

"It took me almost a year to be ready to even consider dating," she said breathlessly. "I turned down a lot of guys. They couldn't begin to compare to Nico." She talked quickly, as if she felt she had to explain herself to me. "But . . . yeah . . . I did finally start dating someone."

"Carli, you don't have to feel bad. You're allowed to be happy."

She surprised me when she teared up. Sniffing she said, "I was so lonely. I tried not to like this guy, but he's so nice and he makes me feel loved and safe." She wiped at her eyes roughly. "Sorry. I'm so emotional. I think it's seeing you again that's making me like this."

Again, guilt nudged me because I'd upset her. I'd been selfish asking her something like that just so she'd stop focusing on me. "I think it's great that you can move on. Please don't think I look down on you for that."

"I was depressed for so long. I really was. But then I decided I either needed to live, or give up," she whispered. "I decided to live."

"I'm glad. You made the right choice."

She lifted her chin. "I'm back on track now and doing something I love."

"You'll be a great nurse," I said. "You're very warm and kindhearted, Carli."

"I don't know about that." She sighed and returned to her food cart. She shifted some juice cartons around. "Helping people makes me feel better. Gives me a reason to live."

I met her sad gaze. "I'm glad. You deserve to be happy."

She said softly, "You do too, Lorenzo."

"Sure." I forced a smile, hoping I looked like I believed her. I didn't really. My face felt tight and stiff as I met her gaze.

"Well, I should get back to work." She gave a sweet smile. "It was wonderful seeing you again, Lorenzo."

"You too."

She left the room, and I set the brownie back on the tray. Seeing her had jarred me. Over the past five years, I'd convinced myself that being stuck in grief was normal. Of course I was still frozen in time from my heartache. I'd told myself no one would be able to move on after tragically losing someone they loved. But Carli had moved on. My parents had moved on. The entire fucking world went on just as it had before as if nothing horrendous had ever happened.

As I lay there with my heart aching, a chilling thought hit me; maybe Nico didn't talk to me because he'd moved on too.

CHAPTER FIVE

As promised, Ian showed up to my hospital room the next day to give me a ride home. He looked relaxed in jeans and a baby blue T-shirt as he entered my hospital room. I was dressed and eager to get the hell out of the hospital. More spirits had joined the first three and I'd already thrown up twice and I had a raging headache. I'd waited to take my pain pill, thinking I might need it while walking out of the hospital. That had been a mistake. With my body cleared of the drugs, the spirits had descended on me with great enthusiasm.

There was one spirit in particular that was draining the life out of me. He was a young Hispanic guy who'd died in the psych ward upstairs. He was convinced his death had been a set up. Apparently, I was lucky enough to be a dead ringer for his old doctor, so he wouldn't leave my side. His energy was strong. Malevolent. He kept trying to invade my body without permission, which I was able to fend off, but it took a lot of energy. Needless to say, I couldn't wait to leave the hospital.

Ian stopped in front of me. "You look green."

I swallowed my precious pain pill, washed it down with water, and pressed my fingers to my temple. "Can we just get out of here, please?"

"Okay." He frowned and led the way out of the hospital.

As we approached his car I inhaled the fresh sea breeze. The briny air was an uplifting change after being cooped up in the hospital for three days. I'd endured nothing but antiseptic scents and whiffs of horrible hospital food.

Johnson Memorial Hospital was situated at the top of a hill that overlooked the small coastal town of Fox Harbor. The town was nestled along Highway 1, with a plethora of restaurants and shops that catered to visitors during the tourist season. Even if visitors didn't like shopping or eating out, they could still enjoy the breathtaking views of the majestic Pacific Ocean.

After helping me settle in the passenger seat of his BMW, Ian slid behind the wheel with a sigh. He slipped on a pair of sunglasses and started the car. "How are you feeling today?" he asked.

"I'll feel fine once the pain pills kick in." His car smelled of coconut and lime, and it was spotless. Not a speck of dust anywhere in sight. I ran my hand over the smooth arm rest, positive it was leather and not cheap vinyl like in my car.

"Why did you wait to take them?" Ian asked.

I sighed. "I miscalculated. I thought they'd do me more good getting in and out of the car."

"Makes sense," he said.

"Yes, you would think so. Except the spirits that roam the hospital came calling. Many of them came at once, and my body can't handle it."

He glanced over at me. "You're saying the hospital has ghosts?"

"Ghosts are everywhere. But hospitals, morgues, and cemeteries have them in large numbers. I avoid those places when possible because it's overwhelming."

He shivered. "You're kind of giving me the creeps."

"Sorry. You asked."

"I guess I did." He hesitated. "They're not in the car with us, right?"

I laughed. "No." I stared out the window, watching a few sail boats tacking into the harbor, their brightly colored sails whipping in the stiff breeze. "I don't like taking drugs ordinarily."

"That's unusual. Most people can't get enough."

"I guess I'm not most people." I frowned at my reflection in the window. My hair looked oily and my face haggard. I was wishing I had a pair of sunglasses. I hadn't had a shower since my surgery. Ian looked like handsome perfection, while I resembled a hobo.

"No, you're a little different from the average Joe." He glanced over, a little smirk on his lips.

"I'm sure you mean that in a good way."

"Naturally."

I sighed. "Thanks again for the ride."

"Of course."

I fiddled with the sun visor and then turned to him abruptly. "Why did you offer?"

He flicked on the turn signal and pulled onto the highway that hugged the coast line. "I thought we ironed this out yesterday. You needed a ride, so I offered."

"But you don't do this on a regular basis?" When I'd first met him I thought he was an arrogant prick. But guys like that didn't give patients rides home from the hospital on their day off. Did he have more depth than I'd originally given him credit for?

"No, I don't usually do this. You're the only patient I've ever given a ride home from the hospital. Well, I take that back. I did offer Mrs. Beckom a ride once when she'd had cataract surgery." He flashed an inquisitive smile. "Why are you so suspicious of my reason?"

"I don't love accepting help from strangers," I murmured.

"We're not really strangers."

I huffed. "The main thing I know about you is you dismiss my psychic abilities."

"Not anymore." He grimaced. "At least, I'm willing to admit you seem to have a gift."

"I guess that's something."

He hesitated. "Have you always had your psychic ability?"

I nodded. "As long as I can remember, but it's become stronger with age."

"Does the psychic thing run in your family?"

I wrinkled my brow. "It does, but it skips around a lot. My parents hated my gift. They felt it went against their religious views. They thought I was possessed by a demon."

"Damn."

"It was pretty awkward. I couldn't control it, especially when I was a kid. My parents didn't understand what was happening. To be honest, neither did I at first. I had one aunt on my mother's side who was also clairvoyant, but I only saw her in person once before she died. My mother didn't want her around and she lived in another state. Aunt Helen tried to help me hone my skills over the phone, but as you can imagine, it wasn't optimal."

"I wouldn't think so." Ian sighed. "Sounds rough."

"It was, but now it's fine. I understand how to deal with my . . . skills better now."

We rode in silence for a bit, and then he asked, "When you were younger, did you ever use your gift to play pranks on people?"

"No. My skills don't really lend themselves to that sort of thing. Like I said sometimes I can read a person's mind. But mostly I . . . uh, just talk to dead people."

"Right."

"Eerie, I know." It wasn't macabre to me, but I knew the average person found the concept of communicating with the dead disturbing.

"So, even as a kid talking to dead people didn't freak you out?" He shivered.

"When it first started happening, yeah, it did. Now? Not really."

He said, "I'd have had to sleep with a light on all the time."

"Oh, the light doesn't stop them from visiting."

"God. Really?" He sounded startled.

I winced. "Sorry. I'll stop talking."

He smiled. "No. I think I get it. I'm the same way about blood. Other people are fainting left and right, and I'm just like, 'What's the big deal? It's just blood.'"

"Exactly." I nodded, glad he understood.

"I know you said your parents live out of state. Do you have any brothers or sisters?"

It was an innocent question. Absolutely nothing wrong with asking something like that. And yet it made my stomach drop like an elephant jumping off a high rise. I considered not answering, or maybe changing the subject. But a part of me just wanted to answer him honestly. I wasn't the first person to lose a sibling, and I wouldn't be the last. So why was it so hard for me to answer a simple question the way anyone else would?

Guilt.

Yes. Whether it was reasonable or not, I still felt responsible for Nico's death. There were many reasons why, but none I wanted to think about. I tried to pull together a sentence that wasn't too defensive, or off putting. Finally, I said, "I had one brother. How about you? Do you have any siblings?"

He gave a curt laugh as if he'd noticed my awkwardness. He didn't call me out though. Instead he responded politely, "I have a younger brother, Toby."

"How old is he?" Hopefully he'd just keep answering my questions so I didn't have to talk about myself.

"Seventeen."

Nico had been the same age at the time of his death. "Is your family local?" With any luck we'd get to my house before he could ask me anything personal.

"Yes." He glanced at me. "Remember my dad was Mrs. Beckom's doctor before I took over?"

"Oh, that's right." I fiddled with the air vent trying to think of another question to keep him talking. "Is he anything like you?"

"Nope. Toby's the wild child. Or he was. I went to college and medical school like an obedient son. I was pretty boring and straitlaced. But my younger brother's always been rebellious. He almost dropped out of high school about a hundred times. He drank a bunch and got in fights. He was a real problem until about a year ago."

"He saw the light?" I asked.

He gripped the wheel tighter and his jaw tensed. "He got in a car wreck and almost died."

I winced. "Damn."

"Yeah, it was pretty scary," he said. "But it woke him up."

I nodded. "That's good. Sounds like he caught himself in time. You don't want him turning into one of those forty-year-old men who still act like they're in high school."

He shuddered. "I have an uncle like that. He's the life of the party, according to him. Mostly we all avoid him at family functions." I laughed, and he gave me a pleased look. "You should laugh more often, it's nice."

I grunted, keeping my gaze focused on the shimmering sea. I looked forward to being home and sleeping in my own bed. I was also jazzed about taking a shower. I knew I had to be careful about the stitches, but there was no way I wasn't showering.

He cleared his throat. "The other day, when you were trying to find Princess, what happened?"

"What do you mean?" I frowned.

"During the reading. You looked like you were struggling." He slowed down to turn onto the street that would take us to my shop. "I'm no expert on psychic stuff, but you seemed stressed."

Remembering Aunt Agatha's unusual tenacity, I shivered. "It wasn't anything I couldn't handle, but Aunt Agatha's spirit didn't want to leave."

"Leave?" A line formed between his brows.

"My body. She wanted to cling to this world," I said.

"Oh. That explains why you were white as a ghost."

"Yeah." I nodded. "Although, ghosts aren't white. They're really more translucent than anything."

"Uh . . . you're a real stickler for details."

I sighed. "People always get that wrong. It bugs me."

"You wouldn't be trying to change the subject, would you?"

"Me? Change the subject?" I asked coyly.

He smiled. "You don't seem to like divulging much about yourself."

"I don't mind talking about myself," I lied.

"I'm not trying to criticize you or say you don't know how to do your job. I'm just curious why you seemed to struggle with Aunt Agatha. Was it a physical strain? Your pulse was elevated and your body seemed stressed overall."

"It wasn't any big deal," I murmured. "Like I said, she didn't want to leave. She wanted to stay in this world."

He raised his brows in surprise. "Can she do that?"

"No. But she can try," I said. "She'd have to leave eventually, but it could have been a few rough hours for me. I'd have been very ill until she left, but she would have to leave." I still didn't know why his touching me had helped drive her spirit from my body. But it had. "I haven't had a spirit try that in a long time."

"How did you get rid of her?" His voice was soft and filled with curiosity.

Twisting my lips, I considered whether or not to be honest with him. I didn't like giving him the idea that I couldn't do my job. But at the same time, he had helped me, and he deserved to know that. "When you touched me, she left."

"Seriously?" He widened his eyes.

"Yep. You touched me and—" I snapped my fingers. "She left. Just like that."

"She reacted to my touching you?"

"Don't get too big of a head," I said. "It was probably a coincidence." I felt a twinge of guilt at leaving out the part about me stealing some of his energy. But what he didn't know wouldn't hurt him.

"Wow. Maybe I'm like the ghost whisperer." He smirked.

I rolled my eyes. "I'd have ejected her one way or another. I have my ways." Rubbing lavender and Roman chamomile on my body helped rid stubborn spirits, as did burning sage and practicing conscious breathing. But I truly hadn't had to do any of that since I was a kid. Aunt Agatha's tenacity had been unusual. There had been a split second where I'd worried she might win.

"Are you concerned that could happen again?" he asked.

I shrugged. "Not really. I can't go into a reading fearful. The spirits will sense that and take advantage."

"Hmmm. Interesting."

I peered out the window as we pulled up to my little yellow house. I felt like I'd been away for weeks. When the car came to a stop, I reached for the handle. I was about to thank him for the ride as I climbed from the car, but his hand on my arm stopped me. His firm fingers were warm on the bare skin of my arm, and I glanced at him warily, shivering.

He seemed to notice, and he let go of me. "Sorry," he said.

"No. It's okay." I held his apologetic gaze, feeling uncertain. "Did you need something?"

Clearing his throat, he said, "I was wondering . . . would you have dinner with me sometime?"

I blinked at him, shocked at the question. Was he asking me out on a date? I hadn't been on a date in so long, I couldn't even remember the last guy's name. Since Nico's death, I'd been disinterested in spending time with humans who weren't paying me for my time. My best friend Claire and the pizza delivery guy were the main humans who I saw on a regular basis.

"You're asking me to dinner?" My voice wobbled.

"Yes." He laughed nervously. "I'd like to take you to dinner sometime this week."

"Why?"

He frowned. "Well, why not?"

"Because."

He laughed. "That's not really a reason."

My eyes slid to my house longingly. "I'm not a social person."

To put it mildly.

"I'm just talking about a quiet dinner. Nowhere fancy." Ian lifted one shoulder. "I want to be sure you heal properly. I get the feeling you don't have a lot of people in your life who check on you."

"I . . . I have people."

"Do you?" He sounded doubtful. "According to the nurses no one came to visit you while you were in the hospital."

My face warmed. "I wasn't there very long."

He frowned. "No, but usually someone comes the first night at least. From what I understand, no one came ever."

"Is that really any of your business?" I huffed. "Were you all gossiping about me or something?" Would Carli have talked about me behind my back? The thought of that hurt.

"God, no. I simply overheard the nurses discussing the fact you hadn't had any visitors. They weren't judging you. They just felt bad."

"That's worse," I said. "I don't need anyone's pity. Is that why you asked me to dinner? Because you pity me?"

He winced. "I'm making a huge mess of this. I didn't ask out of pity. Not at all. I simply thought we might enjoy having a meal together. And at the same time, I could check on your progress. You know, to be sure you're doing okay."

"And why wouldn't I be?" I wrinkled my brow.

"You've just had surgery. Someone should check on you to be sure you have everything you need to heal."

I said, "I have my diet and wound care instructions right here. I'll be fine."

"You experienced a traumatic event." He frowned. "You almost died. Do you not realize that?"

"I didn't die. I'm fine." My voice was hard.

"I'd like to keep you that way," he said stubbornly.

"Ian, being on my own isn't a problem. I'm used to taking care of myself." I tried to soften my tone a little because I suspected he meant well. "I know you think it's weird I had no visitors, but I prefer it that way."

"All I'm suggesting is a casual dinner."

I sighed. "I'll bet you were the kind of kid who brought home stray dogs."

"I'm a doctor. Helping is kind of in my DNA."

His concern was real. It ebbed and flowed around me, leaving me little doubt he truly was worried about me relapsing. But I didn't need a babysitter. "I appreciate your concern, truly I do."

"Why do I feel like there's a 'but' coming?"

I lifted one shoulder and gestured to the sheet the nurse had given me. "I don't think I can eat out with you unless you're taking me to the hospital cafeteria."

He frowned and then smiled contritely. "Oh, right. Only small bland meals for you for a few more days."

"See, it just isn't in the cards, Ian."

"Hmmm." He frowned and then he said, "Oh, I know. I'll cook for you. I'll whip up the most boring food you've ever tasted."

"Uh . . . "

"Look, I'm a good guy. Check your crystal ball if you don't believe me. We can just hang out and have a tasteless meal together."

"You really know how to sell yourself."

He tugged his cell from his pocket. "Give me your number."

"Why?"

"Because whether you have dinner with me or not, I'm calling to check on you. Someone has to watch out for you, whether you know it or not. People need other people, Lorenzo. I'm not going a week without checking in on you."

"Seriously?"

"Someone has to."

"Not really."

"Lorenzo," he rumbled.

"God," I growled, "you're so annoying and weird."

"So are you. You talk to dead people." He leaned toward me. "What's your number? Don't make me look it up from your records."

"You can't do that."

He looked sheepish. "I know. Come on, just give me your number. You don't want me to worry, right?"

"You don't have to worry about me."

"But I will. It's just how I am. Take pity on me."

"Fine." I grudgingly gave him my phone number and then opened the car door. He got out too and came around to assist me. I shrugged off his attempt to help me out of the car. "I'm fine, Ian." I stepped onto the cobblestone path that led to my house. "You can go now."

"I'll go when you're in your house."

"I'm an adult. Why are you treating me like a child?" I hobbled up the walkway scowling.

He followed. "I don't know why someone caring about you is so insulting to you."

"I'm not insulted," I mumbled as I reached the door. I slipped my key into the lock and pushed open the door. He reached up to hold the door open for me, and I got a whiff of his spicy cologne. "There. I'm safe now."

He nodded. "I'll call you tomorrow and check in."

"So soon?"

He frowned. "This is your first night home. I need to be sure you survive."

"I feel so sorry for your mom." I closed the screen door and studied him through the mesh. "I'll bet when you wanted something as a child you were a pain in the ass."

He pointed his finger at me and winked. "You know it baby."

I laughed in spite of myself. "God, I find you incredibly annoying, but I guess I should thank you for the ride home."

"It was my pleasure."

I felt weird shutting the door in his face, but he wasn't walking away, so he wasn't giving me much choice. "Night." I closed the door halfway, and when I peeked he was still standing there. I opened it again. "You have to go now."

He grinned. "I will. Don't worry about it."

I sighed. "Okay, well, I really am closing it now."

"That's fine."

I shut the door. Through the wood I heard his chuckle, and a few moments later, the sound of his engine starting as he drove away. I leaned against the door feeling oddly lighthearted. At first, I didn't recognize what the feeling was because I hadn't felt it in so long.

Ian was definitely not who I'd thought he was. That first meeting had made me think he was an arrogant jerk, but now I recognized his boorish behavior for what it had actually been. He'd been looking out for Mrs. Beckom. Someone he cared about. He was a man who cared about others, and he didn't just say that, he acted on it.

He intrigued me. I didn't want to be curious about him, but he had a warm, uplifting energy. I was drawn to him in spite of myself. I had no doubt he'd check on me just as he'd promised. At the thought of seeing him again, I felt another long-forgotten emotion: anticipation.

CHAPTER SIX

The next morning, as I attempted to eat a bland breakfast of oatmeal, my best friend Claire called to check up on me and chat about her vacation.

"I go away for one week and you have an emergency appendectomy?" Claire's tone was disbelieving. We'd known each other since high school and grown even closer after Nico died. Claire was the one person in this world I truly believed cared about me.

I sighed and adjusted the phone against my ear. "I'm fine. I promise. I shouldn't have even told you because now all you'll do is worry."

"You'd better not keep that kind of thing a secret from me."

"Well, if you're going to get upset . . . "

"I'm concerned. It's allowed." She exhaled.

"I know. I know," I said guiltily. I struggled with the worry that people's concern was truly pity. I hated pity. But I needed to remember this was Claire, and she actually cared about me on a deeper level. "My hospital stay was a drag. Not because of the nurses or anything but because there were so many damn ghosts circling me."

"Oh, dear. That's not good."

"No. I haven't puked that much in years. There were so many of them, it was impossible to time my pain medication to keep them out of my head." I shivered. "Some of the spirits pissed me off with their whining, but some of them were so tragic, it was hard not to feel depressed." Memories of the little girl ghost made my chest ache. She'd been so young and needy, and there was absolutely nothing I could do to help her.

"Gosh, Lorenzo, I'm so sorry you had to go through that. I know how much you hate hospitals."

"Yeah. Well, I'm home now." I stirred the oatmeal, trying to force myself to take a bite. I grabbed the bottle of honey on the table and poured a big glob on top, hoping that might help the boring flavor.

"You said some doctor gave you a ride home?"

"Yes." I tasted the oatmeal, grimacing. The honey wasn't helping. It might even have made it worse because now it was cold *and* sticky.

"But you don't know him?"

"Not really. We met once before my hospital trip." I laughed. "He was with a client at my shop. He thought I was trying to swindle her."

"Were you trying to swindle her?" She sounded amused.

I grimaced. "She got her money's worth. There was no swindling."

"I'm teasing, but I know business is slow this time of year."

"Yes." I glanced down at the bowl of plain oatmeal congealing before me. "I need to advertise or something, but it's so expensive."

"I could loan you some money," she said brightly.

I winced. "No, thank you."

"You're too prideful. There's nothing wrong with loaning a friend money."

"I know. If I need money, I'll ask. Okay?" As I spoke my eyes settled on the stack of unpaid bills on the kitchen table.

"No you won't," she grumbled. "We both know you won't."

"Come on, Claire," I complained. "Can't we have a nice conversation? I don't want to talk about money right now."

"Fine." She sighed. "So, if this doctor guy thought you were a crook, why would he offer you a ride home?"

"He changed his mind about me."

"Did he?" She sounded surprised.

"Yes. His friend found her cat, safe and sound as promised. He had no choice other than to admit my dazzling talent is legit. He even apologized."

She laughed. "Wow."

"Well, he saw up close and personal that I still have a tube TV and not a flat screen. I'm not cleaning out people's bank accounts or conning them."

"No. That would be Weston Bartholomew's MO, not yours."

I leaned back in my chair. "Maybe I should take a cue from Weston. He's obviously doing better than me. He even has ads on bus benches now. The best I can do is pass out fliers at the grocery store."

"Don't even jest. You have too much integrity to ever go down that road."

I pinched the skin between my eyes. "You can't eat integrity."

"No, but you'd hate yourself if you did anything more than stretch out sessions occasionally."

"True." I stood and took my half-eaten bowl of oatmeal to the sink. I washed it down the drain, shuddering. I didn't love oatmeal on the best of days, but cold oatmeal was an abomination. "I wish you were here. I miss you."

Her voice gentled. "I miss you too. I'm sorry I'm on vacation, Lorenzo. I should have been there to help out. Instead you needed a stranger to help you."

"It was fine. It was just a ride home."

"I know. I also know you don't like trusting strangers."

"No. I don't. But I'm not a little kid anymore," I said quietly. "I can handle myself now. He . . . he was just being a nice guy. Okay?"

"Okay."

"Yes, there are a lot of horrible people in the world. I . . . I know that better than anyone. But he did nothing wrong. He just wanted to help me."

She hesitated. "If he was a creep would you be able to sense that?

"I think so." I grimaced. "He's not a creep though. He's a respected doctor. He was simply being kind."

"I just worry about you."

"Yeah, I know." Claire had always been protective of me, ever since we were kids. But while I appreciated her concern, I didn't want to only talk about myself. "Tell me about your trip. Are you having fun?"

She groaned. "Kind of?"

"Oh, no. What's wrong?"

"Well, Steven is driving me crazy." Claire lowered her voice. "He's acting all jealous and stuff. We took surfing lessons this morning, and he acted like the instructor was trying to run off with me."

I grinned. "Were you flirting with the guy?" Odds were she had been. Claire couldn't help flirting, and she went through men like tissues.

"No. I don't think so."

"Come on. You can tell me the truth. You were flirting, weren't you?"

She gave a guilty laugh. "The surfing instructor was so hot. Blond, tanned and blue eyed. He was yummy. You'd have loved him." She laughed even harder. "Okay, maybe I was flirting a little."

"Well, knock it off. You have a man already. Leave some for the rest of us."

"Pfft. As if you're in the market."

"You never know." I thought about Ian and his warm brown eyes. "Maybe one day I'll end my self-imposed dry spell." Not that I had any plans to make a move on

Ian anytime soon. Besides, for all I knew his concern for me was purely platonic. He was a caring guy. Wanting to check on me didn't equal romantic interest. Which was a good thing because I didn't want romance in my life. Right? Besides, who was I kidding? Ian was way out of my league. If he was into me, sex might be fun, but I didn't have the energy to become emotionally invested in anything.

"So tell me more about this doctor slash hero."

I definitely didn't want to encourage her interest in Ian, so I ignored her question and instead said, "I got the weirdest phone call while I was in the hospital."

I sensed her frustration through the phone that I was avoiding her question, but she went with it. "Did you?"

"Yeah, it was some old man who was babbling about a prophesy or something. I felt kind of bad for him because while he sounded crazy, he obviously believed what he was saying."

"What did he want from you?"

"I'm not exactly sure." I filled the tea kettle as I spoke, deciding a soothing cup of chamomile tea was just what I needed after trying to choke down cold oatmeal. "He was mostly warning me."

"About what?"

"He seemed to think I was in danger, but he sounded so scattered, I couldn't make sense of what he was saying."

"Do you think it was a wrong number?"

"No. He knew my name."

She sighed. "Oh. Well, if he calls again maybe you should block his number."

"Yeah, good idea."

She cleared her throat. "So anyway, tell me more about the hunky doctor guy."

I winced. I'd foolishly hoped she'd taken the hint, but apparently not. "What do you want to know?" I asked in a resigned voice.

"You said he's going to check up on you? What does that mean?"

The tea kettle whistled and I turned off the gas. "Simply that he's going to call me and see if I'm alive. He's just being a doctor. It's no big deal." I poured hot water into a mug and grabbed a box of tea from the cupboard over the stove. Tearing open the little paper packet, I dunked the bag into the steaming water, inhaling the refreshing lemon-and-chamomile-scented tea.

"That's it? He just wants to check on you for impersonal reasons?" She sounded skeptical. "I'm not buying it. Come on. Spill it, Lorenzo."

I exhaled tiredly. "Fine. He wants to have dinner sometime. Once I'm able to eat something other than rice and glorified baby food."

"I knew it." She sounded smug.

"It's nothing big. You're making too much of it. It's just dinner."

"Stop playing it down. I think he likes you." She had a smile in her voice.

"This isn't grade school, Claire."

Ignoring me, she said, "A rich doctor boyfriend could do wonders for you."

"It's dinner. He doesn't want to be my *boyfriend*." I gave an embarrassed laughed. "God. This conversation is ridiculous."

"No, it's not. It would be good for you to have a relationship. It's been far too long. You're going to turn into a bitter recluse if you don't open yourself up to other people."

"I'm not looking for a relationship. You know that." My tone was flat. "I *might* be open to sleeping with someone, but a relationship isn't in the cards for me at the moment."

"But if one falls in your lap you should give it a chance."

"Come on, Claire," I mumbled.

She sighed. "Lorenzo, you can't just shut yourself off from the world forever."

"Wanna bet?" My call waiting beeped and I glanced down at the number. I didn't recognize it, so I hit ignore. If it was a client calling they'd be able to leave a message.

"I say give him a chance."

"Of course you do," I muttered.

"What could it hurt to have dinner?"

"If he keeps asking, I will have dinner. But that's probably where it will end."

"Oh, poo," she grumbled. "I want to meet him."

I laughed gruffly. "How did we go from me maybe having dinner with him to you meeting him? By the time you get back he'll have moved on to his next conquest." I cleared my throat. "Not . . . not that I plan on being a conquest."

"Ha. I think that was some sort of Freudian slip."

"No."

"But you do think he's attractive?"

"Well, that's just a fact. Anyone would think he's attractive." I sighed. "But he knows he's sexy. He's too . . . sure of himself. He may be sexy, but he's not really my type."

She huffed. "You don't have a type anymore. You haven't had a real relationship in years."

"Doesn't Jay count?"

"Seriously? He was a jerk and you two weren't really even together."

"No, but that was why I didn't mind what we had. No strings. No promises. No expectations."

"And no depth."

"Yeah, just as I wanted. The sex was good and that was enough."

"Lorenzo," she said sounding exasperated, "that isn't healthy."

"Says who?"

"Everyone." She sighed. "Even if what you had with Jay was fantastic, which I'd argue it wasn't, that was over years ago. You haven't been with anyone since. That's so sad."

"I had a date."

"Did you? With who?"

I grimaced. "I can't remember his name."

"Oh, boy." She sighed. "I've got to do something drastic."

I clenched my jaw. "You know why I'm the way I am."

"I know." Her voice was gentle. "But it's time to move on and rejoin the living."

"I get along better with the dead."

"You always say that shit, but I remember the guy who had dudes running after him in high school."

Hanging my head, I shrugged. "None of them meant anything to me. You know that. It was just sex."

"I know, but you had a lot of fun. You used to like fun."

"That's ancient history. I'm not the same."

"You don't have to be. You just have to be open to quality guys should they come along. This doctor sounds like a good guy. I mean, he drove you home and knew for a fact he wasn't getting any."

I grimaced. "Very funny."

She gave a snort of a laugh. "Sorry. I couldn't resist."

My call waiting beeped again, and when I checked, it was that same strange number. "Somebody keeps calling me."

"It's probably someone wanting to talk to you about your car warranty expiring." She sighed. "I get one of those calls at least once a week."

"The warranty on my junker expired two decades ago."

"Yeah. I'm surprised your car still runs."

"Me too." I sat down at the table, sipping my tea. I winced because it was so hot and said, "I had the strangest thing happen the other day during a reading."

"Did you?" Claire sounded curious.

"It was the reading where Ian was there. The spirit didn't want to leave my body. I had to force her out. To be honest, I was scared for a minute she was going to win."

"Good Lord, really?" she squeaked. "Has that ever happened before?"

"Not really. Not since I was a kid, and never to that extent."

"But she did leave," Claire said. "How did you get rid of her?"

I fingered the little paper tag on my tea bag. "Ian touched me, and she left."

"Really?" She sounded surprised. "Why would touching you make the ghost leave?"

"I don't know." Guilt nudged me as I confessed, "But I stole some of his energy because I felt so weak."

"Did you?"

"His energy was so beautifully pure and intoxicating." I laughed sheepishly.

She sounded amused as she said, "How sexy."

My cheeks warmed. "He can never know. I couldn't help myself. He'd probably hate me if he knew I did that."

"Or maybe he'd let you *drain* him some other way." She laughed.

"God, be quiet." The heat in my face increased.

"I'm just sayin'." She put her hand over the mouthpiece, and I heard muffled voices. Then she came back on the line. "Damn. I have to go. Steven wants to go get breakfast to soothe his massive hang over."

I laughed. "Fair enough."

"I'll call you tomorrow. Stay safe."

"I will." I hung up and went to my computer to work. I had four people waiting for me in a chat room on the psychic network website I worked for. Since I didn't want to be interrupted, I turned off my cell and grabbed a stack of tarot cards.

I shuffled the deck as I chatted with the first client. She was a young girl struggling with a breakup. I tried to concentrate on her problems and give her insight, but when The Tower card continually came up, I couldn't help but feel that card was more directed at me than her.

Once she'd left the chat room, I shuffled the deck several times. When The Tower card once more appeared, uneasiness rippled through me. I studied the colorful card in my hand. The Tower card depicted an ominous black tower being struck by bolts of lightning. The Tower appeared to be crumbling, and many psychics interpreted that to symbolize unexpected upheavals or disruptions in one's life.

For whatever reason, my thoughts immediately went to the weird phone call I'd received in the hospital. While I felt silly even contemplating for one second whether the old man's warning about a prophesy could be true, I couldn't shake the feeling the card was connected to his phone call. I was unsettled by why that particular card had continuously surfaced during the reading with the young girl and even after she'd left. Even shuffling hadn't helped.

Of course, The Tower card wasn't *necessarily* negative. It wasn't definitively warning me of doom heading my way. The card could also be interpreted as a card of change and necessary transformation. Was the universe hinting to me, not-so-subtly, that I was stuck in a rut? That I needed to embrace change? Was Claire right about me needing to open myself up to people more? Or was the universe telling me to give up my psychic gig and instead get a job at Walmart?

With a groan I set the cards face down. Psychoanalyzing myself wouldn't put food on the table. I needed to get some actual work done. I'd worry about possible messages to me from the other side later, after I'd made some money.

I spent the next two hours helping a grieving widower, a woman going through a divorce, and a young man who wasn't sure he should take a job offer. By the time I'd helped all of my clients, my head ached and my stitches hurt. But at least I'd made some money.

I shut down my laptop and went into the kitchen to make myself something to eat. I was staring into my mostly empty fridge when the doorbell rang. I glanced down at my skimpy boxers. I'd never changed out of what I slept in since I hadn't planned on interacting in person with the living today.

I crept toward the door, hoping I could peek out the front window and see who it was without being seen. My unwelcome visitor knocked on the door and rang the bell again several more times. I frowned, feeling grumpy that anyone was bothering me when I felt this shitty.

I looked through the blinds but whoever it was seemed to be just out of sight. They knocked and rang the bell some more, and I moved back toward the kitchen wondering if I should go get my robe on and answer the door or just continue to ignore them.

"Lorenzo? Are you all right?" A muffled male voice called through the door.

I was shocked to recognize Ian's voice. I approached the door and unlocked it, opening it a tiny crack. "Ian?"

His jaw was tight. "Why didn't you answer your phone?"

I studied him, taking in his frazzled appearance. "My phone?"

"Yes. I tried calling you a bunch of times."

"Oh." I frowned. "You did?"

"Yes." He raked his hand through his blond hair. "But you didn't answer. You scared me."

"Sorry. I was talking to a friend. I didn't know it was you calling." I grimaced. "Then I shut my phone off so I could work."

His worried gaze scanned my face. "I'm so glad you're okay."

"I am. I'm fine." I was self-conscious about being half-dressed, but I felt bad leaving him standing out on the porch. "Um . . . did you want to come in?"

Shrugging, he looked down at his shoes. "I don't want to intrude."

Hesitating, I looked over my shoulder toward my bedroom. "I need to get some clothes on. I wasn't expecting visitors."

He nodded and his gaze dropped to my bare chest. "Okay." A warm rush rolled through me at the interested look in his eyes, but then he looked over my head instead. "I'll just wait here."

"Be right back." I hurried away and headed through the beaded curtain to my bedroom. I grabbed a T-shirt that was hung on a chair and pulled it over my head. Feeling breathless, I tugged on jeans and raked my hands through my messy hair. I wasn't sure why I felt so flustered. I guess it had been a long time since a guy had come to my house for anything other than a psychic reading. It was weird to think Ian had been so worried about me.

When I opened the front door I found Ian waiting patiently, leaning against a pillar on the front porch. "I'm decent now," I joked.

He smiled and cautiously entered the house. "I'm sorry to barge in on you. I really was just going to call you to check on you. When you didn't answer . . . I started picturing you surrounded by ghosts and you being too weak to fend them off. Kind of triggered anxiety in me. Even though I'm still not sure I believe in the whole supernatural thing, I couldn't stop worrying."

"It's okay. I'm sorry I made you worry. I had my phone turned off. To be completely honest, I didn't expect you to really call."

He frowned. "But I said I would."

"Yes." I grimaced. "I thought you were just being polite."

"Oh." He rubbed the back of his neck. "Uh . . . no. I said I'd call to check on you because I truly intended to do that."

"Okay, well, I . . . I'm sorry you came all the way over here for nothing."

He winced. "Thank goodness it was for nothing. The alternative is not good."

"Oh, yeah. Of course that's true."

"I'm just glad you're okay. I had visions of you slipping in the shower." He grimaced. "God. That sounded so pervy. I don't mean that I was envisioning you in the shower." His laugh was awkward. "I'm making it worse, aren't I?"

I held up my fingers as if measuring something. "Little bit." I smiled. "I just made a pot of coffee. Would you like some?"

He looked relieved to change the subject. "Yes, please." He followed me into the tiny kitchen just off my main work space.

His expression was impartial as he took in the earthy brown, tan, and orange tones of the linoleum tile. He next examined the worn oak cabinets and the avocado green stove and fridge. The top of the fridge housed an embarrassing number of boxes of Captain Crunch cereal. But thankfully, he made no comment about my guilty pleasure. He gazed up at the floating shelf over the sink where herbs grew in small ceramic pots.

"I keep meaning to grow my own herbs," he said.

"They taste better than the dried stuff." It was cheaper to grow my own herbs too, but I didn't bother mentioning that.

He peered out the window above the sink, and I hoped he didn't notice the dirty dishes stacked in the rack. "This street is such a weird mix of businesses and houses," he said.

"Yeah. It's zoned commercial and residential, although the city wants to buy up the homes. Mayor Spears wants to revamp the area into just businesses, but not sure she'll be successful. Some of the people have lived here for decades." I stood on my tip toes to grab him a mug out of the cupboard—and winced. The movement pulled my stiches a bit.

"Most of the houses look fairly run down."

"Yeah. It's really just elderly people living in them mostly. It's kind of a shame. It used to be a really nice street with lots of families and healthy green lawns." A smile touched my lips. "I remember kids riding their bikes on the sidewalk, and the ice cream truck used to park up at the end of the lane, playing the same song over and over."

"Sounds nice."

I poured his coffee into a big yellow mug. "It was." I looked up. "Cream or sugar?"

"Just cream."

I added the dairy product and stirred. "I guess that's just how life is—full of change."

"Yeah." He took the cup from me and our fingers brushed. "But sometimes that's a good thing."

"Maybe." I sipped my coffee and studied his angular features. He had an aristocratic look about him, with high cheek bones and a long slender nose. His blond hair brushed his collar, and his white shirt hugged his lean torso. My stomach tightened when he glanced up and caught me looking at him.

"It must be pretty deserted here at night. Don't you ever feel nervous all alone on this street?"

I shook my head. "No. Not really." Although, I had to admit after that strange incident with the green stone, and my run-in with that malevolent spirit down the street, I did feel less secure lately. But no one else had tried coming in my house since. At least, not that I was aware of.

He took a drink from his beverage and after he swallowed he asked, "And you do live alone, right?"

I smirked. "Well, except for my boyfriend, Guido. I keep him in the closet. Would you like to meet him?"

He laughed sheepishly. "Was it too obvious I was fishing to see if you have a boyfriend?"

"Kind of. But I'm not worried about being here alone, and you shouldn't worry either. I'm a big boy. I can take care of myself."

"I'm sure you can." He set his coffee on the counter. "Why are you single?"

I stiffened at his bluntness and countered, "Why are *you* single?"

He smiled. "Touché."

"And really, can you ask me that knowing I'm a professional psychic? I hang out with dead people. That's not exactly something that would make me popular on a dating app. Anyway, being single isn't so bad." I stood a little straighter. "It beats sitting through dinner, making boring conversation with a stranger."

"I agree. But I get the feeling that isn't actually why you're single."

I stiffened. "No?"

"No." He narrowed his eyes. "I think there's something much deeper going on with you."

I avoided his gaze. "I'm just not in a place in my life where I want or need a relationship."

"How old are you?"

I faked a gasp. "How dare you, sir."

His lips twitched. "Here, let me go first. I'm thirty."

"God, you're ancient."

He laughed. "Now it's your turn." His expression was expectant.

I tapped my finger on the side of my coffee cup. "I'm twenty-five."

"You look younger."

"Well, at least your momma raised you with manners."

He smiled and gestured to the kitchen chairs. "Do you mind if I sit?"

"Not at all."

He sat at the small kitchen table, crossing his legs. "How about you tell me about yourself?"

I laughed. "Really? What is this, an interview?"

"Don't mock me." He fake-pouted. "I just want to get to know you. Don't make me work so hard. It'll hurt my delicate feelings."

I leaned against the counter across from him, trying not to smile. His confidence was attractive. I found myself drawn in even though that was the last thing I wanted. "You definitely don't have low self-esteem."

"That's a good thing. The last thing you want is a doctor with poor self-esteem."

"Good point." We held each other's gaze.

"I wasn't always the confident stud you see before you." He smirked. "In high school I too had the usual insecurities. I assumed nobody would ever love me for me."

"Really?"

"Yes. My high school experience wasn't completely perfect."

"Please tell me you at least had acne."

He shook his head. "No. But I had braces. Does that help?"

"It's a start."

"I was more serious than most kids in my class. I was driven. Even at that age I knew exactly what I wanted to do with my life." He stared off into space. "Socially, I was popular, maybe because my family had money." He laughed. "But I never knew if kids liked me for me or because they wanted to swim in my pool and play video games on my Play Station console."

"Poor baby."

He shot me a narrowed glance. "Be nice."

"I'll try." I stood and took my empty cup to the sink. "It must have been great to know what you wanted your life to look like at such a young age."

"Not really my whole life. Just my career."

"So you're not your job?" I leaned against the counter and crossed my arms.

"Of course there are things about me as a person that make me good at what I do." He shrugged. "I'm someone who thinks things through and analyzes stuff. It's my personality. But those same qualities that might make me a good doctor interfere with me finding a significant other."

I tilted my head, interested in what he was saying. "Why?"

"Because I have trouble just going with the flow." He waved his hand, and the green jewel in his ring caught my eye. "You know, just letting things go where they will."

"Is that a nice way of saying you're controlling?"

He frowned. "I don't think I'm controlling. But I like a plan. I like structure."

"And that's why you're single?"

"Maybe."

"So you want a real relationship?" I arched one brow.

He shrugged and studied his cuticles. "I'm open to the idea."

I snorted. "Bullshit. That isn't what the nurses at your hospital say."

His face tinted pink. "Excuse me?"

"While I was in the hospital I heard a lot about you. Whether I wanted to or not."

He uncrossed his legs and leaned forward, looking horrified. "What are you talking about?"

I laughed outright because he looked so mortified. "The nurses noticed that you came to see me a few times. It sparked some interesting conversations."

"With you?"

"Yep."

Standing, he approached me. His obvious shock made me regret mentioning the conversations I'd had with the nurses. But after all the little stories I'd heard about him being commitment-phobic, it had been impossible to keep my mouth shut when he was sitting there pretending to be open to a serious relationship.

"What kind of interesting conversations?" he asked.

His close proximity made me nervous. His eyes seemed to look through me, and I could feel the heat of his body only inches from mine. "Well . . . maybe conversation is the wrong word. I didn't really say much. They just told me a few stories."

"Why would they gossip about me? I'm perfectly nice to them." His jaw tensed. "Yet they were talking about me behind my back?"

I twisted my lips. "I shouldn't have said anything. Sorry. They weren't being mean or anything. They really like you."

"What did they say exactly?"

"Does it really matter?" I winced.

"Yes. It does to me. If it wasn't mean, as you say, then why not tell me?"

"Fine." I sighed. "The consensus is you don't want a serious relationship. A few of them said you've dated some really cool guys in the last year, but you always found fault with them."

He frowned and his cheeks turned pink again. "Just because someone is 'cool' doesn't mean they're right for you long term."

"I agree." I felt a little breathless when he turned his intense gaze back onto me. "But they think you have a check list. If the person doesn't meet every criterion, then you dump them."

"That's absurd." He frowned.

My laugh was awkward. "Really this isn't any of my business. Like I said, they just volunteered stuff because you came to see me a few times."

Being so close to him was doing weird things to my knees. But before I could put any space between us, he grabbed my wrist. His hard fingers sank into my skin making me even more breathless.

He had a funny look on his face. "I don't have a check-list."

I swallowed nervously. "We all have things we need." I grimaced. "I mean in another person. Nobody wants to just settle."

"Exactly." He nodded.

"Nothing wrong with that," I said softly.

"Not at all." His voice was hushed.

I licked my lips. "We want what we want."

"Yeah. We want . . . what we want." He tugged me gently against his body and I pulled in a sharp breath. His other hand pressed the small of my back, and his eyes narrowed. "Why do I feel like I know you?"

"No idea." I knew he wanted to kiss me. Maybe I should have pushed him away, but I was curious. Tempted. I wanted to know what he tasted like, and I didn't seem able to think of any reasons why we shouldn't kiss.

He lowered his head, his mouth just inches from mine. His breath was warm and infused with coffee, and my body tingled with anticipation. It felt like this had always been inevitable. I had no idea why I felt that, especially considering how he'd been when we first met. But since that day, I'd had trouble getting him out of my mind.

He hesitated as if he was uncertain about kissing me. I think I surprised us both when I raised up on my toes and pressed my mouth to his. With a little groan, he gave in and claimed my mouth.

CHAPTER SEVEN

The kiss was good. Really fucking nice. His warm mouth was insistent without being aggressive. There was just a hint of tongue, but enough that it turned me on. I pressed closer, wanting more even though I knew this was nuts. We hardly knew each other, and yet his taste was almost familiar.

He broke the kiss first, looking embarrassed. "I'm sorry."

"Don't be sorry," I mumbled, cheeks hot. I was embarrassed I'd kissed him because I was sending him mixed signals. I didn't want to get involved with him. That wasn't what I was looking for. But sticking my tongue in his mouth probably wasn't getting that point across.

Wincing, he said huskily, "I swear I only came by to check on you. Not to hit on you."

"Look, I'm not mad or upset," I said. "We're both adults. But I don't want that. I don't . . . need that. I'm sorry I kissed you. I shouldn't have. Listen, I've thought over your dinner invitation, and I don't think it's a good idea. It has nothing to do with the kiss. I'm just not in a good place for anything. It's not personal. I simply don't want to get involved with you or anyone."

He narrowed his eyes. "What's the big deal?"

"I know. It's not a big deal." I avoided his gaze. "I just think the timing is off."

"Why do I get the feeling there would be no right time?"

"I'm sure you have lots of other options. If the nurses are anything to go by, that is a certainty. I appreciate you giving me a ride home from the hospital. I appreciate you coming to check on me, although it wasn't necessary. But I think it's best to just drop things here."

"Is this the brush-off?"

I moved away from him and said, "Come on, Ian. We don't exactly run in the same circles. I can't even think why you'd want to have dinner with me. It's illogical."

He lifted one shoulder. "I like you. I didn't at first. Well, that's not really true. I didn't trust you at first. But I do now. I'd like to know you better."

"That's flattering and all," I rumbled, "but I just don't think it's a good idea." I did find him attractive. There was no denying that. However, I just didn't want to invest time and energy getting closer to him. It had no future.

Isn't that what I like? No strings. No future.

"I don't give up easy," he said with a stubborn jut to his jaw.

I smiled unwillingly. "Why are you so persistent?"

He wrinkled his brow. "I don't really know. I just feel like I'm supposed to be in your life."

I chuffed. "So now you're a psychic?"

He grimaced. "No. It's just a feeling I can't shake."

His sincerity washed over me. He wasn't lying. He truly did feel that way, I could read it. But why would he feel that way? It made no sense. "I'll . . . I'll think about it some more. Maybe I'll change my mind." I moved to the door as I spoke.

"Are you just saying that to get rid of me?" he asked suspiciously.

I gave a guilty laugh. "No." I opened the door. "But I am tired and I have work to do."

"Okay, I can take a hint." He stepped out onto the porch, but he hesitated. "Don't believe everything you hear, Lorenzo. Nurses are huge gossips."

"I'll keep that in mind."

"And keep your phone on in case I want to check on you," he said.

I sighed. "Ian, listen, you don't need to panic if you call and I don't answer. I shut my phone off when I work."

He frowned. "Maybe you should just put it on vibrate."

I laughed. "Maybe you should just calm the hell down and not assume the worst."

He walked down the steps with a self-conscious grin. "I'm a doctor. We always assume the worst."

"Have a good day, Doc." I closed the door and leaned against it. The memory of his warm mouth against mine still lingered. That familiarity still persisted.

I went back to my laptop and picked up my tarot deck, choosing a card at random: The Ace of Cups, signifying the awakening of new feelings.

Ian said he felt driven to know me better. Why? What cosmic force was compelling him to pursue me, when it was so clear we weren't a good fit?

Scowling, I slid the card back into the deck. I'd wasted enough time on Ian. With a grunt, I headed to my computer to see if I had any online clients waiting. Work was what I needed to focus on. Not men who confused me and made me feel things I didn't want to feel.

A week later I sat with a new client, Mr. Piddleson. He'd been referred to me by Mrs. Beckom. I was thrilled she'd recommended me to one of her friends, until I found out he was yet another lost pet case. Mr. Piddleson was a man in his fifties with a bald head so shiny I was sure he waxed it. His eyes were a muddy brown, and he was a fidgety guy, always shifting in his seat and flicking his eyes around the room.

"Tweetie wouldn't just fly away for no reason." Mr. Piddleson clasped his hands and leaned forward. "Something happened to scare him away like that."

I nodded. "But . . . um . . . you say Tweetie is a wild bird?"

"Yes, but we're buddies. He always stays right near the birdbath. The most he does is fly to the corner of the yard to eat some of the apples when they're in season." His hands trembled, showing he was obviously agitated.

I wanted to help him if I could, but I wasn't sure how to locate the bird. If it were even still alive. Generally, I could hunt down the animals because the client had someone who had passed, someone who was close to the lost animal. By contacting them, I could often find where the lost pet was hiding. I suspected that wouldn't work in this case because the bird wasn't his actual pet, and Mr. Piddleson was clearly still alive.

"Do you have something of his?" I felt stupid even asking. It wasn't like I could talk to the bird directly, but an item of his might give me an idea if the bird was alive or not.

He held out a tiny bell tied to a red string. "This is what he wore to my Christmas party."

I took the bell from him. "You dressed him up?"

He widened his eyes. "Well, it was a party, Lorenzo. Everybody was dressed up."

"Of course. Forgive me. I was just surprised a wild bird would let you that close."

"But I told you. We're buddies." He reached into his pocket and tugged out his wallet. "See, here's a photo of Tweetie. Isn't he a handsome bird?"

I studied the crinkled photo of what appeared to be a European Starling. Its striking green, purple, and blue plumage was easy to identify because they were very common in the area. "He's very—er—handsome."

Mr. Piddleson sighed. "I miss him so much. Please help me find him. Life just isn't the same without him around."

"I'll do my best." I cleared my throat. "Just give me a moment to see if I get anything off of the bell."

"Certainly. Do your thing." He sat back, clasping his hands over his round belly.

I closed my eyes, praying I got a glimpse of something. I wasn't sure I could get Mr. Piddleson out of here if I didn't at least throw him a bone.

"Anything at all?" he asked.

I opened one eye. "Give me just a sec. I need a little more time." I closed my eyes and opened my mind to any spirits that might know Mr. Piddleson and by default, Tweetie. There was a faint tugging at the edges of my mind. "I think I'm getting something."

"Oh, good."

As the energy grew stronger, I recognized it was a child. "Can you help me?" I asked softly. "We're trying to find Tweetie." My chest tingled as the child's spirit crawled inside of me like a human jungle gym.

"Jasper got him." The little boy spoke gruffly through me. "He grabbed her in his mouth."

Damn. I hated giving clients bad news.

Mr. Piddleson gasped. "No. Jasper hasn't been around for months."

I wasn't sure who Jasper was—a dog or a cat maybe? But spirits rarely lied, and if this child's ghost said Jasper got Tweetie, then Jasper got Tweetie. I felt the child trying to speak through me again so I relaxed my throat muscles. "He ain't dead. He's hiding in the bushes."

Mr. Piddleson jumped up, and the child's spirit receded. "Where? What bush?" He grasped his head. "I have many bushes in my yard."

Irritation prickled me. He needed to calm down or the child wouldn't come back. But I couldn't speak yet to tell him that because the child was half-in and half-out of me. Finally the warm energy seeped back in. "Her wing is hurt. She's hiding in the yellow."

"In the yellow?" Mr. Piddleson scratched his jaw.

"Yep."

"I don't understand." Mr. Piddleson wrinkled his brow.

"In the little yellow bells, bells, bells," I sang in a sing-song voice. I felt silly, but if this was how the spirit of the kid chose to communicate, there wasn't much I could do about it.

Mr. Piddleson looked befuddled. "The yellow … hmmm."

"I suck on them, and the sweet stuff gets in my mouth." I laughed gleefully and waved my hands at the behest of my visitor. "They're so good."

"There's nothing like that in the yard right now." Mr. Piddleson sighed. "In the spring I have honeysuckle." He leaned toward me. "Do you mean the honeysuckle, child?"

"In the yellow." The child began to leave me, and my energy drained with him.

"But the honeysuckle isn't in bloom." He pulled his brows together.

I slumped as the spirit left me completely. My body was chilled, and I trembled as I rested my elbows on the table. "Maybe they were blooming when he was alive." I straightened and sucked in a cleansing breath. "Maybe the child was too young to understand seasons."

"It really was a child's spirit that you spoke to?"

"Yes."

"Who was he?"

I shrugged. "I don't know. I reached out and he was there."

He squinted. "I don't remember any kids dying on my street."

"This spirit could have been from any era. He's just around your home."

Mr. Piddleson nodded, looking a little unsettled. "Really? He's just *lingering* there?"

"That's what many spirits do."

"I see." He shivered. "Well . . . it . . . it was kind of him to help me."

"Yes. He's harmless. You didn't know he was there before, and you won't see him now."

"Okay. Good." He seemed relieved, but then he straightened suddenly. "I must get home." With shaking hands, he opened his wallet and tossed down some cash. "If that child is right then Tweetie needs me!" He raced to the front door and slammed it behind him.

I sat where I was for a little while, allowing time for some of my strength to seep back. There was no rush. Mr. Piddleson was my only in-person client of the day. When I didn't feel like I'd collapse if I stood, I went into the kitchen and made some coffee. Scooping the grounds and pouring the water was soothing. I always felt slightly depressed after a spirit used my body. I leaned on the sink and stared in a daze at the dark coffee brewing into the pot.

The doorbell rang and, stifling a groan, I forced myself to go answer. When I found Ian standing on my doorstep, the rush of excitement that shot through me was unsettling. No matter how many times I told myself I had no interest in him, my body didn't seem to agree. Tonight, he looked even hotter than usual in a cream-colored Bottega Veneta V-neck polo sweater and dark jeans.

"Hey." My gaze dropped to the crock pot he held. "What are you doing here?"

"I brought dinner." He smiled and gestured with his chin to his coat pocket where a bottle of wine was nestled. "And beverages."

"What?" I blinked at him. "Why?"

"You need to eat."

I frowned. "I do eat."

"Oh, yeah? Me too. How about we eat together?"

I couldn't help laughing at how unfazed he was.

"Truth is, I wanted to see you." He winced and glanced down at the crockpot. "Any chance I can come in? My fingers are about to fall off."

"Oh. Sorry. Come in." I stepped back and he brushed past me. The scent of his ginger-lemon cologne made my stomach flip-flop. Rejecting him would have been so much easier if I wasn't attracted to him.

"It's been a week, and I haven't heard a thing from you." He set the crockpot on the counter and pulled the wine from his jacket. Then he faced me. "Sorry for barging in. But I knew if I left it up to you, I'd never see you again."

I lifted my shoulder. "I just wouldn't want to lead you on."

He narrowed his eyes and approached. When he was a foot from me he stopped. "People need other people."

"Do they?"

"That's what the magazines say."

"I like being alone." I did too. It was much easier being on my own. Only caring about my own needs.

"Sure, but I know you enjoy my company."

I laughed gruffly. "Oh, really?"

His lips twitched. "There's no point in denying it. Let's just have a nice dinner and find out some stuff about one another."

"You mean, let's do the very thing I told you I didn't want to do?"

"Come on, Lorenzo. It's a meal and some conversation. What could it hurt?"

I was too tired to fight him. "Fine."

"Excellent." He didn't seem at all concerned about my lack of enthusiasm.

I gestured to the coffee pot. "Would you like some? I just made a fresh pot."

"If it's all the same to you, I'd rather have some wine."
He frowned. "You drink a lot of coffee."

"It helps give me energy. The spirits drain me."

"In what way?" Ian asked.

"Well, hosting them in my body or interacting with them even outside of my body sucks my energy, both physically and mentally. Holding the connection is exhausting. Necessary, but very tiring."

He appeared unsure of how to respond to that, but then said, "Still, too much caffeine isn't good for you."

"Some might say any alcohol is too much alcohol."

Ian grimaced. "Fair enough. Some of my colleagues would say that. I happen to think a little bit of red wine on occasion is okay."

I laughed. "Yeah, me too."

"Then join me in a glass of wine."

I shrugged. "Okay."

He smiled. Do you have a bottle opener?"

"No. I usually just chew the cork off with my teeth." I smirked, pointing to the wine opener hanging from a nail near the sink.

"Smart ass."

"Who? Me?" I got two glasses from the cupboard. "I don't know what you mean."

"Uh huh." He widened his eyes as he looked at the glasses I set down in front of him. "Are those *Moser* glasses?"

"Moser?" I stroked the stem of one glass, admiring the iridescent green color of the goblet. "I have no idea. I got them at a garage sale."

"What?" He looked bewildered as he picked up the blue version. "Are you serious? Moser is a prestigious Czech glass manufacturer. If those are authentic Moser glasses, they're very expensive."

"They are? I just thought they were pretty," I murmured. "I like pretty things, even though I can't usually afford them."

He peered at the glass closely. "It has the acid stamp. I think these are authentic Moser."

I blinked at him, almost uneasy at the thought the glasses were valuable. "Now I'm afraid I'll break one. I never thought twice about that before."

He laughed, still looking surprised. "Well, count yourself lucky because those are a rare find at a garage sale."

My hand shook slightly as I poured wine into the glasses. "I'll guard them with my life."

"Well, don't do that."

I smiled and handed him his wine.

He took it, still admiring the beauty of the glass. Eventually he lost interest in the glassware and he met my gaze. "How was your day?"

"Fine. I just got finished reuniting a lonely old man with his pet bird, Tweetie. At least, I hope they'll be reunited."

"I see." He narrowed his eyes. "I'm sorry, did you say you were trying to locate a bird named . . . *Tweetie*?"

"You're jealous of my exciting life, aren't you?"

"Totally." He sipped his wine, his expression thoughtful. "I still can't wrap my head around you . . . channeling spirits. Although, the idea of it does fascinate me. I know you believe you have powers, and I have no way to prove you don't, so . . . I'm willing to entertain the option that they're real. Sort of. But I'm not fully convinced."

I studied him. "Then why do you want to know me better? It makes no sense. If my psychic ability isn't real then I'm either nuts, or a shyster."

"I told you before, I feel like I'm supposed to watch out for you."

I chuffed and moved away from him. "I don't need watching over. Least of all from a skeptic."

He sighed and opened his mouth to respond, when someone banged on the front door.

Frowning, I stared at the door. "Who could that be?"

"You're not expecting anyone?" Ian asked.

"No. And I don't take drop-in clients at night." I moved to the door, feeling a vague sense of uneasiness. I didn't know whoever was on the other side of the door, but I did feel they were agitated. "Maybe it's a late day delivery."

"Maybe an emergency drop shipment of tarot cards?" Ian said sardonically.

I gave him a dirty look and then opened the door.

On the porch stood an elderly man. His stark white hair was unkempt and his bloodshot eyes wide. He wore a rumpled green suit and white tennis shoes. He glanced around nervously, and when his gaze landed on me he whispered, "It's really you."

"Can I . . . help you?" The sensation of uneasiness intensified as I met his pale gaze.

"You don't remember me?"

I hesitated. "I'm sorry. No." His voice was vaguely familiar. "Wait. Did you call me recently?"

"Yes," he responded, looking pleased. "You remember that?"

"Uh, yes?" I laughed awkwardly, taking a step back. He seemed to think remembering the call was a good thing. In truth, it simply made me believe he might be a stalker.

He licked his lips, wincing slightly. "I must speak to you. It's urgent."

I flinched as his raw anxiety prickled over my skin and through my head like thousands of tiny needles. "Well . . . if you'd like to make an appointment for tomorrow—"

"Tomorrow will be too late," he rasped, wiping perspiration from his face with a white cotton handkerchief. "He's closing in. He knows I have it."

I was relieved when Ian approached us. He didn't say anything, but just having him there as backup relaxed me.

"Who is closing in?" I murmured, trying to understand what the old man was talking about. "Who is 'he'?"

"Sableth, of course."

I scowled. "Who?"

"I don't have time to explain everything. If only you remembered." He panted, slumping against the doorjamb. "He's probably watching us now." He groaned. "In fact, I'm sure he is."

It didn't take psychic powers to see this man was very ill. He was deteriorating right in front of me. His skin was the color of gray putty and his lips tinged with blue. "You're obviously sick. Maybe I should call an ambulance?" I glanced over my shoulder at Ian. "In fact, my friend here is a doctor."

Ian spoke up. "Is there anything I can do to help?"

The old man's frazzled gaze settled on Ian. "Do not fail him."

I met Ian's bewildered gaze as he muttered, "Fail him? What in the world?"

"Remember," the man whispered, coughing raggedly. "Sableth revels in anguish and despair."

"Sir, I . . . you . . . do you want to sit down?" I gestured to a wicker chair on the porch.

"No. I'm fine." The old man wiped at his sweaty face.

He was definitely not fine. His gray color was really beginning to worry me. "Let me get you a drink of water."

"I don't have time for that. You're our last hope," he cried, breathing heavily. "He's found you. Don't you understand? He knows you've returned as prophesied."

I wasn't sure what to say. He was obviously unhinged. Even if he believed every word he was saying, he had to be insane.

Moving closer, Ian said, "Sir, you should try to calm down."

"Yeah." I nodded. "I'll call someone to come get you. Do you have any friends or family I can contact?"

"No." He grabbed hold of my shirt and tugged me closer. "Please just listen. Try and remember. You must try." His breath had a hint of chemicals and garlic. "This time he'll get his way if you don't heed my warning."

I managed to pull away and took two steps back. "Listen, I'm not sure what's going on here, but—"

"You can't imagine the havoc he'll wreak if he gets his hands on you this time. He won't stop until he gets what he wants. You must fight him. Use the Mossfire Stone. It's the only way," he hissed. Then, in a performance worthy of a horror movie, he gave a gut-wrenching gasp and lurched forward. Staggering, he fell face-forward onto the floor at my feet.

CHAPTER EIGHT

"Oh, my God." I stared down at him, frozen in horror.

Ian moved swiftly, kneeling over the still body of the man. He pressed his fingers to the side of the man's throat, searching for a pulse. Eventually he grunted and looked up grimly.

My mouth moved wordlessly, but then I finally croaked, "Is he dead?"

Ignoring my question, he rasped, "Call 911."

Ian moved swiftly, rolling the man onto his back. He tugged a packet from his wallet, unfolded it, and inserted something into the man's mouth. He began performing chest compressions, leaning down to puff two breaths into the thing between the man's lips every now and then.

Feeling dazed, I did as he requested. As I dialed the phone with shaking hands, I watched Ian from the kitchen.

Once my phone call ended, the only sounds in the room were those of Ian's grunts and breaths. While the spirit of the man didn't approach me to communicate, I felt him around us. I wanted to tell Ian it was too late, but suspected trying to save the man was how he was dealing with the situation.

Sirens in the distance grew louder, and then two burly paramedics tromped into my house through the open door. The next ten minutes were a blur of strangers crowding into my small home. In addition to the paramedics, two patrol officers also showed up. After giving my statement, I mostly stayed in the kitchen, trying not to get in the way. One of the cops knew Ian from the ER, and they had a quiet conversation near the body. After a bit, Ian joined me in the kitchen.

"He's deceased," he said quietly.

"Yes. I . . . I know."

He nodded, staring down at the floor. Shame radiated off of him, and his thoughts were all about what he could have done better.

"You did your best," I said softly. He probably didn't want my platitudes, but his guilt was so intense, I had to say something.

Ian's expression was grim and I was still in shock. While I spent a lot of time with the dead, I'd rarely seen an actual dead body. I felt queasy and did my best to avoid looking over to where the old man lay. I prayed his spirit wouldn't linger once they removed the corpse. It was a distinct possibility though.

"Something's not right," Ian muttered.

My nerves jangled at his words, but I wasn't exactly surprised at his comment. After all the cryptic things the old man had said, his death felt way too suspicious.

"Were you the one who called the police?" I asked.

He glanced at me. "I did. That was no ordinary heart attack."

"Oh."

While I knew calling the police had been the right thing to do, I dreaded them snooping around my home. I didn't have the best relationship with the cops. I'd had a problem last year when they had received an anonymous complaint about me, accusing me of petty theft. The charges had been bogus and ultimately dropped, but the cops didn't always agree with what cases the DA pursued. It was a small town and the odds of maybe running into an officer who knew about the petty theft charge wasn't out of the realm of possibility.

"We had to call them," Ian said.

"Yeah, I know." I gave the remaining cops a wary glance. "If that wasn't a heart attack, then all the things he told us could be connected to his death."

Ian frowned. "You don't think maybe he was just rambling because he was so sick?"

"He seemed convinced he was in danger. What if he wasn't mentally ill? What if someone really was after him?"

A muscle worked in Ian's cheek. "You seriously think a person named Sabath was after him—"

"*Sableth*," I said shortly.

"Whoever. You think his story was true about being chased by someone who revels in anguish and despair?" Ian's voice went up an octave with incredulity.

"I don't know." I grimaced, remembering the chemical scent on the old man's breath. "All I know is, he was scared of something he implied was supernatural, and now he's dead. Isn't that awfully coincidental?"

Ian shifted uneasily. "I can't help but think all the stuff he said was simply his brain misfiring from his impending death."

"It feels like something more," I murmured, shivering as I watched the body being carried out of my home. So far, the spirit of the man didn't seem to be manifesting, and I was relieved about that.

As they exited the house with the corpse, a tall middle-aged man entered the house, looking alert. He had close-cropped silver hair and sharp blue eyes. His polyester suit and the business-like way he carried himself made me think he had to be a cop. He approached us, his expression very serious.

"I'm looking for a Lorenzo Winston?" His tone was brusque.

My stomach clenched with nerves. "I'm Lorenzo."

"I'm Detective Monroe." He flashed credentials. As he tucked them away he studied me, pursing his lips. "How are you this evening, Mr. Winston?"

"Well—" I winced. "A man died in my house. My night could be better."

"Of course."

"I'm Dr. Ian Thatcher," Ian interjected. "I'm the one who called the police."

Detective Monroe studied Ian. "How do you two know each other?"

"Lorenzo and I are friends," Ian said smoothly. "We were about to have dinner when the old man knocked on the door."

Detective Monroe turned his gaze on me. "You didn't know the old man?"

"I have no idea who he was." I left out the part about the old man thinking he knew me. It had always been my experience telling the police less rather than more was the smart thing to do.

"Why do you suppose he knocked on your door?" Detective Monroe frowned.

"I have no idea."

"But you didn't know him?" Detective Monroe tugged a notepad from his suit pocket.

Didn't I just say that?

"No," I said politely, reining in my irritation. "Never saw him before in my life. Maybe he saw the lights on and that's what drew him to my house?"

"Hmmm. Maybe." Detective Monroe scribbled something on his pad.

"The old man said some odd things." Ian rubbed the back of his neck.

"Like what?" Detective Monroe perked up.

Sighing, Ian said, "He implied he was being chased by someone named Sableth."

Detective Monroe grunted. "Come again?"

Ian grimaced. "That's the name he used. He said that person wanted something from him. He also implied Lorenzo might be in danger."

The detective frowned. "What kind of danger?"

Ian rasped, "I think he was babbling because he was dying. I wouldn't take anything he said seriously. I mean, he seemed to think he knew Lorenzo, even though Lorenzo didn't recognize him."

I gave Ian an impatient look. If he kept saying shit like that the detective was going to start thinking I was involved somehow. That I was lying about knowing the old man. "Look, the bottom line is I didn't know the guy. He was dying and he said some crazy things. I'm sure if you ID him and check things out, you'll see there was no connection between us."

"I'll definitely do that." Detective Monroe's blue eyes were shrewd.

"There's a possibility he might have been poisoned," Ian said.

"Is that right?" Detective Monroe flicked his cool gaze to Ian. It struck me he didn't seem surprised. "What makes you think that?"

Ian frowned. "The odor on his breath and the discoloration around his mouth. I've seen plenty of heart attack cases in my career. That was no simple coronary event."

"Interesting." Detective Monroe rocked back on his heels, surveying the small room. "Did he have anything to eat or drink while he was here?"

I narrowed my eyes. "No. We told you what happened. He knocked on my door, said some crazy shit, and then fell dead on the floor. I didn't serve him food or beverages. There wasn't time."

"I had to ask, Mr. Winston," Detective Monroe said. "You two were the last people to see him alive."

"Okay, fair enough," I said tersely. "But we didn't know him and we didn't do anything to him. If he was poisoned, it had to be someone else who did that. Maybe the person who he thought was chasing him."

The detective grunted. "Do you know anyone named Sableth?"

"No, I do not." I was starting to worry Detective Monroe was one of those cops who liked to make the crime fit the person, rather than the other way around.

Detective Monroe glanced at Ian. "How about you? You know anyone by that name? Could be the last name of one of your patients?"

"The name doesn't ring a bell." Ian shrugged.

"Did the old man have any ID on him?" I asked.

"Apparently not." Detective Monroe tucked his pad and pen into the pocket of his suit coat. "We'll figure out who he is."

"I hope so." I was praying the detective was wrapping things up.

"One thing's for sure," Ian said, "Whether he was talking gibberish or not, he was legitimately terrified, and he definitely believed his own story."

"Hmmm. Well, once we identify him, we'll look into his phone records and texts to see if there was anyone threatening him."

I froze as I suddenly remembered the phone call I'd received in the hospital. Were the police going to see that he'd called my cell and think I was lying about knowing him? I didn't know him. But that phone call could make me look guilty. Was it better to bring it up and get ahead of it or not mention it, hoping they didn't even see that he'd called me? Was it wrong of me to hope the Fox Harbor Police Department did shoddy work so that they'd miss that phone call to me?

I focused on Detective Monroe, wishing I could get a sense of where his head was at. Did he really suspect I was involved, or was he just sniffing around because that was his job?

Unfortunately, Detective Monroe wasn't someone I could read easily. Nothing about me and this case came to me. All I could get was a vague sense that his feet hurt because his shoes were too small, and he was looking forward to taking a hot shower when he got home after his shift ended.

"I'll undoubtedly have more questions for you two," Detective Monroe said.

"That's fine." Ian nodded agreeably.

Not feeling nearly as affable as Ian, I didn't respond.

"We're releasing the scene to you, Mr. Winston." Detective Monroe knitted his salt and pepper brows. "If you remember anything else, call me." He handed me a card as he spoke. "If I don't get back to you immediately, be patient. Our little city has had more than its share of violent crime lately, and our department is small."

Detective Monroe stepped out onto the porch. Moths dive bombed him as they circled the yellow bug light above his head. He tugged the collar of his peacoat tighter around his neck and met my gaze. His eyes reflected the light oddly, appearing to almost glow like a cat's. But then he looked away, and I assumed I'd imagined it. "I advise you to lock your doors."

"Okay." I shivered, glancing around uneasily.

Ian and I watched the detective drive away, and we went back inside. I gave the spot near the door where the old man had died a wide berth and headed into the kitchen. Ian joined me.

"Do you want me to go?" he asked.

Since I hadn't invited him to begin with, I should have wanted him to leave. But after what had happened, I really didn't want to be alone. I found his calm presence reassuring. "Why don't you stay for a bit? We can have a drink."

Ian smiled, appearing happy that I wanted him to stay. "Shall I pour more wine?"

"How about something stronger than wine?" I suggested.

Ian's eyes brightened. "Sure."

I went to the small pantry and found the bottle of single malt twelve-year-old whiskey Claire had given me for my birthday. I set the bottle on the table and went to grab two crystal tumblers. "I was saving this for a special occasion, but I don't think I've ever needed a good strong drink more."

Ian winced. "It's been a weird evening. Not what I expected when I came here tonight."

"No." I sat down, grabbing the bottle and uncorking it. "I'm still in shock."

"Me too." Ian watched me, his expression thoughtful.

I poured us each a generous serving of the amber liquid. I held my glass up and said, "Cin, cin."

"What's that mean?"

"It's Italian for cheers."

He bumped his glass gently with mine. "I'll drink to that." He sipped his whiskey and nodded. "That's nice."

"It is," I agreed.

He studied me. "You look like you have Italian heritage, but your last name is English."

"Yeah, my mother is of Italian descent. Dad is English."

"But you mentioned before you're not close to them?"

I dropped my gaze. "Nope."

He took another drink and set the tumbler down. "Can I ask you something?"

"Yes."

"Why didn't you mention the phone call?"

My stomach tensed. "Phone call?" I'd assumed he was going to ask me more personal questions about my family, so I was thrown.

"Yeah, the call from the old man. I overheard you and the old man talking about him calling you before. Why didn't you mention the phone call to Detective Monroe?"

I avoided his gaze. "It didn't seem important."

"Seriously?" He narrowed his eyes.

Stalling, I tasted my drink, letting the notes of brown sugar and oaky vanilla bathe my tongue. Once I'd swallowed, I said, "I didn't need Detective Monroe any more interested in me than he already was."

"But that call could be an important clue."

"How?" I frowned. "I didn't know him, Ian. I have no idea why he called me."

"Sure, but the fact remains that he did call you."

"He did. Yes. But I'm still not convinced he actually knew me. I certainly didn't recognize him. Maybe it was a case of mistaken identity. Or maybe he was a crazy stalker."

"You really think he was stalking you?" His tone said he didn't necessarily agree.

"All I know is I have no idea who he was. All that nonsense about Sableth bringing anguish and despair. The guy was obviously not right in the head."

"He did sound demented," murmured Ian, rolling his whiskey around in his glass.

Trying to change the subject I glanced at the long-forgotten crockpot on the counter. "I'm sorry you went to all the trouble of making dinner and then we never ate. It's been sitting out for hours at room temperature. I'd be afraid to eat it."

"No. Death by crock pot is definitely not how I want to go. Besides, it wasn't much trouble really. It was just some simple chicken casserole kind of thing I found on the internet."

I couldn't help smiling. "Awww, you looked up a recipe for me?"

He shrugged. "I needed an excuse to come see you."

His willingness to be open about his interest in me intrigued me. In the past, when I'd bothered to date, I'd gravitated to game player types. He was very different.

Warmer. That familiar attraction I felt for him fluttered through me. While I didn't want to have a relationship with him, or anyone for that matter, sometimes I was tempted to just start something sexual with him. He'd be a fun distraction. I had no doubt he'd be good in bed. His confidence was too high for someone who sucked at sex.

"What did the old man say to you on the phone?" Ian asked quietly.

"We're back to that again?"

"Yes."

I sighed. "I really wish you'd let it go."

"A man died in your home, Lorenzo. I don't see how either of us can let that go. Something is going on, and I worry you're at the center of it."

"If that's true, Detective Monroe will probably come knocking on my door again. Until then, I'd love to put it behind me."

He ignored me and said, "Could all of this be connected to . . . your work?"

"What do you mean?"

He grimaced. "I guess I wonder if maybe you poked your nose into the wrong psychic coffee clutch. Maybe you ruffled some ethereal feathers."

I squinted at him. "Are you asking if I accidentally unleashed the hellhounds or something?"

He laughed sheepishly. "Dabbling in the occult is rumored to be dangerous."

"It's never been dangerous before." I avoided his gaze as memories of that strange entity from the other day came back to me. I'd definitely felt threatened that day.

"What about your session with Aunt Agatha?" He frowned.

"That wasn't really dangerous," I lied. "It was more annoying than anything."

"You sure about that?" He looked unconvinced.

"Yes." I stood because it was easier to avoid his gaze that way. I instead went to look out the window over the sink. The night felt especially dark and oppressive tonight. There was only a sliver of a moon, and it was more humid than usual.

I was surprised when Ian joined me. He stood beside me, his shoulder lightly brushing mine. My pulse stuttered as the heat of his body reached me. It had been a long time since I'd been with a man. My senses were hyperaware of everything about him—his clean male scent, the raspy sound of his whiskey-infused breaths. It was impossible not to think about the kiss we'd shared.

He gulped the rest of his drink and set the glass down on the counter. Turning to me, he said breathlessly, "What would you think about me spending the night?"

CHAPTER NINE

"What?" I asked in strangled voice.

He smiled confidently. "You heard me. I'd like to stay the night."

I blinked at him. "Just like that?"

He lifted one shoulder nonchalantly. "You already know I'm attracted to you. It can't be that much of a surprise I'd like to sleep with you."

"Still . . . " I frowned. He wasn't wrong. I did know he was attracted to me. I was attracted to him too. But I wasn't sure I should take him up on his breathless suggestion, although I was tempted. While it would be nice to lose myself in meaningless sex and just put all the awfulness of the evening to bed, so to speak, did I want to risk getting romantically entangled with Ian?

"You don't think that a man dying here tonight ruins the mood?" I arched one brow.

He sighed. "On the contrary. It reminds me how happy I am to be alive."

"I see." While my outlook on life wasn't nearly as rosy as Ian's, it was true witnessing the old man take his last breaths had rattled me. I felt more vulnerable than I liked. I didn't want to be alone tonight, and Ian's warm, buzzing life force was seductive. I'd had every intention of sending Ian home earlier, but now, I wanted his living energy around me.

His inched closer. "Life is precious. It should be enjoyed while we have it in our grasp."

"Is that right?" I faced him. "Pretty sure I saw that on a coffee mug once."

"Ouch." He laughed. "Here I thought it was hitting just the right note—interested, but also philosophical."

"Oh, yeah?" I smirked. "I've never had sex with a philosopher before."

His gaze settled on my mouth, sending heat through me. "May it be enlightening?"

I said softly, "You're very confident. Almost irritatingly so."

"Playing coy has never been my thing."

"Finally, we have something in common."

He murmured, "That sounds promising."

I stepped into him, and he smiled. I slipped my arms around his waist, taking note he was already hard through his jeans. "Did you think I was a sure thing?"

He huffed a laugh. "Nothing about you is a sure thing, Lorenzo." His eyes glittered with arousal and he put his hands on my hips. "But if I didn't ask, I'd never get what I want."

"It's confirmed. You definitely missed your calling. Instead of that pesky doctor gig, you should have opened a gift shop with corny mugs and T-shirts."

"That's not nice. I'm putting myself out there, and you're being mean."

I squeezed his ass through his jeans. "I'm called 'The Great' Lorenzo, not 'The Nice' Lorenzo."

"Even more promising." He leaned into me. "So what do you say? Shall I stay?"

"No strings or expectations?" I narrowed my eyes.

"Not a one."

I nodded approvingly and then kissed him in a slow hungry slide of lips and tongue. He responded, his hands gripping tighter to my body. It was surprising how much I wanted him. Especially after the grim events of the night. But Ian was a welcome distraction. I didn't want to think about old men dying in my house or bills that needed paying. Ian's mouth on mine helped the real world fade into the background as desired.

He gave a needy little groan, and pulling my mouth from his, I whispered, "How about we take this into the bedroom?"

"Yes, please." His pupils were dilated, and he looked happy. "I'm glad you didn't send me home."

"Me too." I pulled him toward my room. The orange and yellow beads clacked as we passed through the beaded curtain. I was glad I'd burned some incense earlier in the day, otherwise my room might have smelled of dirty socks.

He stood in the middle of the small bedroom, taking in the barren décor. "What is that—a full-sized bed?"

I grimaced. "The room's too small for much else. You're lucky it's not a futon. That's what I used to sleep on." I pulled my T-shirt off over my head and tossed it over the small chair near the tiny desk in the corner where my laptop was.

"I guess I expected The Great Lorenzo to have stone lions guarding a king-sized canopy bed and astrology charts and crystal balls everywhere," Ian murmured. "This is surprisingly. . . sterile."

"Is it that bad?" I looked around the room trying to see it through Ian's eyes. A brass lamp on the nightstand cast a stark light over the small space. The headboard-less bed was admittedly lackluster with a plain white comforter and pillows. The oak floorboards were worn and a bit creaky. The walls were a boring gray, adorned with a series of storm-swept seascapes where a local artist had done his best to capture the tumultuous dance of sea and sky off the coast of Fox Harbor. The paintings were the best thing about the room. It was definitely an uninspiring space, but I didn't spend a lot of time in here. "It gets the job done."

"I suppose it does."

I frowned. "Is my bedroom décor a deal breaker?"

He laughed. "Hell, no."

"Then why are you still wearing clothes?" As I spoke, I pushed my jeans down to my ankles, along with my underwear. I stepped out of them, giving him a challenging look.

Unbuttoning his shirt, he scanned my naked body. "You probably think I'm a snob."

"I know you're a snob. I knew that the first day I met you." I grabbed the lube and a condom from the small black nightstand next to the bed. "But I don't care about that because this is just sex."

"And you don't have to like me to fuck me?"

I shrugged and got on the bed. "I have to like your body." I skimmed my gaze over his lean, muscular torso. "So far, so good."

His smile was a cross between flattered and bewildered. He didn't respond, he simply finished undressing.

There was no denying he had a beautiful body. Of the two of us, he was more defined and well-developed. My body was lean, and I naturally had muscle, but I could tell he hit the gym regularly. Looking at his tanned perfection, I had a momentary twinge of insecurity. Then the lust glittering in his eyes reassured me he liked what he saw. His gaze paused briefly on the simplistic black tattoo of a butterfly I had on my left pec. But he didn't ask about it, and I didn't volunteer anything.

Apparently he'd gotten over the pitiful décor because he moved onto the bed and immediately began kissing me. I once more admired his choice of cologne, pleased it wasn't heavy or cloyingly sweet. His touch was gentle but confident. Our kisses were those of two people who didn't know what the other liked yet. But we were both eager to please, and I liked kissing Ian a whole heck of a lot. His lips were full and soft against mine, and his tongue teasing. Playful.

I broke the kiss, panting. "I want you to fuck me."

"Your wish is my command," he whispered.

Before we'd come into the bedroom, I'd wondered if he was the type of lover who just jumped on top and went for it. He wasn't. He was more exploratory and patient than I'd have guessed. His hands were smooth and practiced as they stroked and sought the tender spots that made me respond the best. He seemed eager to taste every inch of my skin. He licked at the small star-shaped birthmark on my left shoulder and nibbled at my nipples until they hardened against his seeking tongue.

Slowly the hunger we'd held in check gave way, and the kisses became more demanding. A fire burned in my belly as he settled between my thighs and took my dick into his hot mouth. Arching my back, I tangled my fingers in his silky wheat-colored hair. He seemed to enjoy sucking me as much as I enjoyed receiving his attention. His fingers caressed my swollen nut sack as he stroked and licked my aching length.

"S'good," I mumbled, trying my best not to thrust too deep into his throat. Maybe if we did this again sometime, and I knew him better, I'd be a little more aggressive. For now, I'd be on my best behavior.

By the time he pulled his mouth off of me and kissed his way up my body, I was more than ready. He tore open the condom with his teeth, eyes never leaving me. Once he was sheathed, he lay on top of me. I gave a happy groan at the feel of his warm flesh against mine. He used his knee to nudge my thighs wider and then he slipped a slick finger inside me.

I threw my head back, absorbing the careful invasion with little whimpers. While I felt slightly impatient with how cautious he was being, I also appreciated his thoughtfulness. I couldn't remember the last time I'd slept with a guy who took his time with me. Even if this was a one-off, Ian wasn't treating me like it was. He was showing me respect, and that made my chest ache oddly.

I tried to show him my gratitude with my kisses and touch. I traced the bumps and ridges of muscle as I rubbed my hands down his back to cup his firm ass. His kisses became more heated, and I spread my thighs wider in invitation. That was all the encouragement he needed. He pulled his fingers from my body and I felt the wide head of his dick pressing my hole.

Our eyes met as he slowly pushed inside me, making the moment almost too intimate. I initially winced as the tight muscles gave way to that invasion of hard flesh. Then the burning glide was so delicious I couldn't keep quiet. I moaned my appreciation and wrapped my legs around his body, meeting his thrusts. He gave a feral growl and drove his hips forward, and I dug my nails into his back. I could feel the pulsing of his thigh muscles as he thrust into me, pumping in and out. The gentleness was gone now, replaced by an instinctive need to take what he needed.

He kissed me, swallowing my moans and then burying his face in my shoulder. His breaths were hot and ragged against my skin. His body trembled, and I sensed he was holding back. Trying not to give into his baser instincts to use me—to use my body only for his own pleasure. The idea of him wanting that excited me. I didn't mind a little selfishness in my lovers, so long as they got me where I needed to go.

"Harder," I whispered, tugging at his hips. "You can fuck me as hard as you want."

"Yeah?" There was a desperation in his voice as he lifted his head.

"Feels good."

He gritted his teeth. "You feel fucking amazing." His eyes burned with a need that was exhilarating. I felt seen. Worshipped. Such bizarre emotions considering I wasn't sure I'd ever see him again after tonight. He let go of his control a little, his hips speeding up, lips parting.

He pumped in and out of me, eyes intense and watchful. I was embarrassed by how noisy I was, but he felt so fucking good inside me. I pulled his head down, feasting on his mouth. His excitement grew and his thrusts intensified. I dug my feet into the mattress, trying to hold onto my need just a little longer. But every stroke inside of me coaxed me closer to the edge.

He groaned and his hips stuttered. "Shit. I'm gonna come."

"Me too," I whimpered, my body aching for release.

"Fuck," Ian rasped, his cheeks flushed and his muscles taut.

As our eyes met for the hundredth time, I had the strongest sense we'd done this before. Of course, that was impossible, but the moment felt both new and familiar. He gripped my thigh as his orgasm hit, and the clunky silver ring on his finger caught the light. The green jewel seemed to glow with a brilliance that hurt my eyes, and then I was coming. A hot flush of pure bliss washed through me, and my toes curled as I cried out his name.

My vision blurred and I felt like I was falling, tumbling down a wormhole of ecstasy. There was only his husky voice, and our bodies undulating and trembling with pure pleasure. I spilled hot release between us, and his dick swelled inside me. I held tight to him, body quaking and shuddering as he finished inside me. I was dazed by the force of my climax, and he seemed equally disoriented.

We were both breathless and covered in perspiration by the time we stopped moving. We held each other, little jolts of pleasure pinging through me every few seconds. Once he'd caught his breath, he carefully pulled out of me.

Ian gave a gruff laugh, avoiding my gaze. I wondered if maybe he'd just grab his clothes and bolt now that we'd finished, but he didn't. Instead, he disposed of the condom and wiped my stomach down with tissues from the nightstand. I watched him as he gently cleaned me off, feeling puzzled. The biggest surprise of all was when he climbed back on the bed with me.

He sat cross-legged beside me, wearing a little smirk. "You thought I was gonna leave, didn't you?"

I hesitated. "Yeah. I did."

"Because you think I'm a snob."

I frowned and scooted up to rest my back against the pillows. "What is it you want me to say, Ian? You want me to apologize for calling you a snob earlier?"

"Not really." He sighed. "I can be a snob sometimes. But I'm a nice guy too."

"Did I say you weren't?" I pulled the comforter up so that it covered my lower half. It was chilly tonight, but that wasn't why I covered my body. It felt too almost intimate to lay naked in bed with him, even though we'd just had sex. I really hadn't expected him to stay once he'd gotten off. The fact he wanted to made me jittery and borderline shy. Not something I usually felt around another man.

"No." His gaze was assessing.

"You've been very nice to me," I admitted. He had been too, ever since my little trip to the hospital he'd been the complete opposite of the man I met that first day. "In fact, you've been surprisingly kind."

He didn't respond immediately. Then he said, "That's because I like you, Lorenzo. I'd like to see you again. Maybe I could take you out to dinner sometime."

"You don't have to do that." Did he feel obligated to wine and dine me because we'd slept together? Probably not. He didn't strike me as a man who did what he didn't feel like doing. That could only mean he actually wanted to take me out to dinner. That felt way too much like the beginnings of a relationship, and I wanted no part of that.

"I know I don't have to take you out to dinner. But is there some reason I shouldn't?" Confusion glittered in his eyes. I got the distinct impression he found it difficult to accept I didn't want to have dinner with him.

I grimaced. "I don't really date."

He wrinkled his brow. "No?"

"We said no expectations, right?"

His gaze flickered. "We did."

"It's not that I'm opposed to doing this again," I said hesitantly. "This was . . . fun."

"Dinner could be fun too."

"I know, but it feels more like a date." I'd hoped he'd take the hint easier. Had he never been turned down before?

"I see." His gaze was assessing. "So, we can do things together, so long as we don't call it dating?"

I shrugged.

"Dating is just a term for seeing someone," he said quietly. "It's not a marriage proposal."

"I know."

When he laughed, I gave him a wary look.

His smile was indulgent. "You don't have to look so stressed, Lorenzo. All I'm suggesting is the occasional dinner, and maybe sleeping together if you're in the mood. You can call it whatever you like."

I nodded slowly. "Okay. I can do that." His summation of what he wanted sounded fairly casual.

"Good. I'm glad to hear it." He looked pleased and he joined me up by the headboard. "You're hard to read. You have a great poker face."

"It's a necessary evil with my job. I read other people, but they're not supposed to read me."

"I guess that's true." He turned his head and studied me. "Why are you like this?"

My face warmed. "Like what?"

His brown eyes were more curious than judgmental. "Closed off. Afraid of human connections."

I tugged at a thread poking out on the edge of the comforter. "You sleep with me once and now you're an expert on me?"

"No. Not even close. But I too have to read people in my line of work. I deduce that something happened in your past that has made you very wary and untrusting of others."

I clamped my jaw tight.

"Am I wrong?" he asked.

I shifted away from him. "Look, just because we had sex, that doesn't mean now I want to spill my guts to you. The sex was fun. That's all you're getting out of me."

"Oh, boy. Prickly. Prickly." He was distracted when his phone buzzed across the room where his pants were hung over the chair. He scowled. "Crap."

"What's wrong?"

He got off the bed and went to check his phone. "Judging by the time, I'm sure it's the hospital."

"Are you on call?" That surprised me because he'd drank the whiskey with me. He didn't strike me as the type of professional who'd drink and go to work.

"No. I'm not officially on call, but they'll still try to bring me in if they need me." He read the text message, and a muscle worked in his cheek. "Damn. They're hoping I'll come in."

"You can't, right?" I was surprised to discover I wanted him to stay longer. I didn't want anything serious with him, but I did enjoy his company. Plus, the events of the evening still had me craving human companionship.

"Nope." He sighed. "I don't drink and then play doctor. I feel guilty though. We've had an unusually high number of assault victims lately, and we're short-staffed. I know they wouldn't try to call me in if they didn't really need me."

"I guess I shouldn't have served you that whiskey."

He glanced over. "I'm glad you did. It was delicious and I was having a nice time. I was on a date after all." He winced. "I mean a non-date . . . thing. It was most definitely not a date."

I smiled grudgingly.

He shot off a text and crawled back on the bed. I widened my eyes when he laid his head in my lap. "What's this?" I asked.

"After-sex snuggles."

I wrinkled my brow. "You're cuddlier than I predicted." I hesitated for a moment but then fluttered my fingers through his hair. "You're not easily discouraged, are you?"

"Nah." He glanced up at me, grinning. "I go after what I want."

I grabbed his hair tight. "Stop trying to make this more than it is."

"Ouch." He laughed. "Careful with the hair. At my age I need to keep every strand."

"Oh, please. You have great hair."

He sighed. "I know, right?"

I bit my lip to keep from smiling. "God, you're an egomaniac."

"Well, that's not very nice."

"Hey, you're the nice one here. I never said I was nice." His warm chuckle made my chest tighten oddly. I truly did enjoy Ian's company. It continually surprised me because we seemed so different.

When his stomach growled, he laughed. "Sorry."

"We never ate dinner." I leaned over and noticed the clock said a bit after midnight. "You must be starving."

"I'll live."

His stomach growled again, only louder, and I laughed and said, "I could make you a grilled cheese sandwich? I don't have much else in the way of groceries at the moment."

He sat up, his expression eager. "You sure it's not too much trouble?"

I opened my mouth to make a smartass comment when the room was plunged into darkness.

CHAPTER TEN

My first thought was I'd forgotten to pay the electric bill. But I distinctly remembered paying it online. Had a circuit breaker blown? Had mice eaten through the wires in the attic? Perhaps it was as simple as the lightbulb burning out.

"It's probably just the bulb," I suggested. "It's one of those LED type that are supposed to last ten years, but they never do."

"Did you shut the lights off in the other room before we came in here?"

I frowned, trying to remember. "No." I'd been too distracted by kissing Ian to even think about the lights.

"Well, they're off too, so it's not the lightbulb."

"Oh." A chill went down my spine, which made little sense. There was nothing particularly sinister about the lights going out. Inconvenient? Yes. Sinister? No. "Maybe it's a blackout."

The mattress jiggled as Ian got off the bed. He tried clicking the lamp switch a few times and then moved to the small window. "It looks like your neighbors still have electricity."

"Really?" I frowned.

Ian asked, "Do you have a flashlight? My phone battery is low or I'd just use that."

I nodded, but then realized he couldn't see me. The moon was too weak tonight to be of much help. "Yes. Hold on." Hopefully I'd put the flashlight back after using it the last time seeing as my phone was almost always drained.

I got off the bed and fluttered my fingers over the smooth wood grain of the nightstand, searching for the small drawer. I found it and slid it open, grasping around among the loose jewelry, books, and pill bottles for the flashlight. Feeling cool metal, I grabbed the flashlight and pulled it from the drawer. Clicking it on, Ian winced as the light illuminated his face.

"Sorry." I flicked the light away.

"It's just a circuit breaker, most likely." As he spoke, he pulled on his underwear and jeans. "I'll go check it out. What side of the house is the electrical panel on?"

"It's not on the outside of the house. It's inside the garage."

"Really?" He frowned, slipping into his shirt. "It's inside? I thought California code required breaker boxes be outside the houses?"

I shrugged. "I have no idea what the code is. I just know the breaker panel is in the little garage against the house."

"That's unusual. Somebody must have bribed somebody at the city a few decades ago." He held out his hand for the flashlight.

"I can go." I ignored his hand and set the flashlight down on the bed. I found my clothes, wiggling into them quickly. "It's my house, after all."

"Just trying to be helpful."

Guilt nudged me. "I know. I . . . uh . . . appreciate that." I zipped up my jeans, grabbed my hoodie, and snatched up the flashlight. "I'll be back in a minute."

He touched my arm, his smile hesitant. "How about we go together?"

I laughed. "Why? Do you think Sableth is out there waiting to get me?"

"No. But one can never be too careful." The flashlight illuminated his very serious expression. "Especially after what happened here tonight."

"I understand that the events of the evening have you rattled, but I'm sure it's fine. It's an older building. The lights going out is no big deal." I spoke firmly because I wasn't wrong. This wasn't the first time the power had gone off at my shop. It didn't happen often, but it did happen.

He ignored me and said, "Lead the way to the electrical panel."

"Ian—" I began in exasperation.

"Is there some reason I shouldn't go with you? What does it hurt if I come along?"

"But there's no need."

"If I don't mind, why do you?"

"Fine. We'll both go." Rolling my eyes, I pushed through the beaded curtain. For all my bravado, the house did feel eerily silent. There was no humming of the fridge, and the furnace had gone quiet. A smoke alarm beeped every few minutes in the living room, and my nerves jangled with each chirp.

I slowly made my way to the front door, Ian close on my heels. Once outside, the air was cool but muggy, and the light of the slivered moon muted. The small building I called a garage wasn't actually a garage. It was a small shed built onto the side of the house, not even big enough for a car to fit inside. I used it for storage mostly and parked my car on the street.

Reaching for my keys in my back pocket, I unlocked the padlock that kept the shed secured. The door squeaked as I opened it, and I shined the flashlight inside the shed before entering. Since the shed had been locked, I had no reason to think someone was inside the little building, but the hairs on my nape stiffened all the same. The torch illuminated old zodiac posters and a rusty bicycle I hadn't ridden in years. There was a push lawn mower I never used and an old burgundy velvet couch.

Everything appeared untouched, but my stomach churned with an instinctive feeling of uneasiness. When I caught a hint of star anise in the air, I stopped in the doorway. Ian bumped into me, putting his hands on my hips.

"What's wrong?" he asked.

"Do you smell that?" I inhaled the musty air of the shed, positive it was tainted with the tobacco aroma from the other day.

Sniffing, Ian hesitated. "I smell tobacco."

"Yes." I wasn't sure whether to be alarmed or glad he smelled the tobacco too. "I . . . I don't smoke."

"Maybe the last tenant smoked."

"I've leased this spot for years, and the scent is fresh," I murmured, chills shifting through me. I tried to sense if anyone was inside the building, but I didn't pick up a presence. "Whoever it was, they're gone."

"You actually think someone was inside here?" Ian sounded alarmed. "But it was locked."

"I know." I met his glittery gaze in the dim light. The flashlight cast sinister shadows over his angular features. "I didn't tell you this, but someone was in my house the other day."

His eyes widened ever so slightly. "Excuse me?"

I grimaced. "It was a few weeks ago actually. The weird thing is, they didn't actually break in. There was no damage to the windows or doors, but I'm positive someone was there because they stole something from me. A stone that only had sentimental value. I didn't mention it before because it was really no big deal. I didn't even bother calling the cops."

He held up his hands. "Hold on a second. You—you had an intruder in your house? But you didn't report that to the police?"

"No."

"No?" His voice was sharp. "Why not?"

His anxiety washed over me like a heated wave, and I grunted at the intensity. "Like I said, they only took that one item and I got it back."

"How did you get it back?" He looked confused.

I exhaled, regretting my honesty. "I shouldn't have said anything. It's not a big deal. I changed the locks and installed an alarm."

He hissed in a breath and I could see he was trying to stay calm. "Lorenzo, someone got into your house, and you're acting like it's nothing."

"Because it is nothing. Nothing else has happened since. I smelled tobacco that day as well. I . . . I just wondered if you smelled the tobacco scent tonight too, or if I was losing my mind." It was disconcerting to keep smelling that elusive scent. Especially since there didn't appear to be anyone around. Was someone lurking around the back of the businesses lately? Was that why I kept smelling that specific tobacco? If so, why was there no other tangible trace of them? There was always just the lingering scent of their cigarettes.

He pressed his lips tight, a line deepening between his brows. "Okay but I did smell the tobacco. So, it's real and someone must have been in here, right? Who else has a key to your home and this shed?"

"No one."

He narrowed his eyes. "Someone obviously has both."

I shook my head, frustrated he didn't seem to be listening. "I don't know how that would be possible. I don't hand out my key to people. And even if I did for some reason give a person a key to my home, why would I ever give them a key to my shed?"

"But the lock wasn't broken," Ian insisted stubbornly.

"I know." I frowned. "I'm not sure how this person gets in without damaging anything. If they're even getting in. Maybe they're just standing outside smoking."

He gave an exasperated sigh. "Are you going to call the police now?"

"And tell them what? That I smell tobacco?"

He scowled. "How can you be so nonchalant about this? If you think someone is getting into your house or shed, you obviously need to call the cops. Especially if you suspect strangers were in your house."

"You're overreacting. I told you, I handled it. I got the item back and I put in an alarm."

"How? How did you get your stone back?" As he spoke, he slipped around me, so that he was now in front.

"It was left on the ground outside down the street." I tried to reclaim the front spot, but he blocked me with his body.

He rubbed his jaw. "Really?"

I tried to tamp down my frustration at him obstructing my way. "Yep. Whoever took it, discarded it. I'm sure it was kids."

"Kids?"

"Probably."

He pulled his brows together. "Random kids got into your home without leaving a trace? That seems plausible to you?"

I shrugged.

"Hmmm." He appeared unconvinced.

Grimacing, I said, "Shouldn't we check the circuit breakers? It's chilly out here and I'd rather get this over with."

His mouth twitched with frustration but all he said was, "Where's the panel?"

I lifted the flashlight, illuminating the far wall. The yellow light showed a small electrical panel at the end of a narrow path winding between the stored items. Without a word, Ian headed toward the electrical panel, careful not to knock things over as he passed. I followed, annoyed he was being so bossy and taking the lead.

"It's awkward to hold the light above your shoulders," I grumbled. "You should have let me go first."

"It wouldn't be a problem if you'd given me the flashlight."

I scowled, muttering under my breath.

"What's that?" He sounded amused. "Did you say, 'Thank you for being my hero, Ian?'"

"I don't need a hero. I need you out of my way."

He chuckled and stopped at the electrical panel. He brushed off the cobwebs without flinching and yanked open the metal door. Inside the circuits looked fine. Nothing was tripped, and there was no smell of burning wire. Ian began to systematically flip each switch on and off.

"They all seem fine," I said softly as he reached the last one.

"Yeah. Weird." He stood back, crossing his arms. "Is your power cable overhead or underground?"

"Underground."

He nodded and moved past me. "It's possible the meter is malfunctioning." As he finished speaking, the bare bulb overhead illuminated.

"Oh," I squeaked. "The power is back on."

"It would seem so." He squinted up at the bulb. "I wonder if you have a short somewhere in the electrical line."

"God, don't say that." I shuddered. Electrical issues were expensive and time consuming. Even if the landlord would have to pay for the repairs, my shop would have to be closed while they worked. That would spell financial disaster for me.

His smile was sheepish. "Sorry."

I shivered. "Let's go inside and warm up."

"Sure. I like the sound of that."

I flicked off the flashlight, flustered by his flirtatious tone.

We'd had sex already, so why was I getting rattled?

There was something about Ian that did get to me though. Something about the way his eyes intensified as they held mine. He wasn't simply the snob or the flirty Casanova I'd originally pegged him for. He had layers. He was funny, protective, thoughtful. Layers could make people more interesting, and I didn't want to be interested in him for anything other than sex.

Without responding to him, I left the shed and went back to the house. As I pushed open the door, a feeling of foreboding swept through me. It was like a punch in the gut so profound I actually grunted as if in pain.

Shock slammed me as I took in the chaotic state of the front room. The table where I usually did my readings was turned over, as were the chairs. The books were out of the bookshelf, strewn on the floor. The beaded curtain that separated my bedroom from my work area was down, and little orange and yellow beads were sprinkled all over the wooden floor.

Behind me, Ian swore under his breath. "What the hell happened?"

I gaped in confusion at what I was seeing. We'd probably only been gone ten minutes at most. Yet, through the doorways to my bedroom and kitchen I could see that the chaos continued. Torn bed linens in the bedroom and broken dishes in the kitchen. It appeared that in the space of minutes, someone had ransacked the entire house.

Ian grabbed my arm and pulled me back outside. "We're calling the cops."

Dazed, I didn't argue. While he spoke on the phone, I tried to wrap my head around how a person could possibly create that huge of a mess in that short of time. It didn't seem physically possible. Had there been more than one person? How come we hadn't heard anything?

Things became clearer as I stood at the bottom of the porch. My skin prickled and my vision blurred as I sensed a lingering energy hovering in the atmosphere in and around the home. A putrid scent descended, permeating the house and yard. It wasn't the nutmeg and star anise scent though; this was a rancid scent of rotting fruit mixed with sulfur. I felt nauseous and hot, as if I had a fever. I couldn't shake the sensation that something wicked was reaching out for me and poisoning my body.

I'd never had anything from beyond reach out to me and try to enter my body that I hadn't reached out first. Shivering, I gritted my teeth, resisting the chilled probing of something trying to slither inside me. I shuddered and took more steps back from the house, until the sensation stopped. Ian gave me a curious glance but continued talking on the phone. Eventually he joined me on the front lawn.

"The police are on the way," he said. "They said not to touch anything and to stay outside."

I nodded, still trying to figure out how to tell Ian what I suspected was happening. There was a good possibility if I told him I suspected a malevolent spirit had plundered my house, he'd drop me off at the psych ward. Not to be confused with the psychic ward. But Ian had surprised me in other ways this evening. Perhaps he'd surprise me again by being open-minded. After all, he'd witnessed the old man's death and heard the stuff about Sableth.

I said softly, "I . . . I don't think the police are going to be much help."

"Why not?"

I cleared my throat but didn't continue. I was losing my nerve. I didn't want him to mock me or think poorly of me. I wasn't sure why his opinion of me mattered so much, but it did seem to.

He peered at me. "Why don't you think the police can help you, Lorenzo?"

Feeling jittery with nerves, I met his questioning gaze. "I'm trying to think of how to word things so that you don't think I'm insane."

He narrowed his eyes. "What? Why would I think that?"

I swallowed hard. "If you want me to talk to you, Ian, you'll have to be open-minded, okay?"

He hesitated. "Okay." He moved closer, putting a hand on my arm. "You can talk to me. I promise I won't judge you."

My stomach churned because I wanted that to be true. However, I realized he'd only said that because he had no idea what I was about to say. Still, even knowing he'd probably reject me, I felt compelled to tell him what I suspected had happened. "I don't think it was a person in my home tonight."

"What?" He looked confused.

I said hoarsely "I think whatever was in my home tonight, it wasn't . . . human."

He laughed as if he thought I was joking, but when I didn't laugh, his smile faded. "Are you serious?"

I nodded. "I can feel it. I can sense evil."

He blinked at me. "You can sense—" He lifted his brows. "Are you saying you think a ghost made that mess?"

I glanced back at the wreckage inside my home. "I definitely don't think it was a person." The street felt unusually deserted of cars tonight, probably because of the late hour. There were only a few houses with lights on, making it seem even more desolate. The chilled, salty breeze made me shiver as it blew in off the ocean.

Ian's lips moved but no sound came out.

I winced at his bewildered expression. "I realize that must be shocking for you to hear."

"Yes," he whispered, wrinkling his brow. "It's beyond shocking that you think something inhuman caused that mess."

"It's hard to grasp, I know." I grimaced. "I'm wondering if perhaps the death of the old man was the catalyst."

"Wait," he rasped, pointing toward the house. "You think the spirit of the old man did that?"

"No. But I'm wondering if his death attracted someone else. Something else." I swallowed hard, giving another wary glance toward the house.

Ian narrowed his eyes. "So, you're actually saying you don't believe it was a . . . human who tossed the place?"

"I don't."

He gave a curt laugh. "Lorenzo, of course it was a human. It has to be."

My heart sank at his unwillingness to entertain my theory. "Why?"

Scowling, he rubbed the back of his neck. "Because the alternative is ridiculous. Unacceptable."

"Not to me. Spirits are very real in my world, Ian." He'd been a skeptic since I'd met him. His cynicism shouldn't have surprised me. But a part of me had hoped he'd been softening a little toward the idea of psychic phenomena being real.

Apparently not.

"Look." He raked a hand through his hair, and the green jewel on his ring seemed unusually dull and lifeless. "We left the house in a hurry. You didn't lock the door, right?"

"No." I frowned, wondering where he was going with that.

"Okay then, it makes more sense that some unsavory types stumbled on the open door and went looking for something to steal."

"They just happened along?" I blinked at him. "That's your theory?"

"It makes more sense than a ghost doing it."

Frustrated at his unwillingness to give an inch, I tried again from another angle. "Did you notice the smell? The rotting scent?"

His eyes flickered. "It would be hard not to."

"That wasn't there before, was it? It's not unusual for smell to be a component in spiritual visits. Don't you think it's odd the house is mysteriously ransacked and suddenly there's also a horrible stench?"

"Maybe a sewer line broke. There could be a lot of reasons for that odor."

"And the power going out so suddenly?" I shook my head. "Come on, Ian."

"Sometimes the power goes out, Lorenzo."

I scowled. "Okay, but the power outage is what got us out of the house."

"You think . . . what?" His laugh was harsh. "That a spirit lured us out of the house by turning off the power and then it ransacked the place?"

Cheeks hot, I said, "You said you wouldn't judge me."

Guilt flickered through his eyes. "I'm not judging you . . . it's just . . . I gotta be honest, I don't believe a word you're saying."

"I'm not crazy," I said quietly. When people didn't understand stuff they always wanted to dismiss it as crazy. It was disappointing Ian seemed to be doing the exact same thing.

"I didn't say you were." His face was tense, his mouth pinched. "But you could be imagining things because you're under a lot of stress."

I scowled. "Seriously, Ian? That's bullshit."

"Is it?" He exhaled roughly. "What would this supposed *spirit* even be looking for?"

"I don't know yet."

He avoided my gaze and his uneasiness intensified. "I'm sorry, Lorenzo. I . . . I just can't wrap my head around your theory. It was probably just opportunists."

Before I could respond, a patrol car parked on the street and a middle-aged cop got slowly from the vehicle. He unhurriedly stretched and leisurely put his hat on. It was obvious he felt no sense of urgency about the call. He strolled up the path toward us, looking bored.

"I'm Officer Brent," he called out. "We got a call about a burglary?" He stopped in front of us. "One of you the home owner?"

I nodded. "I am. I rent, but, yeah, it's my place."

Officer Brent shifted is gaze to Ian. "And you are?"

"Just a friend." Ian's voice was stiff. Earlier in the evening, his energy had been warm and open. He was now completely closed off. His desire to get the hell out of the situation wafted off of him like fumes from a car. I couldn't read his actual thoughts, but it seemed obvious he was getting overloaded by negative energy. Whatever was in my house was affecting him, but also what I was asking him to believe was too much for him. He simply couldn't accept it—that was becoming very obvious.

Keeping my expression and voice pleasant, I said, "Ian, you should go home." I was disappointed he hadn't been willing to believe me even a little. But it was only right to let him off the hook. This wasn't his problem. I wasn't his problem. We'd had sex. That's it. He didn't owe me one more minute of his time.

Guilt shifted over his features. "I can't just leave you."

"Sure you can." My smile felt forced, but hopefully it was convincing. "Officer Brent is here now. I'll be fine."

Ian weighed my comment, a line between his brows. His body was tense as if he were fighting an internal battle. His instincts told him to go. That was coming through loud and clear. He'd had enough crazy for one night. But I also sensed embarrassment at abandoning me. "It doesn't feel right to leave."

"Don't be silly," I said. "Once Officer Brent finishes writing his report, I'll go to a motel for the night. I can clean up the mess tomorrow when I have more energy. There's nothing for you to do here. Go on. Go home."

"Promise you'll stay in a motel?" Ian asked. "You can't sleep in that house. It's not safe. Whoever made that mess might come back."

"I'll definitely get a motel room for the night." I wasn't lying. There was no way in Hell I was spending the night inside that house.

Officer Brent cleared his throat. "Mind if I look around inside?" His tone implied he didn't have all day.

"Oh, sorry, yeah. Go for it." I waved him off.

He headed into the house and I turned to Ian again. "You look beat, Ian. Seriously, take off. I'm a big boy."

His shoulders bowed slightly, and he took a step toward his car parked on the curb. Then he stopped and faced me again. "You're definitely not going to spend the night in that house, right? I know money is an issue, but you can't stay there. I can lend you the money for a hotel."

I gritted my teeth. The only thing worse than him thinking I was a loon was his pity. "I don't need your money."

"You wouldn't admit it if you did," he murmured. "You're too proud." He moved back in my direction. "Why don't you stay at my place tonight?"

Shocked at the offer, I immediately shook my head. "God, no."

He exhaled impatiently. "Why can you never just agree to anything I suggest?"

"I'm not staying at your place."

"Why not?"

"Come on, Ian, neither one of us needs or wants that right now. It's been a long, fucking weird evening. Go home." I was a little surprised he was being so stubborn. I knew he couldn't wait to escape. It had to be guilt keeping him here. "If I were in your shoes, I'd have already left."

"I don't believe you."

"You should." I wouldn't have left him, but he didn't need to know that. He was only offering to stay because he felt sorry for me. I didn't want or need that from him. I shrugged. "I'd look out for myself, and that's what you should do too. Don't let misplaced chivalry drag you into something you don't want to be involved in."

Uncertainty fluttered through his eyes.

That's right. Let my words assuage your guilt, Ian.

He narrowed his eyes. "If things were reversed, you'd really just leave me in this situation?"

"In a heartbeat. Why the hell would I hang around? It wouldn't be my problem—it would be yours." I made sure to sound as heartless as possible. He needed to believe me.

"Seriously?" He looked wounded.

"Yep." I winced inwardly at his hurt expression.

He scowled as my callous words seemed to finally convince him. "Fine, then. I . . . I guess I'll go." He shook his head and turned away, heading toward his car. His shoulders were stiff and his gait hurried. It was like he couldn't get away from me fast enough now.

I turned back to the house, stomach swirling with anxiety. While I was disappointed Ian had been unable to believe me, it was safer for him this way. Even from where I stood out front, I could feel something evil in the house, watching me. I sensed it desperately wanted something from me, but I had no idea what.

CHAPTER ELEVEN

In the dream I was a child again, and the old woman was back. Her coal black eyes were wide and her expression unhinged, her pale skin almost blue against her long dark hair. My little brother Nico clung to me, whimpering, and I felt powerless to protect him.

The woman made me drink a thick bitter liquid, and it dribbled down my chin, soaking into my T-shirt. Guilt made it hard to breathe. I'd stupidly gotten Nico into trouble too. I'd just wanted to pet her puppy. She'd promised we could play with her puppy if we helped her carry her bag of groceries home.

"No one in Viridia is strong enough to fight him," she hissed, grabbing a handful of my hair. I cried out as she yanked hard. "Best if you were never born, child. He can't use you if you aren't here in this world."

"I want to go home," Nico wailed, tears streaming down his chubby cheeks.

The woman turned her ugly gaze on him. "Shut up. Shut up!"

I held him tight, terror ripping through me at the thought she'd hurt him.

"Please," I whispered, "Just let us go home." My stomach was burning again. Every time she made me drink that horrible concoction, I got a belly ache. I pushed Nico gently off of me and crawled to the dirty corner of the basement. Retching violently, I was covered in sweat as I heaved up the contents of my stomach.

"No," the old lady screamed. "You must keep it in your belly for it to work."

Body shaking, I began to black out. Behind me Nico continued to sob, and I slumped onto the cold cement, moaning. I'd failed him. I'd failed Nico so many times. No wonder he hated me. No wonder—

I jerked awake, every inch of me soaked with perspiration. I was breathing hard, and the sound of Nico's sobs still rang in my ears. Outside came the noise of the maid's cart rumbling past. My blurry gaze focused on the faded print of pink roses hung on the wall over the bed, and the air conditioner rattled to life.

Hot tears spilled from my eyes, and I rolled over, pressing my face into the flat pillow. I gritted my teeth, trying to get control of my emotions. I hadn't had a dream about the old woman in years. How could she still terrify me? I was a grown man, but the memory of her reduced me to a sniveling seven-year-old again.

I sat up and roughly wiped my face with my shaking hands. "Fuck. Me."

I threw back the covers and stumbled into the bathroom. I used the toilet and then stripped and got in the shower. The hot water loosened my tense muscles and opened up my lungs. I stayed in the shower until the tips of my fingers wrinkled. I got out and dried off with a cotton towel so thin I could see through it.

The Rosewood Motel wasn't high end, but beggars couldn't be choosers. It wasn't the sort of place I wanted to walk barefoot. Even in shoes, the rug didn't seem to want to let go of the bottom of my footwear. There was also a distinctive scent of old tobacco and possibly weed.

Once I was dressed, I went downstairs and consumed a free, stale bagel and bitter over-brewed coffee. I'd already booked the motel for two nights, so I didn't have to check out yet. As I walked to my car, my cell rang. A tiny, pathetic part of me hoped maybe it was Ian calling to check on me, but my stomach dropped when I saw it was Detective Monroe. Uneasiness shifted through me.

Had he already figured out the old man had called me while in the hospital?

Blowing out a shaky breath, I answered. "Hello?"

"Mr. Winston? This is Detective Monroe."

"Right. How are you?"

"Fine." He sounded distracted and rushed. "I need you to come in to the station today to have a little chat. Does that sound like something you could do?"

I closed my eyes, willing my pulse to slow down. "Sure. When?"

"How about an hour from now?" His voice was steely, and I didn't get the feeling the visit was negotiable.

"I can do that."

"Great. See you then." He hung up.

I scowled at my phone and then tucked it away in my jeans. I had a ton of shit to do today.

First on the list was cleaning up my wreck of a house. I'd texted Claire the night before to see if she'd come over to help me later. So far I hadn't heard back. She was no doubt busy with one of her many men. I really didn't have anyone else to call for help besides Claire. I sure as hell wasn't going to call Ian. Just thinking about him made my stomach hurt.

At least I still had my laptop. By some miracle, it hadn't been destroyed the night before when the house had been tossed. It had ended up under the bed, but it still worked. That meant I could continue serving my online clients. I didn't have any in-person consultations scheduled for the week, but eventually I would.

What was I going to do then? The house made me nervous. I didn't feel right working there for now, and I definitely didn't want to live there. I didn't feel safe. But staying in a motel, even a cheap one, could add up fast.

Claire would let me sleep on her sofa if needed, but I hated putting her out like that. No way could I do that long term.

The obvious solution was to do some kind of exorcism of the property. But exorcising spirits wasn't my area of expertise. Not to mention purging the house of spirits was complicated for me. If I worked as a waiter or stock broker, maybe I could go that route. But I made my living inviting spirits to actually visit me at my home-slash-shop. I couldn't do anything that would discourage spirits from coming to talk to their loved ones.

However, I also couldn't live in that house with some evil entity running the show. To be honest, I wasn't sure what I should do. I certainly didn't have the funds to relocate my shop. Plus, if the spirit was after me personally, moving wouldn't necessarily solve my problem.

I needed to talk to an expert on the subject, but the only other "professional" in town was Weston Bartholomew. No way was I going to ask that fake for advice. I also couldn't bring myself to reach out to anyone online. Even though I myself helped people on the internet, many sites were scams simply stealing credit card information. I didn't want to risk that happening. Things were dire enough without being a victim of identity theft.

The library seemed to be my best option for research. I had some time to spare before my meeting with Detective Monroe, so I decided to go. Our local library actually had a healthy inventory of books on the supernatural. I'd probably be able to dig up some reliable information on how to exorcise a specific malevolent spirit from my home. Maybe there was a way to do a partial cleansing. With that in mind, I drove to the old library.

The Fox Harbor library had served as the heart of town for generations, offering both residents and visitors a sanctuary for learning and discovery. The old Victorian building was surrounded by a wrought-iron fence adorned with intricate seashell patterns. Inside the gate there was a lush garden, maintained by volunteers, where roses, lavender, and wildflowers thrived, adding a burst of color and sweet scent to the briny ocean air.

I made my way up the weathered stone path, listening to the sound of seagulls and distant waves blending into a pleasant and familiar melody. The exterior of the quaint structure was sun-bleached brick, with tall arched windows featuring delicate stained glass panels depicting fishermen hauling in their bountiful catch. Above the entrance there was a carved wooden sign bearing the name of the library in elegant calligraphy. The handles on the heavy, oak double doors, were miniature replicas of weathered ship's wheels.

As I approached the doors, yellow crime scene tape flapping in the wind near a small building to the side of the library caught my eye. My admiration for the beauty of the old building evaporated as a chill zipped down my spine.

With everything that had happened, I'd forgotten about the murder that had occurred here. That tape no doubt marked the spot where the headless corpse had been found. I stared at the area, goosebumps rising on my flesh. What a brutal death that must have been. It made me sick just thinking about it.

Shuddering, I hurried inside the big doors. Once in the building, I felt calmer. I was met with the familiar scent of aged paper and lemon-polished wood. The main room was a spacious, high-ceilinged chamber, with a coffered ceiling and rows of ornate brass chandeliers. The room was bathed in natural light, filtering through the expansive arched windows, which offered views of the nearby coastline. Comfortable leather armchairs and plush sofas were scattered around reading nooks, inviting visitors to lose themselves in the pages of their favorite books. There were also a few ancient desktop computers for the patrons to use that had been donated years ago. Odds were they still ran Windows 7 operating system, but they were better than nothing.

Despite being surrounded by so much history and charm, all I could think about was the crime scene tape outside. Murder was rare in Fox Harbor. It wasn't unheard of, but if someone did decide to do their neighbor in, it was usually your basic knock them over the head or shoot them sort of crime. Headless corpses were something new and heinous for our little town. It only added to my anxiety that the police seemed to have no suspects yet. That could only mean that the head-chopping maniac was still on the loose.

Sighing, I glanced over and met the amiable gaze of Mrs. Zoelle, the librarian. Mrs. Zoelle was a slight woman in her forties with bright red hair and dangling earrings. She was the antithesis of the stereotypical librarian found in movies and books. She didn't wear prim wool skirts and high-necked blouses or put her hair up in a prudish bun. She preferred low cut tops and too short skirts. She was bubbly and chatty, and more often than not, people trying to study had to shush her, not the other way around.

She waved at me when she saw me. "Hello, Lorenzo," she called out brightly. "Can I help you with anything?" There were a few irritable glances thrown our way as she finished speaking.

I hurried over to her so that she'd lower her voice. "Is the occult section still in the same place as usual?" I whispered.

In most libraries, you'd never need to ask if things had been moved, but Mrs. Zoelle had a unique way of doing things. She liked to switch things up from time to time. A technique grocery stores used effectively to get shoppers to discover different flavored chips and new and improved laundry detergents, but not something the citizens of Fox Harbor appreciated when trying to find research materials. Mrs. Zoelle also wasn't a fan of the Dewey Decimal System. She felt its focus on numbers was impersonal and unengaging. She preferred to personally help people find things. Unfortunately, more often than not, that was more like the blind leading the blind.

She nodded. "Yep. All those books are still in the Lobster Den. That reminds me, I need to dust in there."

"If you want to hand me a duster, I could get started on that," I teased.

Her laughter rang through the room, and I winced. "Oh, you're so funny, Lorenzo." She leaned forward, resting her chin on her knuckles. "I can't for the life of me figure out why you're still single."

I grimaced. "I like being single." For some reason Mrs. Zoelle always seemed overly concerned with my relationship status. I wasn't sure if she did that with all her unattached visitors or if I gave off some pathetic vibe I wasn't aware of.

She arched one penciled brow. "Do you?"

"Sure. Why not?"

"Don't you ever get lonely?"

"Not really," I lied. I had my moments where I felt depressed and isolated. But for the most part, I was okay with being alone. I pushed away memories of last night when Ian had been in my bed. I'd definitely enjoyed my time with him, but that ship had sailed.

She leaned even further over the mahogany counter, her eyebrows knitted. "Seriously? I hate going out to eat alone. And movies, they're the worst without a date."

I smiled politely. "I guess." I took a half step back, preparing to make my escape. "Anyway . . . I'm just gonna go—"

"You know, I have a friend I could set you up with. He's divine. Drives a nice car too, if you're into that sort of thing."

Oh, God. Please no.

I laughed awkwardly. "I'm good. Thank you for thinking of me though."

She pouted. "You don't want to meet him?"

"Not really." I added quickly, "I'm sure he's very nice. I'm just happy being single for now."

"Okay." She sighed. "You sure? He's got a great personality."

"I'm sure."

She looked disappointed, but then she abruptly changed the subject. "Did you see the crime scene tape out front?"

I nodded, resisting the urge to shiver. "Yes. Creepy."

"Thank goodness the library was closed when that poor soul lost his life . . . and you know, his head." She laughed awkwardly.

"Definitely. Do you feel safe here alone at night?"

"Oh, I'm rarely alone. There are always a few stragglers." She hugged herself, looking around. "Of course, maybe one of my regulars *is* the killer."

"God, that's very true." I didn't want to blow Mrs. Zoelle off, but if I was going to make my appointment with Detective Monroe, I needed to get moving. I took a step away from her desk, preparing to leave. "Good seeing you—"

She leaned on her elbows, apparently settling in for a nice long chat with me. "Maybe I should buy a rape whistle or something."

Gritting my teeth with frustration, I said, "Yeah, that's probably not a bad idea."

"I saw one on Amazon the other day—"

Thankfully, she was cut off when the phone rang. Frowning, she went to answer it.

Breathing a sigh of relief, I headed down the main walkway that led to the smaller chambers dedicated to specialized subjects. The Coral Room was for local history, the Mermaid Lagoon for maritime lore, and the Lobster Den was for all things occult, etc. Unfortunately, the Lobster Den was at the far end of the building, so it was a long walk.

I glanced at my watch and picked up my pace. I still had to meet with Detective Monroe, and time was ticking. My shoes quietly scraped the polished floor as I made my way toward the Lobster Den. I glanced down the long rows of floor to ceiling books on my way, and the further I went into the bowels of the library, the less crowded the rows were with people.

When I reached the Lobster Den, I pushed into the small room through the weighty oak door. It smelled musty, and I suspected Mrs. Zoelle truly hadn't dusted in there in quite some time. The room was longer than it was wide with rows of oak shelves. The walls were adorned with paintings of sailors standing over wire-mesh traps filled with lobsters, and some of the paintings were simply illustrations of lobsters all on their own. Brass wall sconces dotted the walls, but it was the weakly flickering florescent lights overhead that actually lit the room enough to see what you were doing.

I scoured the shelves, looking for anything to do with exorcising spirits from a building. Most of the modern books seemed to be written by religious zealots who thought all things psychic were evil. Their pious condemnation of psychics reminded me a lot of my parents.

Because of the undependability of the information, I'd never researched much about psychic things, relying only on my natural ability. There had been that short time where

I'd talked with Aunt Helen. But she'd mainly been focused on helping me to control my gift, so that I could learn to quiet the voices when needed. She hadn't delved into anything like protecting against evil spirits. She had helped me, though, mostly because she'd had such a positive view of my gift. My parents had shamed me, but Aunt Helen had taught me to accept myself.

I reached into my hoodie pocket to check the time on my phone, and grimaced. I was going to be late for my interview with Detective Monroe if I didn't leave now. As I pushed my phone back into my sweatshirt, the back of my hand brushed against something cool and smooth lodged deep at the bottom of the pocket.

Frowning, I tugged the item out. In my palm lay a green stone about three inches in diameter. I first thought it was the stone Nico had given me, but it was slightly smaller, flatter, and the color more of a brilliant moss green. The light danced across the smooth surface, radiating an energy and vitality that made the stone seem almost alive. I shivered as the stone vibrated against my flesh.

"Where did you come from?" I muttered, smoothing my thumb over the gem.

I stood, and as I did so, the room seemed to shift beneath my feet. I grabbed onto the table, feeling lightheaded. I folded my fingers around the stone so I didn't drop it, and my skull prickled as I began to tremble uncontrollably. Bewildered, I blinked, trying to clear my head. Was I having a stroke? I definitely didn't feel well, and the room suddenly felt stiflingly hot.

The chamber began to fill with a strange hum that reverberated deep into my bones and teeth. If I hadn't had the table to hold on to, I was certain my legs would have given out. I let out a startled gasp as the wall furthest from the door began to glow an astonishing orange and red color.

Heat radiated around me, and while I wanted to run, my feet felt cemented to the floor. The humming sound grew so loud my eardrums ached painfully.

I stared in disbelief at the far wall as it began to glow brighter. When a dark figure formed in the center of the glowing wall, terror jolted through me. I felt as if I was losing my mind.

Or am I dreaming?

If this was a dream, I desperately wanted to wake up. Sweat beaded on my face as the heat in the room increased. I gritted my teeth and tried to move my feet. They felt too heavy, and my muscles trembled with the strain of trying to walk. The blazing air shuddered round me, and panic set in.

The logical side of my brain couldn't believe any of this was real, and yet my skin felt like it was going to blister from the furnace-like temperature. When the faceless shape detached from the wall and stepped into the room, I felt like screaming. The figure's features were still indiscernible, but as he headed toward me, I had no doubt he meant me harm. The humming sound increased, pounding through my head until it seemed to form words in my brain.

Give it to me and let this end. Give it to me and let this end. Give it to me and let this end.

The words curled malevolently around my soul, clawing and scraping.

Give what to it?

The figure held out its hand, and I stared wordlessly. Terrified into silence, I stood frozen, muscles locked. If I didn't move, I'd die. I felt certain. But still, I was unable to run.

The stone clutched in my hand began to vibrate. While the room and my body felt hot, the gem was cold as ice against my palm. The room shook, and books fell off shelves, and I finally managed to move one foot. But as slowly as I was moving, the figure approaching would be on me way before I could reach the door.

Then what? What would that thing do to me?

When the door to the room suddenly flew open, I managed to cock my head just enough to see who stood there. Shock slammed through me as I recognized the slight blond guy standing there.

"Julian?" I whispered in bewilderment.

Without saying a word, he lunged forward, grabbed my arm, and dragged me from the room.

CHAPTER TWELVE

The dragging didn't stop once we were out of the room either. Stunned into silence, I allowed Julian to tug me through the silent library. None of the other people in the library seemed aware a demonic creature was wreaking havoc in the Lobster Den. In fact, the building was as silent as a church.

I was still unable to find words while grappling with whether I'd just had a nightmare, or if the receptionist at Lacquered Labyrinth Nail Salon had actually just saved me from being burned to death in the library.

As we stumbled past the front desk and out of the building, Mrs. Zoelle called out a cheery, "Have a great day!"

Once outside, I finally found my voice. "Julian," I grated, pulling my arm from his grip. "We need to get everybody out of that building."

He skidded to a stop and grabbed at my arm again. "No. It's okay."

I bugged my eyes, eluding his hands. "It's okay? No, it's definitely not okay." I sounded borderline hysterical. I felt borderline hysterical. "That thing—it—we have to warn them."

He exhaled, looking at me as if I was a clueless child. "He won't hurt them. Not yet. He's after you."

"What?" I blinked at him, feeling dizzy. We stood on the sidewalk about ten feet from the entrance to the library.

"It's you he wants."

"Who? Who or what was that?"

He gritted his teeth but didn't speak.

Dazed, I stared at him. My clothes and hair smelled singed, and the bottom of my shoes sticky as if they'd partially melted.

"I . . . I don't understand what's going on," I mumbled. "I don't understand what I just saw."

He winced. "I know. I . . . I get it. But we have to get away from here for now. Please, just listen to me, Lorenzo. We need to get you to the safe space."

After seeing what I'd just seen, I wasn't sure such a place existed.

His expression was pleading. "Just trust me on this. I'm here to help you."

"I barely know you," I said softly, uneasiness eating at me. "Why on earth would I trust you?"

"Because I came for you just now." He gave me an encouraging smile. "If I just wanted to hurt you, would I risk my own life?"

"This can't be real," I muttered. "It just can't be."

"It's very real, I assure you. I'm trying to save you, Lorenzo. Please, put your trust in me just this once. We need to get out of here."

"How did you even know what was happening?" I asked.

"That's not important right now."

I stared at him wordlessly. I had so many questions, I didn't know where to begin.

Giving the library a wary glance, he said, "There's no time to talk. I promise I'll explain later. But for now, we need to go. Quickly."

I didn't really trust him, but on the edge of my hearing that humming sound was beginning to build again.

Was I just imagining the sound because I was so confused and scared?

I wanted to pretend nothing had really happened, but the scent of burnt hair emanating from my body told me otherwise. The memory of the terrifying heat and physical paralysis sent fear spiraling through me once more. What would have happened to me if Julian hadn't come in the room and dragged me out?

"Please, Lorenzo." His gaze glittered with uneasiness. He stiffened when the door to the library creaked open and a couple walked out of the library, but then he turned his full focus on me again. "Time is of the essence."

"Okay," I rasped. "I'll go with you for now."

Relief painted his young face. "Thank goodness. Come on." He grabbed my arm and yanked me after him. We ended up in a sporty red Mini Cooper. Still dazed, I dug my nails into the vinyl armrest as Julian tore out of the parking lot. The taut suspension made for a jittery ride, and it was cramped inside the small vehicle. But the car was quick, and a sense of relief descended as the library shrank into the distance in the side mirror.

Out of the corner of my eye I studied Julian. He'd always had a penchant for wearing leather, but today he seemed to have taken that to a new level. His pants were black leather, the legs tucked into clunky brown suede boots. He also wore a fitted black leather vest, and around his slender throat there was a brown choker. The choker had green jewels set into the dark leather, and on his hip there appeared to be a small silver dagger.

If I hadn't been so freaked out, perhaps I'd have made a joke about him attending Comic Con. But I wasn't really in a joking mood. Once my breathing had calmed enough to speak, I asked, "Can you please explain what's going on? I feel like I'm losing my mind."

"You're not, but I understand why you feel that way."

I clutched the arm rest as he took a corner a little too fast. "Careful, Julian. There's no point in saving me from . . . whatever that was if you're going to kill me in a car crash."

He laughed sheepishly and took his foot off the gas pedal. "Sorry. I'm just so excited to have you with me."

I frowned at his choice of words but decided to let it pass. "What was that thing?" As I spoke, I slipped the green stone into my hoodie pocket once more.

Instinctively, I felt I should hide it. From who or what, I wasn't sure. I simply had an overpowering need to keep it hidden. "That figure seemed to materialize right in front of my eyes." The scenery of beach cottages and shops zipped by as Julian sped out of town, heading north.

A muscle jerked in Julian's cheek, and he seemed to choose his words carefully. "It's difficult to explain this stuff to you without sounding crazy."

"You have to try. I need to understand what just happened back there." I rubbed my hands down my arm, feeling the rough singed hair. As much as I didn't want any of it to be real, my body showed physical signs that something had indeed happened. "That figure, it wasn't human was it?"

"Do I even really need to answer that?"

I exhaled, grimacing. "Yeah. I feel like you do. I need to hear it out loud."

He cleared his throat. "Then no, that wasn't a human."

A chill shivered through me. "What was it? A spirit? A demon? Why is it after me?"

"It's a long story. Perhaps I could explain better when I'm not driving." He gripped the wheel tighter, giving the rearview mirror an uneasy glance. "I'm a bit distracted."

"Where are you taking me?" I peeked nervously behind us. We seemed to be heading out of town. I still wasn't convinced I could trust Julian. Had I been foolish to just get in his car? Why had he locked the doors? To keep something out, or to keep me in?

"There's a place prepared. We always knew this day would come, and we've done what we could to create a place you can't be tracked."

"Tracked?" I asked in a startled voice. "By whom? And who's we?"

He gritted his teeth. "There's so much to explain. You'll be very confused, but that's inevitable."

"How did you know where I was? I didn't tell anyone I was heading to the library. It was a spur of the moment decision."

"Yes."

"Still, you found me."

"I did indeed."

I shook my head, feeling frustrated at his unhelpful responses. "I thought you were a receptionist at a nail salon?"

"I am. But that's not all I am." He gripped the wheel tighter. "I only worked at that nail salon to be close to you, Lorenzo."

Uneasiness returned. I tried probing his mind, if only to see if there was any negative energy there. I couldn't get anything off of him. His mind was like a fortress.

Why had I trusted him and jumped in his car? Was Julian a stalker? A psycho? Had I been set up? But what about what I'd witnessed? Julian couldn't have set something that elaborate up, right?

"You don't have to fear me," he said softly.

Isn't that exactly what a psycho would say?

"I'm not afraid of you," I lied.

He shook his head but said nothing.

I shivered and turned to stare out the window. For some reason my thoughts went to Ian. I had the strongest desire to have him with me. I closed my eyes, remembering how safe and calm he'd made me feel at times. My heart squeezed at the memory of his kisses, and the way he'd tried to watch out for me. Then the memory of his hurt expression as he left last night washed through me.

He was probably the last person in the world who'd want to help me right now.

I opened my eyes again and watched the foamy waves crash on the beach below. The businesses and charming seaside homes had given way to the dense canopy of coast live oak trees and intermittent stretches of empty sandy marshes. My uneasiness intensified the further we got from Fox Harbor. Why was Julian taking me out of town? Wouldn't I be safer around more people, not fewer? For all I knew Julian was the culprit chopping people's heads off. I studied him out of the corner of my eye, but his expression gave nothing away.

If he was a madman, he was a very calm madman.

After about a ten-minute drive, he slowed and pulled into a narrow dirt road. We bumped down the potholed road, the jarring so extreme my teeth rattled. I worried the little car would get stuck in one of the deep ruts, but it somehow made it through. Eventually we reached an open area where there was a cabin.

At first sight the cabin was unremarkable. Dark brown and weathered with patches of florescent green moss and lichen on the roof. Dense, towering redwoods surrounded the small structure, their ancient branches providing a protective canopy. It was when we left the car and made our way onto the porch that details began to stand out.

The rugged exterior was covered with intricately carved protective symbols and sigils. There were ancient rune symbols, featuring arrows pointing upward with two diagonal lines extending from the stem. It was an ancient runic symbol associated with protection, believed to act as a shield against harm and malevolent entities. There were also markings of The Eye of Horus, an ancient Egyptian symbol often depicted as an eye with a teardrop-like marking below it and a curved tail above it. The list went on with pentagrams, The Hamsa Hand, and the Ouroboros, a circular symbol depicting a serpent or dragon devouring its tail.

There were lines of salt across thresholds and windowsills, and small mirrors were placed strategically to reflect negative energies away from the cabin. The handle on the front door was made from silver, a metal thought to repel evil entities. Dreamcatchers hung in narrow arched windows. The glass didn't seem typical though. It had a subtle green tint reminiscent of sea glass.

I stood in awe mingled with trepidation as I took in all the little details. It was obvious great care had been taken to ward every inch of the structure. In fact, the attention to detail was almost obsessive. Julian had referred to this structure as a safe house, but a safe house could just as easily be a prison depending on who you were with. I glanced at Julian, and he was watching me, a little smile hovering on his lips.

"Did you do this?" I asked in a hushed voice.

"Me and the others, yes."

"The others?" I frowned.

He smiled and reached for the handle. "The others are the 'we' you asked about earlier." He stepped into the cabin first, the door creaking as he pushed it open. "The Guardians."

The Guardians?

"After you," Julian said, gesturing for me to enter the cabin.

I stiffened and shook my head. "I'm not going inside until you give me some answers."

He wrinkled his brow. "Why?"

"Why?" I asked incredulously. "Because you're acting weird, Julian. How did you just show up like that? How could you possibly have known I was in danger?" I waved my hands toward the cabin. "This place. It's insane. How can I be sure you're not just a stalker? This entire thing is nuts."

He sighed. "Lorenzo, you've known me for years. Do you really think I'd hurt you?"

Guilt nudged me because he looked wounded. "Not exactly, but I need some information before I can blindly trust you, Julian. To be fair, I don't know you *well*."

"I swear I'll give you all the answers you want. But it's not safe talking outside like this." He gave a wary glance toward the road we'd come in on. "I swear on my life I'd never harm one hair on your head, Lorenzo. Your well-being is all I care about."

While I was still flustered about everything, it was true Julian wasn't a stranger. He'd always been way too flirtatious, but he'd never once made me feel as if he was a danger to me.

"Please, Lorenzo," he pleaded. "I'm begging you to trust me. I promise I'll share all I know with you once we're inside and the others have joined us."

"How do I know I can trust whoever else is coming?" I rasped.

"Because our purpose is to protect you."

"From what? That thing in the library?"

He nodded, his jaw tight. "Please go inside, Lorenzo. Every second you're out in the open is endangering you."

I narrowed my eyes. "This better not be a trick."

"It's not." He pulled the dagger from his hip and held it out to me. "Take this. I have no other weapons on me. If I do anything threatening to you, you can protect yourself with this knife."

I took the knife, somewhat calmed by the hefty weight of the weapon in my hand. *Was* I overreacting? Julian had rescued me from the library at great risk to himself. Perhaps I was being too suspicious of him? Too paranoid? I did know him, after all, and he'd given me his knife.

"I'm worthy of your trust, Lorenzo," he said quietly.

"I hope so." After a few moments of hesitation, I went ahead and stepped over the threshold and entered the cabin.

"Thank God," Julian muttered under his breath as he followed me inside.

Once inside the cabin, I inhaled the pungent scent of sage and rosemary. The inside of the structure was more modern. There were two beige couches, a glass coffee table, and a stereo system in a small mahogany armoire. To the right was a small kitchen with stainless steel appliances. Past that was a narrow hallway with rooms leading off of it.

"There are three bedrooms," Julian said, closing the door. "It's bigger than it looks from the outside."

"Do you expect me to stay here?"

He frowned, fingering the piercing in his lip. "Well, I brought you here to hide you from him. We need to keep you safe. Now that he knows you have it, he won't stop."

"He, who?" I grimaced. "What is it I have?"

He had a pained expression as he glanced toward the door. "I was really hoping they'd be here by now. I don't like being the only one who explains things."

"You hoped who would be here?" Alarm rippled through me.

"The other Guardians."

"Oh, right." I held his gaze, feeling uneasy.

He slumped. "Look, I know this is all very overwhelming. I swear, I do. But my hand was forced and I had to act."

"You mean because of what happened at the library?" Had that really even happened? How was it possible any of this was real?

"Yes, I had to move faster than planned to get you here. It had been my hope to explain things to you so that you wouldn't be quite so freaked out by this situation. I suppose that was never really a possibility because the predicament we find ourselves in truly is insane."

"Definitely," I murmured. I opened my mouth to ask him another question when the sound of a car engine outside caught my attention.

There was the sound of boots on gravel, and then hurried steps clomping up the porch. Alarmed at the sudden arrival of someone, I spun around to face the door, clutching the dagger. The door opened and a slender blonde girl stood there, eyes bugged. When she saw me she let out a shaky breath and exclaimed, "Oh, thank goodness. You're not dead."

"Huh?" I narrowed my eyes.

Behind me Julian gave a nervous laugh. "Not the best way to introduce yourself, Irene."

The girl winced and shut the door firmly behind her. She wore dark sweats and boots, a baggy pink hoodie, and her long lank hair tumbled around her narrow shoulders. "Sorry I'm late. I heard about what happened at the library from Thomas, and I rushed right over. You made good time, Julian. Good job."

"Thanks." Julian moved closer to me. "We need to explain some things to Lorenzo. He's definitely confused and freaked out right now."

Irene sighed, her gaze empathetic. "Of course he is."

"Where shall we begin do you think?" Julian asked.

Irene sighed. "Not sure. No matter what we tell him, he'll be shocked."

While I was dying to hear some answers, I wished they'd stop talking about me like I wasn't in the room. "Why don't we start with what that was in the library?" I asked quietly. "Maybe then explain why it was interested in me, and how you knew where I was."

She glanced at the silver watch on her wrist. "Should we wait for Thomas to begin?"

Her mention of the time made me stiffen. "Shit." I grabbed my cell from my pocket, but unfortunately without a signal the time wasn't accurate. There was a clock in the small kitchen, and I was horrified to see it was past the time I'd been scheduled to meet with Detective Monroe. "I missed my appointment to talk with the police. They're going to think I did that on purpose."

"You were meeting with the police?" Irene frowned.

"They wanted to ask me questions about—" It occurred to me most people probably wouldn't know about the old man dying in my house yet. "Something awful happened at my house last night."

Julian winced. "Yes. We . . . know."

"Do you?" I narrowed my eyes. "What do you know?"

Meeting my gaze, Julian said solemnly, "We know about the man who died."

"So quickly?" I frowned.

"Yes, he was working with us." Julian sighed. "He was a brilliant man."

That wasn't how I'd have described the old man. Were we talking about the same person? I shook myself, trying to focus. "Either way, I have to call Detective Monroe. He's going to think I'm avoiding him."

"You can't call him." Julian's voice was tense. "It's not possible."

"Why not?" I frowned. "I have to call him. I can't have him thinking I just blew him off."

"I'm not saying you shouldn't call him," Julian responded. "I'm saying you can't call him. Not from here."

"Why not?" I scowled.

Irene said, "We have cellular, wi-fi, and GPS jammers in place. It's for your protection, Lorenzo. Please don't be upset. It's a necessary evil."

"Jammers are illegal in the United States," I said.

"Yeah." Julian raised his brows. "We know."

"You know?"

Irene said, "It's far too easy to track people through electronic devices these days. Steps needed to be taken."

"Uh . . . right." Had I been kidnapped by a group of domestic terrorists? I turned to look at Julian, and he gave me a hesitant smile. Neither he nor Irene looked particularly dangerous. But then, what exactly did a domestic terrorist look like? In the long run, it didn't matter if they were domestic terrorist or crazy cosplayers, I didn't trust them.

Irene moved toward me, her expression earnest. "You don't need to look so worried, Lorenzo. We're here to protect you."

"Are you?" I asked, flicking my eyes to the door. "How is it you know about the old man already? How did Julian just happen to show up at the library? None of this makes sense. Were you watching me? Spying on me?"

She sighed. "I swear, we aren't crazy and neither are you. There's a very real spiritual battle going on."

"A spiritual battle?" I repeated numbly.

Irene winced. "Yes. And unfortunately, Lorenzo, you're at the heart of it."

My stomach clenched. "That's ridiculous. Why would I be at the center of any spiritual battle?"

Julian's gaze was almost worshipping. "You're special, Lorenzo. I promise you that."

His intense gaze made me uncomfortable. "Look, I'm not really sure what's going on here," I muttered, inching toward the door. "But I think I'd feel safer if I went back into town. Maybe I'll just go to the police and tell them what happened at the library and let them handle it. I need to explain myself to Detective Monroe anyway."

"The police will think you're insane if you tell them about what happened at the library." Julian frowned.

"Well, I should at least try," I said, fingers tightening on the dagger. I took another step toward the door, tensing my muscles and preparing for a fight. I'd never stabbed anyone, and I wasn't relishing the idea of that now.

"You can't go back there yet," Irene said firmly.

"At least let us explain what we can to you." Julian's tone was coaxing. "Then, if you still want to leave, we can discuss that."

Irene shot him a sharp glance. "What are you talking about? There can be no discussion. He has to stay here for now. You know that, Julian."

His glance toward her was impatient, but when he looked at me it softened. "Once you know everything, you'll understand why we've brought you here."

"Yeah, I don't think so," I said, anxiety eating at me. I began to mentally plan a way past them. Julian was near me, but Irene was closer to the door. Would she try and stop me if I made a run for it? I got the feeling she might. "Thank you, but I want to go back to town. If you don't want to drive me, I'll walk. But I'm not comfortable staying here."

Irene let out a nervous squeak and she glanced to Julian. "We can't let him go. We need to stop him."

Uneasiness bloomed into outright fear. "Are you saying I'm your prisoner?" I eyed the door, trying not to be too obvious I was about to bolt.

"It's for your own good," Irene said, sounding border-line impatient. "You'll be torn to shreds if you go back into town too soon."

"Be quiet, Irene," Julian said through clenched teeth. "You're making it worse." He turned his flustered gaze on me, and he stepped closer. "I understand completely why you're spooked, Lorenzo. You don't understand anything yet, and you assume we're crazy."

I didn't bother arguing since my expression was probably already giving me away. "You know what? I . . . I don't really care about the answers anymore. I just want to go." I put my hand on the door knob, and Irene let out a whimper.

"Julian, do something. He's going to leave," she cried, wringing her hands.

Julian's calm demeanor slipped, and his expression became more frantic. "Please, Lorenzo, just let us explain. We'll answer all your questions now, okay? You can't go. You absolutely must stay here just a little while longer."

I ignored him and started to open the door, and Irene wailed, "He's not listening."

Before I could actually get the door wide enough to slip through, Julian leapt forward and pushed it shut with a bang. His eyes were apologetic, but his mouth was a grim line. He mumbled, "I'm so sorry, Lorenzo."

"Julian," I rumbled, "Let me out of this cabin this minute."

"I . . . I realize you're confused and upset, but I simply can't let you leave, Lorenzo. I promise you it's not what you think. We have your best interests in mind."

Fear surged through me, but I couldn't quite bring myself to stab Julian. Instead, I decided to try and weaken him so that I could get past him. Unlike when I'd done the same thing to Ian, I needed to be more aggressive with Julian. I had to take enough of Julian's energy to actually stun him.

Gritting my teeth, I grabbed hold of him, concentrating on siphoning some of his pure white energy. He grunted and I felt his oozing energy pour into me like hot wax. His eyes glazed over and he shuddered, looking confused.

I took that opportunity to shove him sideways with all my might. I caught him off-guard, and he fell, landing on his ass. He stared up at me with wide-eyed shock. He looked so hurt, I felt a nudge of guilt. But since he didn't seem injured, just offended and muddled, I raced out of the cabin and practically fell down the steps on the porch in my hurry to escape.

Just as I reached the bottom, Julian yelled hoarsely, "Lorenzo, please stop. I'm begging you." There was raw panic in his voice as he cried out, "If you don't help us, Sableth will destroy this world and everyone in it."

CHAPTER THIRTEEN

Sableth.

That one word stopped me in my tracks. I turned slowly, the sound of the wind swooshing through the tall trees as I stared up at Julian. He was on his knees at the top of the steps, face flushed and eyes glittering.

I grated, "What did you say?"

Julian scrambled to his feet. "Please, come back inside and we can talk." He glanced around uneasily. "It's safer inside."

"How do you know that name?" I demanded.

Julian held out a hand. "Come inside. I'll tell you anything you want to know. But we shouldn't do it out here."

Part of me just wanted to run and put as much distance between me and them as possible. I wanted to pretend none of this was real, and that what had happened earlier in the library was all in my head. But the instinctive terror I felt at the mention of the name Sableth forced me to acknowledge something more was going on here. I grudgingly moved up the steps, my hand gliding along the smooth pine railing.

When I reached the top, I said gruffly, "Tell me how you know that name."

"Of course. Just come back inside." Julian said, stepping back into the building. He gave me a coaxing smile as he beckoned to me.

I hesitated, but then gritting my teeth, I followed. I hovered near the door, still wary of what they were up to. Irene stood a few feet away with hands clenched, watching me as if I were a pin-less grenade.

Julian cleared his throat. "If you'd be so kind as to close

the door, Lorenzo? It will be safer that way."

I narrowed my eyes, uneasiness eating at me. I didn't trust either of them as far as I could throw them, but I needed answers. I grudgingly closed the door, but I stayed near it. "So talk. How do you know about Sableth?"

Julian said, "I learned about him from the man who died at your home last night."

"Who was that old man?"

Pain rippled through Julian's eyes. "His name was Professor David Buckler. He was my teacher and friend."

"Teacher? What kind of teacher?" I frowned.

"He taught Folklore and Mythology at Fox Harbor junior college. I was one of his students." Julian hung his head. "Decades ago, he's the one who first recognized the prophesy. He spent his life studying the stories that told of your birth and what would happen next."

Fear rose in my throat as I asked, "Foretold my birth? That's a little hard to swallow. But, let's say he was able to do that. What exactly is supposed to happen?"

Irene said softly, "That's kind of up to you, Lorenzo."

I blinked at her. "None of this makes sense. I can assure you, I'm nothing special."

"You're so wrong," Julian murmured, his eyes fixed on me intently. "We know it and Sableth knows it."

"Who or what is Sableth and why would he be after me?" I felt foolish even asking that. "Is he the thing from the library?"

"Yes." Julian dropped his gaze. "To understand what I'm about to tell you, you'll need to be open to the idea of other dimensions, Lorenzo." A line deepened between his light brows. "I'm hopeful that being a psychic, you'll already understand that's a reality."

I rubbed my jaw. "I know that there is the physical world and the spiritual world, yes."

Raising his eyes to mine, Julian said, "There are more worlds as well. Worlds that exist at the same time as ours. They're also real worlds."

I frowned, trying to wrap my head around what he was saying.

Irene leaned forward. "Our worlds don't usually intersect. They aren't meant to. But thanks to Sableth and his scheming, they're colliding."

"How?" I frowned.

"Sableth has broken through to our world," Julian said. "To be more accurate, his spirit has broken through. Sableth's mortal body died long ago."

I gave a harsh laugh. "Okay, let's say this is true. Show me some proof."

Julian didn't seem offended. "Some people think your psychic abilities are insane and fake, but they're not, are they?"

I hesitated. "No, they're very real."

"Then why can you accept the unseen when it comes to that, but mock what we're telling you?" Irene asked, frowning.

"Because I'm not the one trying to make you stay in some psycho cabin, so the burden of proof is on you to convince me that what you're saying is true." I frowned. "And when it comes to my powers I just do what I do. I can't stop it from happening. Spirits reach out to me whether I like it or not."

"Yes, they do," said Julian. "And Sableth is reaching out to you too."

I couldn't control the shudder that ran through me. "Why? Why would he want anything to do with me? Because of the professor's supposed prophesy?"

"That has everything to do with Sableth's interest in you, yes." Julian gestured to the couches. "Shall we sit? This isn't a short story."

"No, I'll stay here. But feel free to make yourselves comfortable." I felt calmer now. I didn't necessarily believe what they were saying, but I also didn't feel they wanted to hurt me. I was ready to hear them out. If only so we could get it over with.

Irene sat next to Julian, while I stayed in the walkway between the sitting area and the door.

"Why would Sableth's spirit be after me?" I asked.

Julian crossed his hands on his lap. "First, I'll tell you a bit about Sableth."

"Okay, that would be great." I nodded.

"According to the lore, Sableth was a powerful, twisted psychic born to a noble family in Viridia."

I wrinkled my brow. "Viridia? I assume that's one of your other worlds?"

Julian sighed. "They're not my worlds, Lorenzo. This is my world. My home."

"Right." I grimaced.

"Anyway," Julian continued, "Sableth wasn't normal from birth. Even as a teen he was mean-spirited. Cruel. He burned animals to death with his powers. His parents had no control over him. Some even suspected he used his powers to kill other people, but no one could prove it. He was protected by his money and his family name."

I exhaled. "This sounds like a fairytale."

"It's not," Irene said firmly. "Sableth is very real."

"You must admit," I said gruffly, "It all sounds very silly."

Julian's mouth thinned. "There's nothing silly about Sableth. He's horrible and brutal. If you stick your head in the sand, Lorenzo, you'll die. We all will."

It wasn't the anger in his words that got to me, it was the fear. I held his glittery gaze and said, "Go on with your story."

Julian waited a moment then said, "You have to have an open mind, or there's no point in me telling you any of this."

I grimaced. "I'm trying, Julian. But you're not really telling me anything. It's all so vague. I'm hearing a lot of threats of what might happen, but no details. I need you to actually answer my questions. How do I figure into any of this?"

Sitting next to each other, Irene and Julian looked like fair-haired siblings. Their expressions were very serious, but where Julian's eyes were light, Irene's were dark.

He studied me and then he sighed. "I suppose I need to be more patient. I was born knowing my role in the world. You weren't supposed to know until the time was right."

"There you go again. Unless you can tell me why Sableth wants me *personally*, none of this feels real."

Irene clenched her fists. "What happened to you in the library, that was real. You could have died right then and Sableth would have won."

"How would he . . . win . . . by killing me?" I asked.

Julian leaned forward, his eyes bright. "You're the key to it all."

"Tell me how." I shook my head. "Otherwise, it's impossible to accept any of this is true."

"It is true." Irene sounded less patient than Julian.

I straightened, meeting Julian's gaze. "You said the entity coming for me is Sableth's spirit. How did he die? Why is Sableth here now? What does he want?"

Julian said, "He died in his world because he was finally caught in the act of killing. He murdered a young girl who rejected his advances. He was burned to death at the stake, but his spirit still lives."

"So then, nothing can actually stop him?" I asked uneasily. "Not even death?"

"No, he can be stopped," Julian said.

"How?"

Julian looked nervous but determined. "The prophesy Professor Buckler discovered spoke about Sableth's breaking through to another world. Our world. His vengeful spirit goes on a rampage spreading anguish and despair. He . . . he will destroy this world unless The Vessel stops him."

I squinted at him. I felt deeply uneasy about where the conversation seemed to be headed. "The Vessel?"

"Yes," Julian said softly. "The prophesy spoke of a dark-haired, dark-eyed young psychic who's called The Vessel."

The way they both stared at me expectantly had my stomach aching with nerves. My mouth was dry and my throat tight as I said hoarsely, "Please tell me you don't think I'm The Vessel."

Irene spoke first, her voice wobbling with excitement. "Of course you are, Lorenzo. We're sure of it. Professor Buckler was positive too."

I let out a shaky breath. "Oh, hell no. You're wrong. I'm definitely not The . . . Vessel."

"I understand your skepticism." Julian was calmer sounding than Irene, but his gaze even more fervent. "However, we can prove it."

I blinked at him. "How?"

He leaned forward eagerly. "Do you have a birthmark in the shape of a star?" When I widened my eyes, he smiled. "You do, right?"

I laughed gruffly. "Is that your only proof? That I might have a star-shaped birthmark?" While it was odd he'd have known that, I was hardly going to take that as definitive proof that I was the savior of the world. "I'll bet there are other people with birthmarks just like mine."

"That's probably true." Julian pursed his lips. "But you also have the ability to speak to the Mossfire Stone."

I frowned. "I don't understand."

"The stone Professor Buckler gave you last night before he died." Pain fluttered through his light green eyes. "That stone is called the Mossfire Stone."

"He didn't give me any stone." I wasn't sure why I was lying, I just felt compelled to keep the stone a secret.

Irene smiled slyly. "He's lying."

"Yes." Julian narrowed his eyes. "I know."

My face warmed. "Says who?"

Julian said, "It's good that you're keeping the stone hidden. It shows you're bonding to the stone."

I had no response.

"I will tell you, though, that the stone is how I found you today at the library," Julian said. "You touched the stone and awakened it. I was able to sense that."

A memory of rubbing my thumb over the green jewel came to me. It was true the stone had seemed to vibrate like a living thing when I'd stroked it. Still I said nothing, driven to keep the stone a secret.

"The Vessel can awaken the Mossfire Stone," Irene said.

Julian's expression was more serious. "The problem is Sableth can sense when the stone is awakened also. That's how he found you at the library."

I said hesitantly, "For argument's sake, let's say I have the stone. Why does Sableth want it? Can it make him more powerful?"

"Yes." Julian nodded. "The stone was made for you, Lorenzo. However, if it doesn't respect you it can choose another master."

I scowled. "Respect me? How would a stone respect me?"

"If you're willing to fight Sableth, the stone will fight with you. But if you're weak or a coward, the stone will turn against you. It will reject you and bond to the next strongest soul, alive or dead. That would no doubt be Sableth. Then with the stone's help, Sableth will be able to do whatever he wants in this world."

"But you said the stone was made to fight Sableth." I frowned. "Why would it bond to him?"

"Because the stone can't help being drawn to the strongest soul," Irene said. "It's a flaw in its design. The witch who created the stone was ambivalent about destroying Sableth. Her doubt crept into the stone when it was formed."

I shuddered thinking of the faceless figure in the library today. "How am I supposed to trust the stone then?"

Irene shrugged. "So long as you remain brave the stone will be loyal. But if you falter." She grimaced. "That's another story."

"Why didn't the stone help me today in the library?" I asked. "I had no power against that thing today. If that was Sableth, I had no ability to fight him."

"The stone isn't a guard dog," Julian said. "You have to tell it what to do."

"Hmmm." I frowned. "What about the fact that Sableth is way bigger and stronger than me?"

"It's not a physical battle, Lorenzo." Irene wrinkled her brow. "It's a psychic battle."

Feeling overwhelmed, I rasped, "I talk to dead spirits. I . . . I help people connect to their loved ones and lost pets. I'm not a warrior. I can't have . . . psychic battles with evil forces." I shook my head, panic setting in. "No, you have the wrong person. I can't do whatever it is you need. I can't."

Irene looked flustered. "Lorenzo, you're stronger than you know."

I inched toward the door, sweat breaking out on my face. "You're wrong. The stone didn't help me today. If Julian hadn't come, I'd have burned to death today. The stone was useless."

"You have to work *with* the stone. You're a team. The stone will help you become stronger, I promise. Irene and I are here to help you. Thomas will help you too when he comes. Your talent is more than just finding lost pets, Lorenzo." Julian sounded frustrated. "That was fine before, but it's time for you to step up and fulfill your role in the prophesy."

"No, no." I moved toward the door, reaching in my pocket for the stone. It was cold as ice as I grabbed it and set it on the small table by the door. "I don't want any part of whatever this is. I'm not a vessel or a savior of any kind. I'm just an average guy with average psychic abilities. I promise you that."

Irene watched me, her face pale. "You're rejecting the stone?"

"You guys can have it. You can use it to . . . fight whoever." I opened the front door, fear driving me. "I'm not a hero. I'm just not. I'm sorry," I mumbled, moving down the steps. "I'm truly sorry, but you have the wrong guy."

"Where are you going, Lorenzo?" Julian called after me.

I had no idea where I was going, I just had to get away from Irene and Julian. They had to be nuts. I wanted no part of the bullshit they were spewing. They could take their vessels and stones and evil entities and shove them up their asses. I had enough problems of my own.

Behind me I could hear Julian calling for me and Irene's higher pitched voice. But the blood was rushing through my head so loudly, I couldn't make out the words. I didn't care what they were saying. It would just be something designed to make me stay, and that wasn't going to happen.

When I was halfway down the dirt road, I heard the sound of the Mini Cooper behind me. The driver beeped the horn a few times and revved the engine.

"Lorenzo, please, at least let me drive you into town," Julian yelled.

I glanced at him over my shoulder. He was alone, and there was no sign of Irene in the car. I slowed down and stopped walking, and he braked and came to a rest beside me. His face was flushed through the windshield, and his eyes glittered with worry.

When he rolled down the passenger side window, I bent over cautiously. "I can just walk," I said gruffly.

"That's silly when I can drive you."

"How do I know you won't take me back to the cabin?"

He sighed. "Just get in, Lorenzo. Come on, you've known me for years. We're not going to chain you up and kidnap you."

"You literally did just kidnap and try to detain me," I pointed out.

"Well, I won't do that again, okay?"

I hesitated, but trying to walk back into town would take me hours. By now Julian had to know if he took me back to the cabin, I wouldn't cooperate. I straightened and opened the door. I slid into the passenger seat, giving him an uneasy glance.

He held out his hand and in his palm was the Mossfire Stone. "Take it."

Scowling, I said, "I don't want it."

"You'll be safer with it than without it," he growled. "Take it, Lorenzo. Don't be an idiot."

My fingers itched to take the stone, even as I dreaded having it back in my possession. I couldn't shake the feeling that it was mine and it belonged with me. I didn't want to accept the strange bond I already seemed to have with the damn stone, but I also knew instinctively I'd feel better if I had it back.

I grabbed the rock and dropped it into my hoodie pocket. "It didn't do me any good in the library."

"That's what you think," he muttered, pressing the gas so that the small car lurched forward. "If I hadn't found you, you'd have died. That rock is how I found you."

"Well, according to you it's also how Sableth found me."

"He's already well aware of you. I'm sure you've sensed his presence. You prefer to bury your head in the sand, but the war is happening whether you want it to or not."

"Are you going to lecture me the entire way home?" I mumbled, staring out the window at the thick trees on my side of the car. "I'm telling you I'm not up to the task. I don't know why you won't listen."

"Because we're all doomed if you don't even try." His voice broke and he gripped the wheel tighter. Once he seemed calmer, he said, "Surely you understand why we're upset. We can't fight him without you. The Mossfire Stone is the only way to destroy him and only you or God forbid, Sableth, can control the stone. You were our only hope. With the professor gone, and now this, I don't know what to do."

Guilt nudged me because he sounded so young and scared. I sighed. "I'm sorry, Julian. But even if I foolishly agreed to what you want, I'd fail anyway."

It was still difficult for me to believe Viridia existed, but both Julian, Irene, and the professor had seemed so completely convinced, I had to at least contemplate that it *might* be real. One thing I could not accept, though, was that I was the hero in this crazy scenario.

"Why do you have such little faith in yourself?" He glanced over. "You're a very skilled psychic."

I gritted my teeth. "You're wasting your breath. I won't change my mind."

"That doesn't make what I've told you untrue."

As we reached the main road, a flurry of missed calls and text messages came in, beeping every few seconds. I tugged my phone out of my pocket and saw several missed calls from Claire and one from Detective Monroe. My stomach ached when I saw the call from the detective.

"Maybe you can drop me off at the police station," I said gruffly. "I need to grovel to the detective in charge of Professor Buckler's death. I'll get my car from the library later."

"Please let me take you back to the cabin."

I shook my head. "No. I'm sorry."

"But we can't keep you safe out there in the real world. You need to be protected. Why can't you understand that?"

"Julian, if you won't drive me to the police station, I'll just walk. I can't just disappear from my life. I'm not going back to the cabin. I'm sorry."

He clenched his jaw, then said, "Fine. I'll drive you. But only because it's safer for you." He pulled out onto the road.

We didn't speak for a few minutes, then I slid my gaze to him. "I'm sorry about the professor. It sounds like you were close."

"Thanks." He stared blankly out the windshield. "I don't know what to do now. You're not cooperating, and he's gone."

My guilt grew, but I couldn't simply agree to whatever they wanted because I felt bad. They had the wrong guy. I wasn't hero material. The professor must have got it wrong.

Julian asked softly, "Did the professor suffer?"

I pressed my lips tight, remembering last night. "A little, yes, I'm sorry. I had a . . . friend with me when he died." I cleared my throat. "He's a doctor, and he suspected the professor was poisoned."

Julian grunted. "Yes. The professor knew he was dying. That's why he went to you. He wanted you to have the stone."

"He should have gone to the hospital, not to me."

"It was too late." He pressed the accelerator to pass another vehicle. "You were what mattered most to him. To all of us."

Shame nipped at me again, but I pushed it down. "I wouldn't have thought poison was something Sableth would need to resort to." I dug my nails into the arm rest as Julian passed yet another vehicle. I was beginning to wonder if I'd have been safer walking after all.

"Sableth will do whatever he must to win."

I glanced at Julian. "Are you sure you're not just dealing with a crazy human? Maybe Professor Buckler had some enemies you don't know about. Maybe he died of a heart attack."

He huffed. "Just because you're in denial doesn't mean we all are, Lorenzo."

"You call it denial," I mumbled, "I call it logic."

He scowled at me. "How can you even say that? After the things you've seen in that library? After how the professor died in your home warning you about Sableth? I know you can sense his evil presence. I know you can."

"I'm not saying something weird isn't happening. I'm not even saying a spiritual battle isn't possibly brewing. I . . . I'm saying I'm not your hero. I'm not the one who can defeat Sableth. I don't believe God or whoever is running things would put me in charge of saving anyone. I'm far more likely to get someone killed than to save them," I muttered.

"That's ridiculous."

"No," I snapped. "Thinking I'm your knight in shining armor is though."

He clammed up after that, occasionally mumbling to himself and gripping the steering wheel tight. We didn't speak again until we reached the police station. I glanced over at his stern profile as I opened the door to exit the car.

"Thanks for the ride," I said.

"You're welcome." His tone was curt.

I sighed. "I'm sorry, Julian. I know you're disappointed in me. But you can't really expect me to just blindly accept the things you've told me today. Perhaps if you or the professor had come to me before and tried explaining this stuff to me, I'd have had time to digest this craziness."

"It wasn't my call to make. The prophesy unfolded as it was supposed to." He didn't look at me as he said, "I'm still hoping you'll come to your senses, Lorenzo. Before it's too late."

"I won't because I'm not the hero you think I am." I got out of the car, and he drove away before I could even close the door all the way.

CHAPTER FOURTEEN

It turned out Detective Monroe wasn't at the station. I was informed he'd been called away and had canceled our interview. I was so relieved I wasn't in trouble, as I walked out of the station I felt like skipping. Then I remembered the bizarre state of my life, and all joy drained away.

I called an Uber to drive me to the library so I could grab my car. I was admittedly nervous as the driver let me out at the library. But everything seemed peaceful, and Sableth or whatever the entity was didn't make an appearance as I got in my car and drove home.

The things Irene and Julian had told me swirled in my head. It was impossible to believe everything they'd said, and it was impossible not to also consider it. The things I'd seen in just the last two days were difficult to explain away. Unless Julian had somehow set me up? I wasn't sure how that would be possible, but so much of this scenario was impossible to accept. I'd definitely faced something terrifying in the library, and I'd sensed something evil in my home yesterday. I'd even tried to convince Ian of that, without success.

Julian didn't seem to understand that I wasn't denying there was an evil spirit hanging around. There definitely was something wicked hovering. It was the part about me being the only hope to save the world that I couldn't swallow. There were people destined to be heroes, and then the rest of us. I was firmly in the latter camp.

How was I supposed to accept the idea of a multi-verse that included a far-off place called Virida on faith alone? Julian's story had lacked details as if he'd come up with it on the spot. But that cabin was another story. All the warding and care that had been taken to make it a safe house hadn't been rushed. It was those conflicting truths that had me going back and forth between believing Julian and definitely not believing him.

Since I was off the hook for now with Detective Monroe, I texted Claire and arranged to meet her at my house to start the cleanup. I was nervous as I pulled up to my house. I really hoped whatever negative spirit had been hanging around the previous day was gone. I hadn't found anything useful at the library about being able to partially cleanse a home of spirits. It seemed to be all or nothing, and that wouldn't work for my type of job. That meant, if the malevolent spirit I'd sensed yesterday was still in my home, I had no idea how to get it to leave.

I parked on the street in front of my house. As I exited my car, I was surprised to see Ian parking behind me. My pulse raced as he got out of his car. I hadn't expected to see him again, especially after how we'd parted last night. His expression as he approached wasn't warm, but it wasn't cold either. He stopped in front of me, and I swallowed nervously.

"Hi," I said. "Didn't expect to see you here."

Or ever again.

Part of me wanted to blurt out everything I'd gone through from the library to being kidnapped by Julian and Irene. But after how dismissive he'd been last night, I didn't want his judgment right now. I was shaken and confused enough.

He shrugged. "I wanted to be sure you were okay."

My stomach warmed and tightened at the obvious concern in his voice. Even after how we'd left things last night, he cared about my safety? That both pleased and confused me. "I'm fine. Just here to clean up the mess from last night."

"Right." He studied me, his jaw tense. "Look, I wanted to say I'm sorry I didn't believe you last night and that I made you feel bad." He grimaced. "I'm sure it's no surprise all this psychic stuff isn't my thing."

"No, it's not a surprise," I murmured. "But I'm not going to apologize that all this psychic stuff is my thing."

"Nor should you."

An uncomfortable silence fell. His crisp cologne floated on the breeze, bringing back many good memories of last night. I wanted to touch him but was too shy to do it in case he rejected me. I hated how things had ended between us the night before, but I wasn't great at apologies. Even if I wanted to, I didn't know how to smooth things over.

He cleared his throat. "Can I help with the clean up?"

Shocked at the offer, I blinked at him. "You want to help?"

He shrugged. "Yeah. Why not?"

"Why not?" I repeated. Weren't there so many reasons why not?

He frowned. "Do you not want my help?"

"It's not that." I took in his expensive suit and tie. "You're not really dressed for menial labor."

He laughed and tugged at his tie, loosening it. "I had a meeting with the hospital chief of staff. I'll just take off the jacket and tie, and I'll be good to go."

"Shouldn't you be at work?"

"I actually have the rest of the day off."

"And cleaning up my house is how you want to spend it?" I laughed because I suddenly felt happier. Ian's energy seemed to be brightening my mood.

"I'm happy to help."

"I believe you." Without giving myself time to overthink it, I slipped my arms around him and kissed him. I didn't care if neighbors or customers coming out of the nail salon saw us kissing. I'd had such a horrible day, and Ian was being so kind and warm, I was drawn to him for comfort.

He was obviously surprised by my actions. His body stiffened, and he took a second to respond, but then he was all in. He put his arms around me too, and the kiss deepened. He slipped his tongue into my mouth, and lust curled in my gut. When the kiss ended, he grinned down at me, looking boyish in the afternoon sun.

"I guess you forgive me for being a clod last night?" he asked, smoothing his hands down my arms.

"You weren't a clod. It was a weird night." I grimaced. "I was a jerk to you."

"Nah."

"Yeah, I was. I said some things I shouldn't have. If our positions were reversed, I . . . I wouldn't have just bailed on you. I only said that so you'd go home without being guilty."

A smile hovered on his full lips. "I'm glad to hear it. It kind of hurt to think you wouldn't care if I needed help."

"I'd care," I said. "You've been really good to me. How could I not?"

He nodded but didn't say anything.

A car horn honked next to us, and I jumped. Glancing over I found Claire grinning at us through her white Toyota's window. Her blonde hair was cut in a pixie cut, and her dark eyes glittered with curiosity. She rolled the glass down and waved. "BFF reporting for cleanup up duty," she called out merrily.

"You made it," I said.

"I sure did." Her curious gaze flicked to Ian. "Hello, I'm Claire."

"Ian." He smiled at her.

"Ooh, you're the doctor." She grinned and pulled forward to park against the curb.

My face warmed because her comment made it clear I'd talked about him with her. I guess that wasn't really a bad thing, but I worried Claire might mention something about my pathetic track record with men. She tended to speak her mind a bit too freely.

Ian and I walked up to the porch and Claire joined us. While Claire and Ian introduced themselves more thoroughly, I concentrated on the building, putting out feelers for any negative energy. Whatever had been around last night seemed to be gone now. I unlocked the front door and we stepped inside.

Claire gasped as she took in the mess. To be honest, it was even worse than I remembered. It appeared that every item I owned was on the floor. Every shelf and table had been cleared, and the ground littered with books, candles, and tarot cards. The kitchen had a lot of broken dishes, and we had to be careful not to slip on the loose beads from the little curtain that had been shredded.

"Do the police know who did it yet?" she asked, surveying the mayhem.

Ian frowned. "I doubt it. Even if they were able to find any prints, it's probably too soon for results to be back."

Since I strongly suspected the culprit hadn't been a human, I didn't say anything. Claire was open-minded, but I didn't want to get into a disagreement with Ian again. We'd just patched things up and I wanted to keep it like that for now.

Claire moved to the bedroom. Feathers covered the floor from the slashed comforter and pillows. She shivered and met my gaze. "This feels personal."

"Yeah, it does," Ian agreed, frowning.

Once more, I didn't respond. They were right though. It did seem as if whoever or whatever had thrashed my house had a grudge against me. I shivered as I surveyed the room. The place hadn't just been rifled through; it had been demolished.

Claire sighed. "Where's the broom, in the kitchen?"

"Yeah." I nodded. "Maybe a shovel would be better?"

Claire laughed. "Okay. I'll start in here. This room needs some serious help."

"All the rooms do." I sighed, moving out into the front area again.

Ian followed me. "Where do you want me?"

"Anywhere is fine. I'll probably start on the kitchen."

"Then I'll start cleaning up in here." Ian smiled encouragingly. "Between the three of us, we should have this done in no time."

"Wouldn't that be nice." I bent over and retrieved the green stone my brother had given me from under the couch. I held it in my palm, remembering how the Mossfire Stone had seemed to come alive against my skin. This stone sat still and lifeless, but it meant so much more to me because it was from Nico.

Ian looked over my shoulder. "Pretty."

I glanced up. "It is, right? My brother gave it to me."

His eyes warmed with sympathy. "He had good taste in gifts."

I laughed. "I think this is the only gift he ever gave me."

"That's just how younger brothers are. They don't realize once they're adults, they're supposed to start acting like it." He sighed. "My brother is the same way. He expects gifts, but he's horrible about giving them."

I smiled and slipped the stone into my back pocket. "I'd give anything to have Nico back, gifts or no gifts." The second the words left my mouth, I stiffened. That was an unusually emotional thing for me to say, and I was instantly embarrassed.

But Ian simply smiled and turned away.

Relieved he hadn't immediately started pumping me for more info, I moved into the kitchen.

Anger built in me as I picked up the shards of broken dishes. I didn't have expensive things, but the items I'd accumulated over the years had sentimental value. I growled with frustration as I discovered Nico's favorite cereal bowl shattered. The bottle of whiskey from last night was smashed, and the kitchen smelled of the liquor. Dish after dish had been destroyed, leaving only a few unbroken plates and cups.

The things Julian and Irene had told me earlier today haunted me. I was positive no human had created this mess, but still balked at the idea I was supposed to play the hero in this situation. I knew that Julian believed with all his heart I was The Vessel, but the idea of that left me cold. Scared.

And vaguely disgusted, if was honest.

I didn't want to be at the center of any battle, spiritual or otherwise. The very idea something as vile as Sableth could have its sights set on destroying me was terrifying. I just wanted to pretend none of this was happening.

There was a knock on the front door, which we'd left open. As I walked into the front room, I found Weston Bartholomew standing on the threshold. Shocked to see my arch nemesis on my doorstep, I scowled. He didn't seem to notice my displeasure as he stepped inside, taking in the mess.

"Goodness. Looks like a bomb went off in here." He laughed as he tiptoed over the items strewn on the floor. Weston was the same age as me, but taller and thinner. His face was pale and angular. He wore a long black wool coat, a paisley vest, and leather brown boots that came to his knees. He always dressed like a cross between Paul Revere and a wizard, but that was the thing that least annoyed me about the man.

"What do you want?" I asked, not even feigning politeness.

We'd clashed many times over the years. Weston had a habit of trying to steal my clients. We'd almost come to blows one summer when he'd stood out in front of my shop, handing out flyers for discounts at his place. I wasn't sure why he did things like that to irk me. He had more business than me already. It was as if he simply enjoyed poking at me.

"No friendly hello?" Weston pouted, tucking a bright red strand of hair behind his ear. "I came by to see if you needed anything. I heard about what happened here last night. People dying in your shop isn't going to be good for business."

I frowned as the scent of star anise and nutmeg tobacco filled my nostrils. That's where I'd smelled that scent before—Weston. He sometimes smoked skinny little hand-rolled cigarettes. Had he been in my house the other day when I was out? Why the hell and how the hell would that have happened?

Claire came out of the bedroom, her face flushed and her hair done up in a messy ponytail. "You can drop the act, Weston. You only came here to gloat over Lorenzo's misfortune."

Pressing a hand to his chest dramatically, Weston said, "What? Me gloat? Why, I wouldn't dream of it."

Ian had stopped working and was watching us with curiosity.

I said curtly, "Can you just say why you're here, so we can get back to work? I don't have time for you right now, Weston."

Weston's eyes flickered. "You don't have to be rude. I stopped by to see if you needed anything, Lorenzo."

I somehow stopped myself from blurting out, "Bullshit." Instead, I gave a tight smile and snapped, "No. I'm fine. You can go."

"You sure?" Weston pinned his beady black eyes on me. "I was thinking, maybe I could take over your clients while you sort things out?"

"Seriously?" I gave a humorless laugh. Weston had to be the most obtuse person I'd ever met. It was hard not to grab hold of him and shove him forcefully from the shop.

"Of course I'm serious." His smile didn't reach his eyes. "You need a hand right now, so I'm here to help."

"No, thanks," I said harshly. "I'm not handing my clients over to you, Weston, but nice try."

"You sure?" He sighed, looking around. "Seems to me the energy in here isn't good. My shop has such a better vibe. I think your clients would enjoy it."

"You brazen son of a bi—" Claire began.

"You wouldn't know good energy if it smacked you in the face, Weston," I mumbled, crossing my arms. "I'll be just fine, so don't worry about me. Run along back to your own shop. I don't need your vulture-like presence around here."

"No? well . . ." His eyes scanned the floor almost feverishly. "Perhaps I could help you clean."

I laughed. "Why?"

"Oh, just because." He walked around the room, eyes still pinned to the floor. "Was anything taken?"

"Hard to tell," I said, wondering why he was asking that. Seemed like a bizarre thing to ask.

"We have a lot of work to do, Weston. Maybe you could shove off?" Claire said brightly. "Surely there are people to scam somewhere in town?"

He met her gaze, and his mouth thinned. "Always so protective of your friend, Lorenzo. How sweet."

Ian had moved to stand behind me. He still hadn't spoken, but I could feel the heat of his body and was oddly comforted by it.

Weston rubbed his stubbled jaw, meeting my gaze. "Lorenzo, I've been thinking . . ."

Claire snorted a laugh.

Ignoring her, he continued. "Wouldn't it be wiser to

combine our talents, instead of competing against each other?"

Shocked at the suggestion, I scowled. "What?"

Shrugging, Weston said, "It makes sense if you think about it."

"How so?"

"Well, for one thing, I could bankroll a facelift for your shop." Weston sniffed as he once more glanced around. "Customers these days like a more modern décor. This sort of retro thing went out with the traveling circus. Plus, I could advertise your store. I know you don't have the budget for that. I heard you had surgery recently. Nothing like hospital bills to put a dent in the old wallet. Especially when you're already struggling to pay your bills."

His pitying tone made my face hot. "I'm doing fine. Besides, things will pick up in the summer. They always do."

Ian didn't speak up on my behalf, but he squeezed my shoulder in a silent, reassuring gesture that I appreciated.

"I know," Weston cooed, "But even then, you don't really make enough to save, do you? Plus, the way things are going for you this winter, will you even make it to the summer?"

I squinted at him. "Since when do you care how hard I have it?"

"I've always been rooting for you, Lorenzo. You just don't like me." He sighed. "I'm not sure why."

"You know exactly why," I said. Did he actually think I was buying his compassionate act? I wasn't. Not even a little. He was a selfish, greedy person who only cared about his own business. I wasn't sure why he'd dropped in, but it sure as hell wasn't out of concern for me.

"Not really." His boots crunched on broken glass as he moved slowly around the room. "Is it just jealousy?"

"I'm not jealous of you, Weston. I don't approve of how you do business."

"You mean successfully?" He smirked.

I shook my head. "Just tell me why you're really here. We both know it isn't to help me."

"How can you say that? Didn't I just offer to merge with you?"

"We both know your offer makes no sense. Seems to me that you'd prefer I fail and go out of business."

"Not at all." He bit his lip as if trying not to smile.

"God, you're such a jerk, Weston," Claire hissed.

Weston laughed but didn't respond to her. He flicked his gaze suddenly to Ian who still stood behind me. Recognition seemed to flutter through his eyes. "Don't I know you?"

"I don't think so," Ian said.

Weston tilted his head, his expression thoughtful. "I'm sure I know you."

I glanced at Ian, but there seemed to be no recognition in his eyes.

Ian said, "I work at the hospital. Perhaps you've been a patient of mine."

"Oh, that could be." Despite his words, Weston's tone said he didn't think that was it.

Claire said, "There's no way Lorenzo will ever partner with you, Weston. No damn way. He's a real psychic, and you're a fake."

Weston's eyes glittered maliciously. "Careful, Claire, or I'll sue you for slander."

"Pffft." Claire rolled her eyes.

"Nobody is suing anybody," I said. "And I'm not interested in your offer."

Irritation fluttered across Weston's face. "Don't be a fool, Lorenzo. I'm offering you a lifeline. Without me, you'll be out of business in a few months."

"Maybe so." I lifted one shoulder. "But I still have no interest in partnering with you."

Weston huffed. "You're making a huge mistake."

"I don't think I am."

Claire held up the broom she'd been using in the bedroom. "Run along, Weston, before I sweep you out with the rest of the trash."

Instead of leaving, Weston moved closer to me, his eyes glittering with malice. "I'm destined for amazing things, Lorenzo. Join me and we can do them together."

I stepped back because his energy was so intense. "No thanks. My guess is you're destined for prison."

He rumbled, "This is the last time I'll ask nicely." His facial features seemed to distort and flicker much like a television screen losing the signal. It was only for a split second, and then it was gone.

My heart raced as I tried to process what I'd just seen. Had it been a trick of the light? Uneasiness settled in my gut, and I rasped, "You should go, Weston. I'll never work with you."

Weston's smile was cold and a chill ran through me. "We'll see about that."

As our eyes met, a horrible feeling of hopelessness seemed to shudder through me, but then Ian's hands came down on my shoulders, and his light touch seemed to calm me. Weston flicked his gaze to Ian, and then took a step backward. A silent message seemed to pass between them, and Weston trembled and turned away.

"We can talk about this another time, Lorenzo," Weston grated as he headed for the doorway. "This conversation isn't over."

Bewildered by his persistence, I said, "You're wrong. I want nothing to do with you."

"We'll see." As he left the house, he glanced back over his shoulder. I stiffened as something ugly slithered through his murky eyes.

A heavy silence fell once he was gone.

"Well, that wasn't bizarre at all," Claire muttered finally. "He was even weirder than usual."

"He's not usually so intense?" Ian asked, moving away from me.

I let out a shaky breath. "I've never seen him like that."

"No," Claire agreed. "Me neither."

I wrinkled my brow. "Why would he want to work with me out of the blue? He's done his best to drive me out of business in the past."

"Whatever his reason, you know it isn't to help you." Claire shivered. "Oh, he just gives me the creeps."

Ian looked thoughtful as he moved to the door and watched Weston drive away. I joined him, and he glanced at me. "What could he possibly want from you?"

I frowned. "I have no idea. He seemed almost desperate."

In truth I had a lot of ideas but none that I wanted to share yet. Between finding out the kid from the nail salon was in cahoots with the dead professor, and the ransacking of my house-slash-shop by an evil entity, I already had a lot to process. Was Weston in on what was happening? It seemed he had to be because why else had he suddenly shown up on my doorstep? Was he on Team Sableth? I couldn't imagine he was on the side of good. There was nothing inherently *good* about Weston.

"Perhaps he wants to merge because his business isn't doing as well as he says?" Ian shrugged. "People tend to exaggerate that stuff."

"But he does have a lot of customers," Claire said. "I've seen the cars at his place. He advertises constantly, and his location is closer to the pier where the tourists come in."

"Exactly," I muttered. "He doesn't need me, so why was he offering to work with me?"

Ian moved back into the room. "Maybe he really does just think you both could do more if you worked together."

Claire shook her head. "No. Lorenzo helps people. That isn't what Weston is interested in. He has no actual psychic powers. He's a scam artist." She sighed. "Unfortunately, a very successful one."

I gave a humorless laugh. "It probably would be in my best interests to work with him. I'd make a lot more money."

"Don't you dare even say that," Claire exclaimed. "If I have to hogtie you to stop you, I will."

"Tell me how you really feel, Claire."

She laughed, cheeks pink. "I feel very passionately about this."

"You don't say?" I smiled.

Ian nodded. "It's good that Lorenzo has people to protect him."

People like Julian and Irene?

They'd called themselves The Guardians but then called me the chosen one and tried to lock me up. And now Weston was acting weird as well. My stomach churned at the memory of Weston's malicious gaze and the threat in his voice. I felt like the world had gone mad.

Was it possible I was at the center of some psychic battle? The very idea seemed too ridiculous. I couldn't be the Chosen One, or The Vessel. It was far more believable that I was just a guy who was down on his luck, with a mess of a house to clean. If I didn't engage in all the turmoil going on around me, hopefully it would just pass me by.

CHAPTER FIFTEEN

By dusk the house was in order. Trash bags filled with broken items were neatly lined up outside on the curb. The inside of my house felt like a stranger's. The shelves were half-bare, and what had survived had been put back in the wrong spots. While I wasn't a materialistic person, some things that had been destroyed had held personal significance for me. One of the most sentimental had been a vintage beige crackle pottery cat figurine that Nico had adored as a kid. Seeing the shattered remains on the floor had filled me with rage and sadness. No amount of glue could have repaired it, and there would be no replacing it either. Instead, it was now at the bottom of a trash can.

While the house smelled of lemon polish, and the floor gleamed from Ian and Claire's hard work, I felt no relief that things had been put in order. Inside, my emotions were still as messy as the house had been after being ransacked.

I did gain some comfort from the presence of Claire and Ian though. The three of us were slumped on the couch, recovering from our labor. I was in the middle, sandwiched between Claire and Ian. The warm press of his thigh against mine was nice, and I couldn't help hoping maybe we could sleep together again sometime. He seemed to have forgiven me, so there was a good chance.

"How about I treat us to a pizza?" I offered.

Ian's expression brightened. "I could go for some pizza."

"I would, but I have a date," Claire said without hesitation.

I murmured drolly, "Of course you do."

She laughed. "Hey, don't give me a hard time. I just spent my whole day cleaning your house."

I rested my head on her shoulder. "And I appreciate it. Thank you, Claire."

She grabbed my hand and kissed my knuckles. "My pleasure."

Ian watched us, a smile on his lips. "You two are super close."

"We've known each other since high school." Claire met my gaze. "I probably know Lorenzo the most of anyone."

"True." I gave Claire a conspiratorial wink. "She knows where the bodies are buried."

"That's nice." Ian's smile was wistful. "I don't have any friends from that long ago. We all went in different directions. Most of them moved away."

"But you stayed," Claire said. "How come you didn't go the big city and make a name for yourself, Doc?"

He lifted one shoulder. "I like Fox Harbor. I love living near the sea and being close to family."

"I'm the same," Claire agreed. "I wouldn't move away even if someone paid me. If I ever get serious with anyone, I'm going to make them sign a contract never to move out of Fox Harbor."

Ian elbowed me. "What about you? What keeps you here in Fox Harbor?"

I tensed up and stared at my feet. "Same reasons as you two, I suppose."

Ian studied me, appearing puzzled. "But your family lives in Texas, right?"

"I don't consider them family. They're just the people who fed and clothed me, when they could be bothered." I cleared my throat. "I stay in Fox Harbor because this is where my little brother is buried. He was my family."

Ian stilled. "Oh. I see."

An awkward silence fell, and Claire squeezed my hand. Then she stood and said brightly, "I'm off."

"Have fun on your hot date." My lips twitched.

Claire held up crossed fingers. "The guy I'm seeing tonight isn't my usual type, so wish me luck."

"What's different about him?" I asked.

"He has a brain." She looked like she was trying not to laugh. "You should be proud of me, Lorenzo. He's not just a sexy boy toy. He's a teacher."

"Really?" I stood and walked her to the door. "That is different for you."

She gave a sheepish grin. "Not gonna lie, he's still hot. I have certain standards."

I rolled my eyes. "That they have a pulse?"

"Rude." She waved to Ian. "It was really nice meeting you. I'm impressed by how hard you worked. That earned you a lot of points in my book."

"Oh." Ian looked a bit embarrassed. "Thanks."

I watched her walk to her car and drive away. Then I returned to Ian. The evening shadows were slowly spreading across the small room. I hadn't turned on a light yet, and the room had a hazy pink glow from the reflection of the sunset off the ocean.

I asked, "Do you still want pizza?"

He hesitated. "You don't have to bother if it's just me."

I smiled. "Why? Aren't you worthy of a pizza?"

"I hope I am. At least a slice."

I said, "I think you're worth at least two slices of pizza."

"Yeah?" Heat shifted through his eyes, and a flirty smile hovered.

"I believe so."

He grabbed my hand and tugged me down on his lap. I gave a surprised yelp, but I didn't fight him. I put my arms around his neck, and he leaned in to kiss me. I was surprised at the sudden affection but certainly not opposed to it. His mouth was warm and searching, and my heart raced. He tasted so fucking good, and I just felt so content when I was in his arms. It was like a jolt of pure oxygen when he kissed me and held me. I'd never felt anything like it before. People usually drained me, they didn't give me energy.

When the kiss ended, he said softly, "I thought about you all night. I was worried."

"Yeah?" I frowned. "I was fine."

"I assumed you would be, but last night was so strange." He glanced around, appearing almost apprehensive. "You're not staying here tonight, right?"

"No. I have a room at the Rosewood Motel for another night." I had to admit, it was flattering he seemed so worried about me. I usually hated guys who were super possessive, but his concern didn't annoy me. Perhaps it was because he wasn't trying to control me. He just wanted me safe. We didn't know each other well, but we were definitely forming a bond.

"Okay, good." He nodded approvingly.

"You don't like it here, do you?"

He frowned. "I feel uneasy. I'm not sure why. I didn't used to. When I came with Mrs. Beckom, I didn't have any weird feelings."

"No. You just assumed I was a fake."

He winced. "Yeah. Sorry about that."

I gave an exaggerated sigh. "I forgive you. I even understand why you feel differently about the place too. A lot of weird stuff happened last night. The old man dying alone was shocking, and then the rest . . . well, I see why you're uncomfortable."

"Are you going to move back in here?"

"I kind of have to. I can't stay in a motel forever." I shrugged. "I don't feel anything bad here today. There's no negative energy that I can sense."

"Good to know," he shivered.

He looked sexy, sitting there with mussed hair and flushed cheeks. The memory of last night's sex and the taste of his kiss from a few moments ago on my tongue had me aroused.

"I need a shower," I said nonchalantly, trying to think how to broach the subject of him joining me.

"When we get to the hotel?"

I gave a breathless laugh. "No, I was thinking more of like right now." I met his gaze and said softly, "Would you care to join me?"

His eyes flickered as he realized what I was saying. "So, no pizza?" He didn't look particularly disappointed at the tradeoff.

"Oh, no. We'll still have pizza. I definitely need my pizza fix." I stood and held out my hand. "But first, I think a dirty boy like you needs a hot shower."

He pressed his lips together, giving an eager nod. "I am a very dirty boy. I worked hard today just to please you."

"I am pleased," I said, happy when he took my hand and stood. "Come with me and I'll give you a performance review."

He grinned. "This is an interesting seduction technique, but I'm kind of digging it."

"Excellent. Follow me." I tugged him toward the bedroom. It was weird to enter my bedroom without the familiar clack of beads. It was yet another reminder of how someone or something had violated my sanctuary. Still, I had more important things on my mind at the moment. Namely getting Ian naked, wet, and soapy.

At the far end of my small room there was a tiny shower, mostly hidden in a little alcove behind my computer desk area. Fitting two people would be a tight fit, so we wouldn't be experimenting with the Kama Sutra's Congress of a Cow position, but we could still have some fun.

As I passed my nightstand, I flicked on the brass lamp, remarkably unharmed by the intruder, and grabbed lube and a condom from the drawer.

"Where are you taking me?" Ian asked, sounding amused as we neared my work desk.

I smiled at him over my shoulder. "There's a shower back here."

"Really?" Ian glanced around the small room. "I'm beginning to think the city inspector who checked over this building was drunk."

We rounded the small desk, reaching the shower. The shower stall was clean, but the glass door was frosted glass with years of hard water build up. Scrubbing showers wasn't my thing, and mostly I was just happy to have a shower.

I set the lube and condom on the shelf inside the cubicle and turned to Ian. "Strip," I commanded.

He hesitated, but then began to undo his light blue dress shirt. His nostrils flared as he watched me strip down to nothing. There was definite lust in his brown eyes, and his arousal was even more obvious once he shed his pants and briefs.

I got into the shower first, and he cautiously followed, his expression skeptical. "Are you sure we can both fit in there?"

"Yes." I turned on the water, shivering as the cool water hit me. I'd usually have waited for the water to warm up before stepping in, but Ian was waiting on me, so I was forced to suffer the colder temperatures.

He slid in behind me, and he let out a gasp as the water hit him too. "Holy Hell," he squeaked.

I laughed at his decidedly unmanly sound. "It'll warm up in a second."

"It better or I'll be experiencing the dreaded shrinkage."

"We don't want that," I said, grabbing the bottle of Beast Wash Claire had gotten me last Christmas. I squeezed a healthy amount onto my palm, my elbows bumping against the side of the shower stall.

Ian put his hands on my hips, and his erection pressed the small of my back. I shivered at his touch and smoothed the body wash down my arms. The scent of teakwood, coffee bean, and smoky sandalwood filled my nose.

Ian kissed my shoulder, nipping the skin at the nape of my neck. "This is a nice surprise," he said huskily. "I wanted more of you."

I leaned against him, enjoying the press of his sinewy chest against my back. "I wanted more of you too. I was worried I'd never see you again."

"Were you worried about that?" He rubbed his hands up my soapy abdomen and over my nipples. The flat nubs instantly beaded against his palm, and I let out a guttural moan. "I'm glad to hear it."

I rubbed my ass against his cock, and he released a hot breath that skated over my ear. My dick was already hard, and I knew I probably wasn't going to last long. I was too turned on. "You should fuck me, Ian."

"Yeah?" He sounded excited.

"I need it. Want it fast and hard." I pressed the palms of my hands on the prefab shower wall and arched my back.

"Don't need to ask twice." His voice shook as he grabbed for the condom and lube. He made quick work of both, and soon one slick finger was gliding up inside me.

I pressed my face to the wall, moaning as he worked me, loosening me up with a skilled, teasing touch. He rocked into me, dragging his sheathed dick up and down the crack of my ass.

"You want this, Lorenzo? You want me to fuck you?" He nuzzled my neck, his breath hot against my wet skin.

"Fuck yeah."

He pulled his finger from inside me and clamped his hands my hips, holding me in place as he nudged my legs wider. He pressed the head of his cock against my hole, and with a grunt, he entered me. I groaned as his width filled me, hot and hard. I clawed at the wall, biting my lip to keep from crying out at the delicious invasion.

He was *slightly* rougher this time than the first night, seemingly carried away by his lust. The space was so cramped we were pressed tight together, his body molded into mine.

I bit my forearm as he began to thrust, his movements almost lifting me off my feet. There was no holding in my sounds now, and he wasn't being quiet either.

"Feels so good," he rasped, sensually rolling his hips.

I hung my head, water cascading over my hair and down my face. The sensation of being taken by the beautiful grunting beast of a man behind me while hot water swept down my naked body was exhilarating.

I began to stroke myself, moaning my approval of Ian's assertive performance. I was getting off on this other side of him. After the last few days of stress, this mindless fuck was exactly what I needed.

Ian grunted. "Shit, I'm gonna come."

"Good," I whispered. "Make me come too."

He responded by pounding into me faster and harder. He placed one big hand over mine on the shower wall, and the green jewel of his ring seemed to fill the small space with reflective jade prisms of light.

I leaned my head back against him and he panted in my ear as he pumped in and out of my body. He gave a strangled sound and I felt his dick jerk inside of me. Then I lost track of what was happening with him because I was coming too.

My cock spilled against the wall of the shower, creamy release sliding down to disappear into the drain. My body jolted and trembled as Ian finished inside me, thrusting weakly to the last second.

We were both breathing hard as our orgasms slowly faded away. My legs were shaky and weak, and Ian gave a gruff laugh. His hand still covered mine, but the jewel of his ring seemed duller now.

He carefully pulled out of me, and I turned around and we kissed. He smiled down at me, looking relaxed and happy. His blond hair was plastered to his head, and drops of water hung off his long dark eyelashes.

"That was fucking amazing," he said, wiping water out of his eyes.

"You're definitely getting a raise." I smirked, running my hands down his muscular arms. "You really go that extra mile."

He planted an affectionate kiss on my mouth, and then he proceeded to soap up his body with the Beast Wash. Once we were both cleaned off, I shut off the water, and we got out of the shower. He surprised me by drying me off first with a towel before taking care of himself. That considerate gesture made my chest warm and fuzzy. It was kind of nice to be doted on.

Once we were both dry, we dressed and moved into the bedroom near the bed. When the brass light flickered on and off, Ian gave a wary glance into the other room. The sun had lowered in the sky now, casting dark shadows throughout the house.

Taking pity on Ian's obvious uneasiness at being in my house after sundown, I said, "Let's get going. We'll eat at my motel instead of here. That way you can relax without worrying about the Boogeyman coming to get you."

He looked relieved. "That would be great."

I led the way to the front door. "I'll lock up and then we can head over to the motel."

He stepped out onto the porch, and even though it was apparent he was spooked about being near the house after dark, he didn't rush off to the safety of his BMW. He stayed on the veranda waiting for me. I made sure the shop was closed tight, and we made our way to the cars.

I called out, "You know where the motel is, right?"

"Yep." He nodded and was about to get in his car, but his attention was drawn to two men on the sidewalk who had begun screaming at each other. One of the men raised a cane threateningly at the other. "Hey, hey!" Ian yelled, moving in their direction.

I was surprised to see one of the men was my most immediate residential neighbor.

Ralph was a widower, probably in his eighties. He was one of the nicest people I knew and one of the original homeowners on our street. He grew his own tomatoes and would give me bags of them every season. He invited me to coffee every Tuesday, even though I rarely accepted. He usually puttered in his garden, whistling and talking to the birds. But at the moment, his face was red, and veins bulged in his neck as he roared at the other man.

The other man I didn't know. He was younger than Ralph, probably in his forties, and he too seemed furious. I followed Ian toward the two men, praying they didn't actually start brawling. I'd never seen Ralph looking so angry, and wondered what the hell the other man had done to get him so mad.

"I was just walking to my car, you old coot," the younger man bellowed.

"You picked one of my roses. I saw you." Ralph's face twitched with rage. "Those are my flowers. Who gave you permission to touch my roses? They're mine, not yours!"

Feeling bewildered, I watched as Ralph unraveled. Spittle flew as he cursed at the other man, waving his cane aggressively. The other man was upset too, shoving his face in Ralph's and vowing vengeance if Ralph dared say one more word. What was doubly bewildering about Ralph's behavior was he usually encouraged neighbors to help themselves to his abundant roses.

Ian stepped between the two men, grabbing Ralph's swinging cane.

"What are you doing? You can't just hit him because you're upset," he said.

"I won't be disrespected like that. I won't." Ralph's voice shook with anger, and he tried again to strike the other man with his cane.

Ralph seemed surprisingly strong for his age, so I grabbed the cane too, trying to help Ian. "Ralph," I rasped. "Calm down. What's going on with you?"

Ralph turned his pale blue eyes on me. "Are you on his side?"

"I'm not on anyone's side. I just don't want anyone to get hurt," I panted, struggling to hold onto the cane.

A group of women came out of the nail salon, and before I knew it, two of them were screaming at each other. I met Ian's frazzled gaze, befuddled by what was happening. Linda, the owner of the salon, jumped into the fray with the two customers, trying to calm them down.

The madness continued with a few other people breaking into fights. It felt like an eternity before there was the blip of a police siren, and two patrol cars arrived. The cops broke up the crowd into smaller groups and began questioning people. Ralph was breathing hard, and covered in sweat by the time Ian was able to convince him to sit on the curb. Once he was seated, he seemed more like his old self, only confused.

"Lorenzo, what are you doing here?" he asked, his expression muddled.

I sat beside him, patting his back. I worried perhaps he'd had a stroke. "Are you feeling okay, Ralph? You had me worried."

Ralph wiped at his shiny face, and muttered, "What's going on?"

Ian crouched in front of Ralph, frowning. "Can you smile for me, Ralph?"

Grimacing, Ralph said, "Smile? What for?"

Ian scrutinized the old man's face. "I don't see any drooping of the face." He cleared his throat. "Would you mind lifting both of your arms?"

"My arms?" Ralph wrinkled his brow.

"Ian is a doctor. I think he's checking to see if you had a stroke, Ralph," I said softly.

"Huh?" Ralph looked shocked, but he went ahead and lifted both arms.

"Okay, that's good," murmured Ian. "I still think you should probably go to the hospital to get checked out."

"I don't need to go to the hospital." Ralph scowled. "I'm right as rain."

Ian and I exchanged a glance.

I cleared my throat. "It couldn't hurt to get looked at. You seemed extremely upset, Ralph. You didn't seem like yourself."

Ralph looked around, frowning. "That guy just pissed me off."

"But, why?" I asked.

Looking confused, Ralph said, "I'm not sure. Something about the way he looked at me."

One of the officers walked over to us. He was an older guy, salt and pepper hair, clean shaven. He gave Ralph a chiding look. "What's gotten into you, Ralph? That's not like you to be involved in something like this."

Ralph's cheeks flushed, and he looked embarrassed. "I was angry."

The cop shook his head. "That's no excuse to start brawling."

Ralph gave the cop a sheepish glance. "Yeah, I just lost my temper. Sorry."

The cop sighed, chewing the inside of his cheek. "Well, no one was hurt, so that's a good thing at least. If I let this slide this one time, are you going to behave, Ralph? Mr. Thompson is willing to drop this craziness if you are."

Looking drained, Ralph said, "Yeah. I don't want to fight anymore."

"Okay, then I'll give you a break." The cop wagged a finger at Ralph. "I won't be this nice twice. Remember that."

"I will," mumbled Ralph.

The cop walked away and had a short conversation with the other guy, who I assumed was Mr. Thompson. The guy gave one wary glance in our direction, nodding his head. Then he got in his car and drove away.

"I'm happy to take you to the ER, Ralph." Ian's gaze was sincere. "I can even hangout with you there."

Ralph winced. "Nah. I appreciate the offer, but I'm fine."

Ian didn't look convinced. "Are you sure?"

"There's no need. I'm fine." Ralph got to his feet with a grunt. "Just embarrassed."

I stood too, as did Ian.

"I'm gonna go have a cup of tea and relax." Ralph gave a shamefaced laugh and looked at his cane. "I was mad enough to hit that guy over the head, but I can't for the life of me remember why."

"No?" I frowned.

"Nope." Ralph scratched his sparse white hair." It all seems pretty silly to me now." He turned and ambled toward his home, head down.

The cops had restored order, and most everyone had dispersed. Linda from the nail salon had coaxed her squabbling customers back inside.

Ian said, "Guess there's no reason to hang around."

"Nope. I guess not."

"You sure live on an exciting street, Lorenzo." He laughed gruffly. "Seems like something is always happening."

I gave a weak smile. "It's not usually this much fun." I watched the two cop cars pull away. "After all that excitement, are you still up for pizza?"

He smiled. "Hell, yeah."

Pleased he hadn't been discouraged by the ugliness of that brawl, I smiled. "Then I'll see you at the motel?"

"Yep." He gave me a cursory salute and headed toward his vehicle.

It was a short uneventful drive to the motel. Since it was offseason, there was plenty of parking right in front of the room. I used the key card to let us in, and the stale scent of old carpet and drapes filled my nose. I'd noticed the place wasn't exactly the Ritz last night, but today I saw the room through Ian's eyes. No doubt he'd never stayed in a motel this low-end before. Now that he saw the room, perhaps he'd make a run for it.

I felt embarrassed as I took in the worn carpet that was a mottled gray with mysterious dark spots. The drapes and comforter were orange, which clashed with the pink rose print over the bed. There was a small desk against the far wall, no mirror, and a bathroom the size of a closet. There was no microwave. No minifridge. No movie channels.

Clearing my throat I announced, "I know it's pretty bad. It's just a place to sleep and shower."

Ian grunted but was well-mannered enough not to say anything derogatory about the room. Although he did seem squeamish about sitting on the bed. He dusted it off with his handkerchief before sitting.

I laughed. "Are you going to burn that handkerchief later?"

"Probably not a bad idea."

"It's actually very clean in here," I said, pushing away thoughts of the mysteriously sticky carpet. It's just not luxurious, and a bit dated."

He smiled politely.

"Your snobbery is showing, Ian," I teased. "Would you rather eat in your car?"

He laughed sheepishly. "No. I don't want to get cheese on the seats."

I pulled my phone out and dialed the local pizza place down the street. "Do you have a preference for the type of pizza?" I asked him.

"I'll eat anything."

I ordered a large vegetarian pizza and some beers, which all came within twenty minutes. I toed off my shoes and said, "I want to lie on the bed and relax. Is that okay with you?"

His smile was flirty. "If you're in or on the bed, that's where I want to be."

I narrowed my eyes. "We're just eating. I'm not offering sex."

"The night is young."

"You're insatiable," I muttered.

"You say that like it's a bad thing." Ian's tone was cocky as if he'd never heard the word "no" before in his life.

"Ahhh, there's that confident stud I remember." I set the pizza on the bed along with the ice bucket and the beers.

"You should be flattered." He eyed the bed. "I'm willing to risk disease to be near you."

"I think you're safe. The sheets smelled so strongly of bleach, I doubt anything could survive on them."

He kicked off his shoes and joined me on the bed. "This mattress isn't bad."

"No, it was actually pretty comfortable." I opened the pizza box and my mouth watered as I gazed down at the cheesy goodness. Thankfully, the restaurant had included paper plates and napkins, so I helped myself to two big pieces and a beer. Leaning against the headboard, I sighed.

He laughed. "You seem very content, and you haven't taken a bite."

"I am. The moment before you eat and drink is the

best. In about fifteen minutes, I'll be too full and whining I shouldn't have had that last piece."

"So true." He took a bite of pizza and groaned his appreciation.

I followed suit, and we ate in silence for a while. It was interesting to me that Ian and I could already have comfortable silences together. I usually took way longer to feel at ease around another person.

The beer relaxed me, and with my belly full, I could honestly say I was enjoying the moment. Yes, my life was in turmoil, but everything felt okay right then.

When we'd consumed all we could, I put the mostly empty box on the small desk. I rejoined Ian on the bed. His hair was slightly mussed, and his cheeks had a hint of pink from the alcohol. I couldn't help smiling as I settled next to him, shoulders brushing.

"I was worried you wouldn't want to see me again," he said quietly.

I frowned. "I thought the same of you."

"I didn't want to leave you last night. I kept worrying you wouldn't go to a hotel because of money."

"No. Believe it or not, what happened rattled me as well." I met his curious gaze. "It's actually scarier to believe a malicious spirit is around than it is to believe some low-life humans tried to rob me."

"So . . . you still believe there's an evil entity involved?"

I could sense his uneasiness with the words that he spoke, but at least he didn't outright mock me. "I'm even more certain of it now than I was before."

"Why?" He frowned. "Did something else happen?"

I wasn't about to tell him about the library incident. We might get into another argument, and then he'd probably leave, and I really wanted him to stay. But maybe I could mention the thing with Julian, minus the saving-me-from-a-burning-library part. The conversation with Julian and Irene had been enlightening in many ways. They'd known the identity of the man who'd died in my shop. That was huge. I wanted to be able to talk about that with Ian.

"There was an interesting development," I admitted.

"Was there?"

"I found out who the old man was."

He lifted his brows in surprise. "Did the police ID him so soon?"

I shook my head. "Not that I know of. I uh . . . met some people who knew him. Apparently, he was a professor of folklore and mythology at FHJC."

"Was he?"

"That's what they said."

He wrinkled his brow. "Do you trust the source?"

"I don't know why they'd lie. I could check that out pretty easily. Besides, one of them is a guy named Julian who works next door to my shop at the nail salon. I've known him for years, so I think he's trustworthy."

"I see," he murmured. "How did they find out so quickly? I didn't see anything about the old man's death in the local paper today."

I hadn't checked, and it hadn't occurred to me that Ian would have. "Oh. Um . . . probably he heard it at work."

He studied me. "I feel like you're not telling me something."

"No." My face warmed.

"Promise?"

I didn't respond.

He tapped his finger against the side of his beer bottle. "So, this Julian guy just sought you out to tell you he knew the old man?"

"Kind of, yeah." I avoided his gaze.

"Why?"

"Not sure," I lied.

He sipped his beer and then asked, "Why was the professor at your house? Does Julian know the reason?"

I hesitated. "It had to do with some research the professor had been doing. It was a sort of obsession of his."

"And you were connected to his research?"

I should have known better than to assume Ian wouldn't ask questions. He had an inquisitive mind. I really didn't want to tell him about the bizarre encounter I'd had in the library. Ian was too closed-minded about the psychic stuff and might think I'd lost my marbles.

I grimaced. "It's a long story."

He glanced at me, a line between his brows. "Unless you're kicking me out, I have time to listen."

"Truthfully, I don't think you'll want to hear more than I've told you," I admitted.

He absorbed that comment, looking uncertain. "I'd like to know why he came to your house and warned you about being in danger."

I hesitated. "Even if his reason isn't something you . . . believe in?"

"You mean it's psychic in nature?"

"Yes."

He didn't speak for a few moments. Then he said softly, "It's true I find it difficult to accept the idea you can tap into a spiritual world. I'm a factual kind of guy. I suppose most medical types are. If I can't see it, it's hard for me to believe in it." He paused and then continued. "But last night, after I left you, I couldn't stop thinking about you and how scared you'd seemed. Whether I can wrap my head around a spiritual world or not, your fear was real. That bothered me."

I wasn't sure how to respond.

He took my hand, his thumb rubbing distractedly across my flesh. "Then today, that guy, Weston. There was just something off about him. I felt protective of you, like I had to defend you from some unseen threat he posed. It was weird. I've never felt anything like it."

"Really?" I studied him, remembering the moment when Weston had looked at Ian and backed down.

"I've been saying this since I met you, but I feel like I'm supposed to be near you." He gave an embarrassed laugh. "Like it's my role almost to keep you safe."

"Maybe I remind you of your little brother or something."

He gave me a startled glance. "Uh, no. That is most definitely not it. I don't have brotherly feelings toward you, Lorenzo."

I smiled. "Good."

He shifted to face me, our knees touching. "I think you should tell me everything."

I shook my head immediately. "Hell, no. You won't like it, and I don't want to fight with you again."

He looked almost irritated now. "I can handle it, Lorenzo."

"I'm not sure you can," I murmured.

He chuffed. "What, are you the antichrist or something?"

I scowled. "No. Of course not. To be honest, I don't even believe half of the stuff I heard from Julian. You definitely won't."

"What was his reason for telling you those things?"

I sighed. "To protect me. He . . . he thinks he has to protect me."

"From what?" He sounded breathless, and his eyes seemed more golden brown than usual. The green jewel in his ring glittered as he leaned closer. The stone in my hoodie pocket seemed to vibrate as Ian said softly, "Tell me, Lorenzo, what wants to harm you?"

"It's silly really." I felt almost mesmerized by his gaze, but I tried to shake it off. "The professor read some lore that mentioned a star birthmark and a dark-haired, dark-eyed psychic being born. He thought it was some kind of prophesy." I expected him to laugh, but he didn't. "I'm sure it's nonsense. Lots of people have birthmarks, and dark hair and eyes aren't exactly rare."

"Why would they think it's you in the . . . prophesy?"

"Because of the things I told you."

He wrinkled his brow. "No, there must be more than that."

"I shouldn't have brought any of this up."

I started to move away, but Ian grabbed tighter to my hand. "You must have wanted or needed to talk about it." His gaze softened. "I'm a good listener. I know you don't trust I won't mock you, but I won't. Haven't I been better today than I was yesterday?"

He looked so hopeful, it was hard not to smile. "You have been better, yeah." My smile faded. "But the stuff I'm leaving out—it's difficult for me to swallow." Again the stone vibrated so hard in my pocket, even Ian seemed to notice.

He glanced at the nightstand where my cell rested and then frowned at my pocket. "What's buzzing?"

Before I could respond, there was a loud banging on the motel door. Startled, I got off the bed as did Ian. I stared at the door, trepidation rolling through me. I couldn't sense who it was on the other side of the door, but I could feel raw fear.

"Lorenzo, open the door," Julian shouted through the wood. "Please, hurry."

Driven by the panic in his voice, I moved to open the door. Ian followed me, and when I flung the door wide, Julian and Irene stood there. They were both bruised and bloodied, and Irene held what looked like a double-edged broad sword. The basket hilt was silver with a green stone at the very top.

Eyes wild, Julian growled, "We only have minutes. Sableth is coming. We need to run, now."

CHAPTER SIXTEEN

"What the hell?" Ian rumbled from behind me, taking in the disheveled pair.

In my pocket the Mossfire Stone was vibrating and shuddering, emitting a high-pitched screech. I gritted my teeth against the almost excruciating sound. "What do you mean Sableth is coming?"

Glancing around nervously, Irene lifted the sword. "Are we really going to have a discussion right now?"

"Please, Lorenzo, we must leave," Julian hissed. He held a black knife that also had a green stone on the hilt. "We only have seconds before he's here."

He'd barely finished speaking when the atmosphere of the motel room shifted suddenly. Heat radiated from the corners of the room, and I had a horrifying feeling of déjà vu as I turned around. The room was filled with a roaring hum that seemed to build with every second. Ian turned too, and we stared in shock as near the bed a smoldering spot on the wall began to form. Within seconds it burned through with a searing heat, and white-hot flames sprouted from the wall.

When the ground beneath us shuddered, Ian grabbed me and shoved me out of the room, lunging after me. He slammed the door closed, all the while looking completely bewildered. Julian grabbed hold of my arm, and the four of us sprinted away from the motel. None of us spoke. We simply ran as fast as possible toward a lot at the back of the motel. Ian had his hand on my back as we ran, and Julian led the way. Irene brought up the rear, maybe because she had the sword.

We ran through the vacant lot and out onto a street that ran on the opposite side. My muscles burned, and my lungs ached from running so fast without a break. The stone was still emitting the piercing sound, and Julian scowled over his shoulder.

"We need to keep the stone quiet," Julian hissed.

"I have no idea how it's even making a sound." As I finished speaking, my foot caught on an uneven part of the pavement, and I slammed to the ground onto my knee. I cried out as pain radiated through my leg. "Fuck."

Everyone stopped running, and Ian knelt beside me.

"Is it your knee?" Ian asked, panting.

I nodded. "Yeah."

He gently pressed his fingers to my knee, frowning as he explored the bones and tendons. I winced in pain, breathing hard and covered in sweat.

Irene turned in a circle, watching the dark shadows around us. "We can't stop," she said, her voice trembling. "He's coming. I can feel it."

"Can you stand?" Ian asked me.

"I don't know. I can try." With his help I was able to rise, and when I put weight on the knee, it hurt like hell, but it supported me.

Ian said, "I don't think anything is broken. Probably just very bruised."

"We need to go," Julian said gruffly.

The stone had gone silent when I fell. I had no idea why, and for one minute I thought maybe it had fallen out of my pocket. But when I put my hand inside the pocket, the stone was there. Usually it felt tepid, but at the moment it was very cool to the touch.

"Go. Go," Irene hissed, eyes wide with fear. "I don't want to end up like Thomas and Gordon."

I had no idea what she was talking about, although I recognized the name Thomas. When Julian had taken me to the cabin, Irene had mentioned his name. From what I'd gathered he was one of The Guardians.

"Follow me," Julian said.

We started running again, although I was slower now since my leg hurt. But terror was a great motivator, so I had no desire to stop. We ran for what felt like an hour, sneaking behind buildings and down dark alleys. I could sense Ian's complete confusion, but he didn't ask questions.

At one point we reached what looked like an abandoned warehouse. I eyed the tall fence with barbed wire uneasily, wondering if they expected me to scale that. But then Irene slipped through the fence a few feet down where there was a gap. Relieved, I followed, then Ian, and then Julian.

Julian led us to the side of the big building. I glanced up at the boarded windows and noticed aluminum siding hanging loose from the frame. Julian pulled a key out and opened the lock on a small door, and then we were inside. It smelled of gasoline inside the building, and there were numerous barrels stacked around the open room.

"Will we be safe here?" I asked, my voice echoing in the mostly empty room.

Without addressing my question, Julian said, "Follow me." He led the way to a small room at the far end. As we neared, I noticed similar rune symbols like those at the cabin etched into the outer walls of the room. He unlocked the door to what had probably been an office, and we entered. There was a line of salt at the threshold, and we all took care not to disturb it.

Irene shut the door and slumped. Her pale face was glistening with perspiration, and there was fear in her eyes. "What do we do, Julian? How do we keep him safe?"

"Give me a minute to think." Julian ran a shaky hand through his hair.

The room was empty except for a plastic wrapped case of water against the wall. There were no windows, but Julian flicked a switch near the door, and a florescent light flickered feebly to life. My knee throbbed painfully, so I sat on the floor as far from the door as possible. My heart was racing, and my senses on high alert. At the moment, I didn't sense any heat or hear any humming. I prayed that meant we were safe.

But for how long?

"We can't go back to the cabin. Gordon must have told them where it was." Irene looked like she wanted to cry as she said, "Poor Thomas. He'd never have suspected they'd find the cabin. I'm sure his guard was down."

"We can't think about that right now," Julian snapped. "We have to keep Lorenzo safe while he figures out how to use the stone."

My hand instinctively slipped into my pocket to hold the stone. It throbbed against my palm, and I met Ian's frazzled gaze.

"What is going on?" he mouthed.

I shook my head, feeling nauseated with fear. I felt horrible that he was being dragged into what was happening.

Julian met my gaze, and he moved toward me. "Have you accepted yet that you're The Vessel?"

Ian frowned, but said nothing.

I licked my dry lips. "I still find it hard to believe."

"Even now?" Irene screeched. "You saw Sableth burning through the wall to get to you twice now, but still you reject what we say?"

Ian gave me an alarmed look. "Twice? That's happened before?"

I grimaced but didn't address his question.

"How much longer will you deny the reality of this situation, Lorenzo?" Irene demanded. "What does it take to prove things to you?"

"I know something is happening. I'm just saying I don't see how I can be the one to fix it," I growled. "I have no clue what to do. How would I possibly be the answer?"

When Irene started to speak, Julian held up his hand and gave her a stern look. "I understand why Lorenzo is intimidated. This is terrifying enough when you're not The Vessel."

Ian cleared his throat. "Does anyone mind telling me what the hell is going on?"

I winced. "God, Ian. I'm so sorry you're involved."

"What exactly am I involved in?" he asked.

I whispered, "I don't even know where to begin."

Julian hesitated. "How much do you know, Ian?"

Ian frowned. "I know the old man who died was a professor of lore. I know he seemed worried that Lorenzo was in danger."

"I told Ian about the prophesy but not everything that has to do with me," I admitted.

Julian gave me a quizzical look. "That seems like the most important part. Why leave that out?"

My face warmed. "I didn't believe it myself. Why would I tell him?"

"I know I'm missing a lot of pertinent information." Ian sounded like he was trying hard to stay calm. "For example, how the hell did that wall in the motel room catch on fire, and who are we running from?"

I took a deep breath, and as quickly as possible I ran down everything Julian had told me. Ian listened, his expression skeptical.

Feeling a bit foolish, I added, "According to these two that fire in the motel room was caused by this . . . evil entity, Sableth . . . who wants to kill me to take this supposedly special rock from me." I showed him the Mossfire Stone.

Irene huffed. "Exactly. We're running—so that Sableth and his followers don't chop our heads off too."

I widened my eyes. "What? He has followers? *Human* followers?"

"Oh, yeah, tons of them. They kill whoever Sableth wants killed," she said brightly, but clammed up when Julian gave her a warning look.

I demanded, "The body at the library, is that connected to all of this?"

Julian groaned and leaned against the dingy wall. "Everything is spiraling out of control. It's not supposed to happen like this."

Irene shot a frustrated glance at me. "Everything is going wrong because Lorenzo won't listen. He should already have been training with the stone. Sableth should already be on the verge of defeat. Instead he's growing stronger every day and recruiting followers."

"Don't blame Lorenzo. You didn't even tell him about this insanity until this morning," Ian said. "How could he have possibly been training? If anyone is to blame, it's you two, not Lorenzo."

"Everything would be fine if he'd just do what he's supposed to *do*," groused Irene.

Confusion and guilt shifted through me as Irene and Julian both turned to stare at me. Their disenchantment came through loud and clear. I pulled the Mossfire Stone from my pocket and stared at it. It throbbed in my hand, light dancing across the faceted green surface. Sometimes the surface of the stone shifted and quivered almost like a face making expressions. "If this thing has power, why doesn't it just . . . destroy Sableth? Why does it need me?"

Ian addressed Julian. "That's a fair question. Go ahead, explain how he's supposed to do all the things you're saying with the help of a . . . *rock*."

Julian sighed. "While he refuses to believe it, Lorenzo is what's known as The Vessel. It's prophesied that he would be born to destroy the evil entity Sableth with the Mossfire Stone."

Irene pulled a rag from her pocket and began buffing her sword. "But if The Vessel rejects his role and won't fight, then Sableth can take the stone from him and use it to become immortal."

Her words sent a chill through me. "But he's a spirit, not a human."

Julian hung his head, his expression grim. "He'll be reborn if the Mossfire Stone chooses him. He'll be his human form again, only immortal. Can you imagine the destruction he could cause if he was immortal?"

"And the Mossfire Stone will choose Sableth if you keep being so passive, Lorenzo," Irene wailed. "The Mossfire Stone hates weakness more than anything. It would rather its master be evil than weak."

"I'm not weak," I growled. "I'm simply not made to be the savior of the fucking world."

The stone vibrated in my hand and became almost too hot to hold. "Ouch." I swapped it between my hands, blowing on it.

"You're making it mad," Irene grumbled.

"It's a stone. How can I make it mad?" I winced as the stone burned my skin even hotter. I hurriedly set it on the ground, watching the colors shift and swirl, as if the stone were scowling at me.

Ian's expression was very serious. "What happens if Sableth is reborn?"

Irene shuddered, swinging her sword back and forth. "Nothing good. He's pure evil."

"He'll spread anguish and despair," Julian said in a hushed tone. "We'll all die because we dared to fight against him. But to be honest, he'll torture and torment all humans because he relishes pain. He feeds on terror. Hatred. Anger."

"The stone would allow that? Just because Lorenzo isn't… happy about being…The Vessel?" Ian appeared bewildered.

Julian stared at the stone with an almost apprehensive expression. "The Mossfire Stone is a finicky little thing."

My stomach churned. "If I don't work with the stone and learn how to use it, you're saying the world will be destroyed?" Even as the words left my lips, I felt foolish. But the things I'd seen in the last few days made it impossible to continue to dismiss what Julian said.

Irene nodded. "That's exactly what we're saying. We've been saying that all along, but you won't listen."

"You must admit, this is a lot for Lorenzo to have to swallow. He's had less than a day to try and absorb all you've said to him," Ian remarked. "Is he just supposed to jump into action because you say so?"

"That's not my fault," Irene said. "I wanted to tell him last year."

Julian shot her a surly look. "It wasn't time. How many times do I have to tell you we have to do things the way the prophesy says to do them?"

She muttered, "I still think we should have told him sooner."

I gestured to her sword. "Doesn't that sword work against Sableth?"

"It can't kill him. It can only stun him for a few minutes. That's if I can get close enough before I'm incinerated." She swallowed loudly. "It can kill the humans he recruits to help him, though, and there are plenty of them. There are always many greedy souls willing to do just about anything for money and power."

I shivered at her callous tone. She was nonchalantly admitting she'd killed humans who followed Sableth. That fact certainly didn't make me trust her more. If anything it made me even warier of her. Who made the decision of who should live or die? Would she turn her sword on Ian and me if we didn't do as she wanted?

Julian said softly, "Even if we killed all the humans Sableth sends against us, it wouldn't be enough to save this world. Sableth is too powerful. He can burn us alive within minutes."

Ian frowned. "Is it just you two fighting?"

"With the Mossfire Stone, we don't need numbers." Julian's voice had a hard edge. "But there are others the professor brought in who support the cause. They help us pass messages and warn us of things that are happening all over the city. But we're The Guardians. We were born with the knowledge that it's our duty to protect The Vessel when the time comes." Julian's expression turned grim, and he began to pace. "There were four of us, but two of our own were murdered. They were tortured and beheaded."

"Thomas and Gordon," Irene said, her mouth drooping. "They were good soldiers for the cause."

"So the body at the library was one of your people?" I asked, feeling nauseous.

Julian gave a sharp nod. "Yes. His name was Gordon. Sableth and his followers tortured him until he told them where the cabin was. Then Sableth's people must have found Thomas there." Julian swallowed hard. "He was alone. He never stood a chance."

"Jesus," Ian muttered under his breath.

I could hear the fear in Ian's voice, and it made my heart ache. I was terrified for myself, but the idea of Sableth and his people torturing or harming Ian or Claire in any way made me sick to my stomach. "If Gordon told them about the cabin, who's to say he didn't tell them about this place too?"

Julian's expression was grim. "Because if he had told them, they'd have been here waiting for us, and we'd already be dead."

My nausea intensified. I didn't want to be The Vessel. I wanted to stick my head in the sand and let someone else handle this horrifying mess. But then I looked over and met Ian's golden gaze. I could feel his horror and fear clearly. My chest squeezed painfully, and I knew instantly I had to protect him. I had to protect Claire. I had to at least try to fight, even if the thought of it terrified me to the core.

I gritted my teeth and then said, "I can't believe I'm saying this, and I don't know if I'm up to the task, but I…I'll try to use the stone. I feel like I have no choice but to try."

Irene let out a gasp. "Oh, thank heavens."

Julian's response was much more tempered. He nodded and his expression didn't really change, but his body slumped with relief. "Thank you, Lorenzo."

I sighed. "Don't thank me yet. For all you know I'll fail miserably. So far, the stone hasn't exactly helped me."

"No, it hasn't accepted you yet as it's master." Julian gnawed his bottom lip.

"Are you sure, Lorenzo?" Ian sounded worried.

"What choice do I have? If I don't try, we'll all die." I met Julian's gaze. "How long can we safely stay here?"

"A few days, I think. But we can't call anyone or reach out in any way." There were lines of strain on Julian's bruised face. "I don't even dare try to contact our network of allies. Not yet. Not until you've bonded with the stone."

"So, I can't warn my friend Claire to be careful?" I asked. "Ian can't call his family to be sure they're safe?"

"God, no," Julian said harshly. "Any contact with the outside world could lead Sableth and his followers to us. I'm sorry, but we can't risk it. The best way to keep those we care about safe is for you to learn to use the Mossfire Stone."

"Where will I train?" I frowned.

"We'll train inside this room. We don't need a lot of space. It's really just a matter of you learning to get the stone to do what you need. But if we use the stone outside of this warded room, Sableth will feel the vibrations, and he'll find us within minutes."

"Really?" Ian asked, his voice tense.

"Yes." Julian nodded. "But I suspect Lorenzo and the stone are already bonding. The way the stone reacts to him, that's a good sign."

"Even though the stone seems to dislike me?" I grimaced.

Julian shrugged. "The stone is temperamental. But if it wanted to, it could have already reached out to Sableth."

"It can do that?" I squeaked.

"Yeah." Julian laughed gruffly. "Having the Mossfire Stone is both a curse and a blessing."

"Was it calling out to Sableth earlier? When it made that high-pitched noise?" I asked.

Irene shook her head. "No. It was warning us. Telling us to run."

Julian winced. "If the stone had called to Sableth, you wouldn't have known. He'd have been on you before you even realized it."

"Oh." The more I heard about Sableth, the more disheartened I felt. How would I ever be able to defeat him? He seemed too powerful, and I had no idea what to do or how to make the stone respect me.

"You guys look like you were in a battle." I frowned. "What happened?"

Pain washed through Julian's eyes. "We went to the cabin, and we were ambushed."

Irene's bottom lip quivered. "Thomas fought hard, that was obvious. But in the end, they killed him and then laid in wait for us."

Ian asked, "So, you were attacked by humans?"

Julian nodded. "They're humans under Sableth's control."

"Oh." I shuddered.

"That's why this battle is so difficult," Irene said. "People you know and trust can be under his power, but you'd never realize it until they slit your throat."

"So, Sableth can actually possess people against their will?" I asked, feeling alarmed.

"Yes. If you have the Mossfire Stone, he can't possess you unless you allow it. The Guardians are also impervious to him, but regular humans are fair game," Julian said. "Most of his followers are willing, but he can sometimes enter humans who aren't aware of his existence."

I thought about how out of character my neighbor Ralph had been acting, and the strange shifting expression I'd seen on Weston's face the day he'd visited my shop. Had Sableth gotten to them?

Irene lifted her sword and said grimly, "You really shouldn't trust anyone for now, Lorenzo. Except Julian and I."

Ian frowned. "He can trust me."

Julian glanced at Ian. "Perhaps."

Ian's laugh was hard. "Perhaps? What does that mean?"

"It means perhaps," Julian said curtly. "Perhaps you're trustworthy, and perhaps you're not. It remains to be seen."

"The same could be said of both of you," Ian shot back.

I moved closer to Ian. "I trust Ian."

Ian gave me a grateful smile.

"You haven't seen what we've seen," rumbled Julian. "If you had, you'd be more careful about who you put your faith in."

"I'd never hurt Lorenzo," Ian said quietly.

Julian's cheek twitched. "Perhaps."

Ian's lips thinned, but he didn't respond.

Julian grunted, pushing his hand through his blond hair. There were lines of strain on his face. "Anyway, we should rest. Irene and I are exhausted, and I'm sure you two are as well."

Irene leaned on her sword, looking equally fatigued. "I'd kill for a hot meal and a shower."

I couldn't help but suspect she meant that literally.

"Tomorrow, we'll rise early and Lorenzo can begin training with the stone." Julian moved to the door. "I'll take the first watch, Irene. You can take the second."

Ian said, "I can help. I don't mind taking a watch."

Julian hesitated. "I think for now Irene and I will handle that."

Ian's jaw tensed, but he didn't argue. I'm sure he felt offended that Julian didn't seem to trust him. I was irritated with Julian for being so cold toward Ian, but also understood he'd seen things I couldn't imagine. Still, I felt compelled to reassure Ian that I trusted him.

"Ian, come sleep near me," I said, patting the ground.

He joined me, wincing a bit as he lowered himself onto the hard cement floor. "I haven't slept on the floor since I was a kid."

"Do I show a guy a good time, or what?"

Ian shifted his weight, giving a weak smile. "The Rosewood Motel is starting to seem like the Marriott right about now."

I murmured, "Very true. I wouldn't even mind putting up with the sticky carpet if I could just have that mattress here."

He laid down and turned to face me, resting his head on his folded arms. I did the same, facing him, and we held each other's gaze.

I said quietly, "I'm sorry you got dragged into this."

"It's not your fault."

I sighed. "I feel like it is."

"No. I'm glad I'm here with you. Maybe I can keep you safe."

I didn't bother arguing, but Ian would never be able to protect me from Sableth. That would be like a kitten fighting a dragon. "Julian will come around, don't worry."

"I'm not worried. It's your opinion that matters to me."

"Okay, good."

He gave a wistful smile and whispered, "I wish we'd had more time in the motel."

"Me too."

His eyes flickered. "I wish I could kiss you."

I was able to read his thoughts clearly. He was afraid of what was coming. He wasn't even sure we'd make it through the night. A lump rose in my throat at the hint of regret I saw in his eyes. I realized that, while he wasn't coming right out and saying it, what he really meant was, "I wish I could have kissed you . . . one last time."

CHAPTER SEVENTEEN

The next morning I woke to stiff muscles and a body that ached from sleeping on the hard cement floor. Though I wasn't as chilled as I might have been because during the night Ian and I had gravitated to each other. My head rested on his chest, and his arms encircled me protectively.

For one fleeting moment, I allowed myself to enjoy the feel of his warm hard body against mine. If I closed my eyes and just listened to his even breathing and the steady thump of his heart, I could almost convince myself that we were simply lovers and that everything was normal again.

The intimacy was ruined when Julian and Irene began whispering to each other. Words like "Sableth" and "The Vessel" stood out, making anxiety churn through me. I stirred, and Ian's eyes popped open. He looked briefly disoriented, but then his expression turned grim.

"Morning," I said, my voice thick with sleep.

"Good morning." Ian sat up, running a hand over his messy blond hair. "How's your knee?"

I rubbed my leg. "Sore. Stiff. The swelling has gone down though."

"Good. I'll take a look at it later." He winced and pressed a hand to his spine. "My back hurts. I must be getting old."

"Or maybe sleeping on a cement floor isn't all it's cracked up to be?" I winced, glancing around the barren room. Julian and Irene stood near the door still whispering to each other.

"That might be it." He gave a weak smile.

"Oh, good, you're finally awake." Julian's voice was tense as he turned to address us. The bruising around his eyes and cheek seemed darker this morning, and he looked glum. Irene, however, seemed less morose. Her expression was almost cheerful as she stood leaning on her broadsword, watching Ian and me.

I slowly crawled to my feet, flinching. "I don't suppose there's a continental breakfast at this fine establishment?"

Irene laughed. "No, but we have some delicious bottled water for your enjoyment."

"That will have to do." I was thirsty, my throat and mouth bone dry, so I went over to the case of water and grabbed a couple of bottles for Ian and me. I returned to him, and he took the bottle with a grateful smile.

I drank half the bottle then asked, "How do we handle the bathroom situation? I need to pee."

"There's a porta-potty type of thing behind the warehouse. Be warned—it's scary in there." Julian shuddered. "Lots of spiders and disgusting smells."

"Awesome."

"Also, leave the stone here," Julian said. "It can't leave this room."

"Oh, right." I took the stone out of my pocket and offered it to Ian since he was closest.

He looked uneasy as he hesitantly took it. "Am I allowed to touch this?"

"Why wouldn't you be?" I frowned.

"I don't know. Maybe it will dislike me and burn me to death?" He laughed, but I suspected he was half-serious.

"It won't hurt you." Irene's gaze was assessing as she studied Ian. "It won't even notice you. All the stone cares about is its master. Once it chooses either The Vessel or Sableth, it will only protect its master." She had a faraway look in her eyes as she murmured, "It would be cool, though, if it could also like other people. You know, like maybe if it respected them enough to want to work with them too?"

Julian wrinkled his brow. "That's not how it works, Irene. You know that. The stone can't just be wooed by anyone. It has to bond to its master."

"I'm just saying it would be cool if it liked me. What's wrong with that? Maybe then I wouldn't end up like Gordon or Thomas." She shivered and seemed to tighten her grip on her sword.

Julian rolled his eyes. "That's a silly idea. The stone doesn't care about anyone but the one person it serves."

Irritation twitched across her face. "It's not silly. Who wouldn't want the stone to protect them?"

He exhaled impatiently. "You should focus on what's real, not daydream about what isn't."

She gave him a dirty look but didn't respond.

Ian watched their interaction with mild curiosity. He got to his feet. "You know what? I need to use the facilities too. Maybe one of you could hang on to the stone while we're gone?"

"Absolutely." Irene's eyes lit with excitement. "I'm happy to do it." She moved to Ian, taking the stone. She stared down at it, an expression of wonderment on her face, but then she frowned. "It was so pretty when Lorenzo held it, but now it's so plain when I do."

"Maybe it just needs to warm up to you," Ian suggested.

Julian's expression was grumpy. "Don't encourage her. She shouldn't fixate on the stone. It's not healthy."

Irene said under her breath, "Says the guy who's fixated on Lorenzo."

Julian's cheeks tinted pink. "What?"

"Oh, nothing." Irene batted her eyes innocently.

Ian cleared his throat. "Not to rush you or anything, Lorenzo, but I really need to go."

"Right." I nodded and followed him to the door.

Julian opened it for us and then stepped aside. "Ian,

you should leave your phone here."

Ian frowned. "I won't use it."

"It's just safer if you leave it here." Julian sounded firm.

Reaching into his back pocket, Ian grabbed his phone. He looked annoyed but just said, "I turned it off last night."

"Great." Julian tucked the phone away in his pocket. "Don't take too long. We need to begin training right away, Lorenzo."

I tried not to bristle at his lecturing tone, reminding myself he was just trying to help. "Okay."

We left the small room and walked through the big building to the side door. Stepping out into the fresh air made me instantly happier. The sky was an unblemished blue canopy overhead, and the sun was warm on my face. I inhaled the chilly clean air greedily as I examined the area for the first time in the daylight.

Last night it had been too dark to really see anything, and I'd been so scared I wouldn't have noticed anyway. Now I saw that there were oil barrels stacked along the perimeter of the rusty chain-link fence. There didn't appear to be any other buildings in the vicinity, but thick groves of oak trees and evergreens surrounded the lot.

While the inside of the compound had been cleared of trees, big stumps along the perimeter of the fence remained. Beyond the fence tall evergreens towered. Their crisp, piney scent mingled with the damp, earthy aroma of the forest floor.

Ian groaned, stretching his arms. "God, I needed this. I was feeling claustrophobic in there."

"Me too," I murmured, staring up at the big building we'd just exited.

The structure looked even worse for wear in the daylight. The metal siding was covered in patches of rust and flaking paint. The plywood boards that covered the windows were warped and weathered. The air was tinged with a mix of earthy dust, decaying vegetation, and a hint of metallic tang from the rusty fence, building, and barrels.

The lot itself was uneven, with scattered patches of dry, cracked earth and encroaching weeds claiming space. Wild mustard and yarrow stubbornly thrived in thick clumps along the base of the building. A ground squirrel chirped the alarm somewhere in the trees, and a red-tailed hawk circled gracefully above, probably hoping to make that squirrel his next meal.

Julian wasn't lying about the disgusting state of the porta-potty. Ian bravely went first, and he came out looking green around the gills. I tried not to touch anything or breathe too deeply as I gingerly used the facilities. We then used a bottle of water we'd brought to wash our hands as best we could.

"We should probably get back inside," Ian said, looking forlornly at the blue sky and wispy white clouds that had appeared. "Don't want to ruffle Julian's feathers."

"Let's stay outside for a bit," I suggested. "We need the sun for vitamin D, right?" Plus, I longed for some time alone with Ian while away from Julian's glowering gaze.

"True. Vitamin D is very important." He smiled and slipped his arm around my waist. "As a physician, it's my sworn duty to keep my patients happy and healthy."

I smirked. "Is that right?"

He gave the porta-potty a wary glance. "Let's move location."

"Okay."

He tugged me toward the building. Once there, he pressed me up against the old structure and kissed me. His soft lips teased mine, and then he pushed his tongue into my mouth. I moaned because I'd been craving his taste and touch. It was disconcerting that I could be afraid for my life but still desire Ian's touch. He roamed my body with his hands, caressing and gentle. He leaned more of his weight on me, and his kisses became more passionate. My dick warmed and hardened, and I wished we were somewhere way more private.

When the kiss ended, he whispered, "I wanted to do that all night."

"Same." I slipped my hand under his shirt, running my hands over his warm, smooth skin. "You think Irene and Julian would notice if we had sex up against the building?"

"I think the building might fall down if we lean on it too much." He grimaced. "Plus, Julian would probably slit my throat with Irene's sword."

"What? Why?"

He narrowed his eyes. "Come on, Lorenzo. Surely you know the reason Julian dislikes me is because he likes you."

I hesitated but there was really no reason to lie. I'd always known Julian had a little crush on me. "Well, I don't care because I don't like him like that."

His lips twitched. "No? Who do you like?"

"Take a guess."

"Irene?"

I laughed. "Wrong. I mean, she seems nice and all . . ."

His smile faded. "Well, I like you, Lorenzo. A lot."

My pulse fluttered at how serious he looked. "Usually, if a guy said that to me, I'd want to run."

"Yeah? You don't feel like running?"

"Well, commitment doesn't seem as scary as usual, seeing as we'll probably be dead in a few days."

He frowned. "That's very grim."

Guilt nudged me at his unsettled expression, but I simply said, "The situation is grim."

"True." He sighed and touched my cheek gently, his eyes warm. "Julian may not believe me, but I'll do what I can to protect you, Lorenzo. I hope you know that."

"I believe you. I trust you."

He lifted his brows. "Does that mean you might actually be willing to date me?"

"Well, first I have to save the world, apparently." I glanced up at the swaying treetops, trying to ignore the insecurities clawing at me.

He winced and said gruffly, "Timing really is everything."

"It is." I put my arms around his neck, pressing closer. "But this is nice. Just being out here with you, without Julian hovering."

"I agree." His arms tightened around my waist. "Julian takes his role as Guardian very seriously."

"Yes. He's very young to be under this sort of stress. I'm sure the professor's death has put even more pressure on him."

"I'm sure it has." His expression was thoughtful. "Do you think Julian would let us see the books where the professor discovered the prophesy?"

"I don't know. Do you want to see them?"

"I kind of do. We're just taking everything Julian says as the truth." The light breeze fluttered Ian's blond hair, and his gaze was very serious.

"You don't trust him?" I frowned, unsettled by the idea Ian thought Julian might be lying to us.

"I'm not saying that exactly. Irene obviously trusts him. I get the feeling she follows him blindly."

"You think that's a mistake?"

He grimaced, looking slightly sheepish. "I'm not sure. I guess I'd feel more comfortable if I saw the lore with my own eyes. Julian seems obsessed with you. He's very possessive.

Maybe his feelings are clouding his decisions. He might not be telling us everything."

"What would he be leaving out?"

"I don't know." He bit his bottom lip. "But unless he's hiding something, he shouldn't be opposed to letting us see the lore, right?"

Ian was making sense, but still I hesitated. "I wouldn't know how to bring it up. He might get offended." Things were insane enough. The last thing I needed was to piss off Julian. He was the one person who seemed to have some of the answers I needed.

"But, what's wrong with wanting to see the lore for yourself? If you're The Vessel, it concerns you most of all."

"True," I murmured.

He studied me. "It was just a thought. I guess I'm used to being in charge. It's hard to trust Julian with my life when I can feel he resents me."

"I'm sure he doesn't want anything bad to happen to you."

"I hope not."

I studied him, considering what he'd said. I could understand his hesitation at putting his faith in Julian, considering how Julian was treating him. I wasn't opposed to seeing the lore for myself. In fact, I liked the idea. I simply wasn't sure how to ask Julian without putting his back up. But our lives were at stake, so perhaps I needed to risk upsetting Julian even if it might be incredibly awkward.

"You look worried now." He sighed, guilt rippling through his gaze. "I'm sorry. I didn't mean to stress you out. I'm sure Julian is absolutely trustworthy."

"I understand why you're concerned." I leaned into him, tightening my arms around him. I wanted Ian to feel he wasn't alone. That he could trust me to take his concerns seriously. "The books may not be anywhere we can get to them though. They might have been at the cabin, and we can't go back there."

"True."

"But I agree if we can see the books, we should," I said firmly. "I'll ask Julian later."

"Yeah?"

"Sure. Like you said, I'm The Vessel." I shrugged. "If I'm supposed to save the damn world, I have every right to see that stuff."

"Exactly." He smiled, appearing relieved. "Now, where were we?" He lowered his head and kissed me.

I opened to his seeking tongue, lust nipping at me. The warm breeze carried the scent of sage, and I gave myself to the moment. With the situation we were in, life seemed more precious than ever. The taste of Ian and the feel of his hands sliding down my body made me feel rejuvenated. Hopeful.

When the door squeaked open, Ian and I broke the kiss. However, we still held each other as Julian popped his head out of the door.

When he saw us, his expression hardened. "You've been out here a long time. It might not be safe." He sniffed. "Plus, we need to get started on your training, Lorenzo, ASAP."

Ian looked annoyed as we exchanged a glance.

"We'll be right in, Julian," I said tersely. "Don't worry. I'm going to train as hard as possible. I just needed a moment to center myself."

"Well, hurry up." Julian banged the door closed.

Ian scowled. "See, he's jealous. It's so obvious. He can't even hide it anymore."

"Yeah." Julian's possessiveness was a complication I didn't need.

"Well, it was fun while it lasted." Ian let go of me. "We'd better get you back inside before the warden puts me in a timeout."

Once Ian and I returned to the room inside the building, Julian stood in the center of the room, hunched over, watching me under his lashes. Irene sat perched a few feet away on an upside-down wooden box, polishing her broadsword with a scrap of cloth she kept in her pocket. Ian gravitated to a spot near the door to the room, his gaze pinned on me.

"How do we begin? What should I learn first?" I asked, joining Julian where he stood.

Julian cleared his throat. "With the Mossfire Stone, you can perform illusion manipulations."

"Okay." My voice wobbled, and my stomach churned as I stared at the cool, dark stone in my hand.

"Unfortunately, they won't work on Sableth." Julian winced as he added that little tidbit.

"The illusions won't work on Sableth?" I did my best not to sound as panicked as that information made me feel.

"No." Julian quickly added, "But they will work on his followers."

Ian grunted disapprovingly from his position near the door. His expression was deadly serious as he asked, "The stone only works on his followers? Then what good is the stone to Lorenzo? Isn't Sableth the real problem here?"

Julian appeared confused by the question. "The stone is how Lorenzo will destroy Sableth."

Impatience sparked in Ian's green eyes. "How does that work if the stone has no power over Sableth?"

Julian gave Ian an equally irritable glance. "It does have power over Sableth. That's why Lorenzo will need to master the illusion manipulation technique so that he can destroy Sableth."

I stared at the stone in my hand. "But how? I don't understand. If the illusions don't work on Sableth? How do I destroy him?"

Irene glanced up from polishing her sword. "The key is getting close to Sableth."

Julian pointed at her. "Yes. What she said."

"But, if I'm supposed to get close to him, why do we always run?" I turned the stone over in my palm, observing its flat, lifeless color. There were times when the stone glowed so bright it hurt my eyes, and other times when it was the dullest rock I'd ever seen.

"Ahhh." Julian nodded as if finally understanding my point. "We ran because you aren't bonded to the stone yet. If you're not bonded, Sableth can kill you."

"Oh." I shuddered. "Great."

"That's why Sableth is trying so hard to find you and the stone," Irene said. "He really, really wants you dead before you connect to the stone. He knows you're the only one who can stop him. So long as the stone accepts you."

"And if the stone rejects me?"

Irene and Julian exchanged an uneasy glance.

"Let's think positive." Julian's smile was strained.

I frowned, uneasy at his evasive answer. "But it can refuse me, right?"

"Yeah." Irene's tone was offhand. "It definitely can."

Julian grunted, shooting Irene a chiding glance. "That's not going to happen. According to the lore, the stone wants to accept Lorenzo."

"Sure." Irene shrugged, focusing on polishing the green stone in the hilt of her sword. "But it has to feel Lorenzo is worthy."

"What makes me worthy?" Irene wasn't the most reassuring person, and her nonchalant attitude was beginning to bug me.

"You have to have the strength to take Sableth on." Irene sounded as if the idea of that was as simple as placing an order on Doordash. "You must be brave. The stone hates weakness."

"What if I'm not strong enough? I'm not exactly a he-man."

Julian grimaced. "You'll never be physically strong enough to defeat Sableth. It's not that kind of battle. Your mind is your greatest weapon against Sableth. So long as you have the stone."

Irene glanced up, squinting. "The illusions are for the humans that do Sableth's bidding."

"I see. So then, I'm practicing illusions so that I can get past the humans and close to Sableth?" I hesitated. "But I can't do any of this if the stone rejects me."

"Exactly." Julian appeared relieved that I was finally catching on.

"Sure. Piece of cake understanding all of this, Julian," mumbled Ian, raking a hand through his blond hair.

"Am I guaranteed victory if I have the stone on my side?" My stomach churned waiting for Julian's answer.

He avoided my gaze. "No."

"No?" My voice was sharp.

Ian rasped, "For God's sake. None of this is fair to ask of Lorenzo."

Julian ignored Ian and met my gaze, looking resigned. "The stone gives you an edge, but ultimately, you have to be psychically strong enough to enter Sableth's spirit with the stone in your possession, and explode him into oblivion."

An awkward silence followed his statement.

I cleared my throat. "I'm sorry, what? You expect me to …enter his spirit and do what now?"

"This is insanity," muttered Ian. "Absolute lunacy."

Julian gave him an impatient glance. "It's a battle, Ian. There are no guarantees in battle."

"Yeah," snapped Ian. "A battle you want Lorenzo to fight alone."

"Alone?" Julian bugged his eyes. "I'm standing right here, aren't I?"

"Sure, but when the time comes, where will you be?" Ian grated out angrily.

I appreciated Ian defending me. Julian and Irene seemed only too happy to let me go into battle with nothing but a rock in my hand. "So, I'm supposed to trust that the stone has my back, and even then I might fail because I'm not psychically strong enough to defeat Sableth?" I gave a humorless laugh. "Why in the hell would I do any of that?"

"Exactly," Ian said forcefully.

"Because if you don't we'll all die anyway," snapped Julian. "It's true there's no guarantee you'll succeed, but if you don't even try, it's guaranteed the world as you know it will end."

Sweat broke out on my upper lip. "Why the hell would all of this be on me? What lunatic thought that was a good idea?" I raked a shaky hand through my hair, and I began pacing back and forth. "This makes no sense. I'm nobody."

"You're so much stronger than you realize, Lorenzo." Julian's voice was plaintive. "If you can get the Mossfire Stone to bond with you, I truly believe in my heart you'll be successful."

"And if you're wrong, he'll die." Ian's voice was harsh and his eyes glittered with anger.

Julian snapped, "As I said, we'll all die regardless if he doesn't try."

Irene shrugged. "Julian is saying you have nothing to lose, Lorenzo, because it might already be lost."

"I know you don't want to believe this is real," Julian shook his head. "But this has been building your entire life. This is your destiny. The Guardians have always known this day would come, and the dark side has too."

"The dark side," I mumbled mockingly. "How do I know you're not the dark side?"

Julian winced. "I'm here to protect you."

"Right." I shook my head, feeling panicked. I met Ian's serious gaze and I turned to Julian and blurted, "I want to see the books."

Julian blinked at me, appearing confused. "What books?"

"The lore," Ian interjected. "Is there some reason you can't show Lorenzo the books? He's supposed to just blindly believe what you're saying is true?"

Julian said angrily, "Are you calling me a liar?"

I held his gaze, stomach clenched with stress. "I don't see anything wrong with wanting to see in writing the things you're telling me are true."

"Exactly." Ian nodded, giving me an encouraging look. "Lorenzo has every right to see the actual books. You're asking a lot of him to blindly believe you. Don't you think?"

Irene met Julian's frazzled gaze. "We can't show you the books," she mumbled.

"Why not?" I demanded. "If I'm The Vessel, why can't I see the lore?"

"Because we don't have the books," Julian said harshly, his cheeks flushed pink. "The professor hid them for safe keeping, but we don't know where he put them."

Ian gave a dismissive huff. "Seriously? We're supposed to believe that?"

"Yeah," I muttered. "That's awfully convenient."

"Actually," snapped Julian, "It's extremely inconvenient."

Irene nodded, looking frustrated. "You think we wouldn't love to have those books with us right now? Maybe they could make all of this less confusing for all of us."

"If you can't produce the books, I'm not sure I can just blindly go along with all of this." The idea that even if the Mossfire Stone accepted me I could still fail had me hyperventilating.

"So if we can't produce the books, you're just going to bail on us?" Julian sounded frustrated. Hurt.

"You're asking me to risk my *life*, Julian. Without any proof you just want me to accept I'm The Vessel and that all this craziness is true."

Julian watched me for a moment, then said softly, "Lorenzo, do you remember the old woman?"

Shock rolled through me at his question. "What?"

"Do you remember the old woman who took you and your brother, Nico?" Julian's eyes glittered. "The woman who held you captive and tortured you."

"How could you possibly know about that?" I whispered.

"Because all of what I'm telling you is true. We know everything about you," Julian said.

"How?" I demanded.

A muscle worked in Julian's cheek. "The story of your kidnapping in the newspaper all those years ago is what alerted Professor Buckler to your existence. You'd have only been seven at the time you were kidnapped. But you remember, don't you?"

My heart raced as I held his gaze. "So what if I do?"

Julian said, "It was no fluke that you were the one that woman kidnapped. That old woman poisoned you hoping if you died Sableth wouldn't come. She failed, thankfully, but even all the way back when you were a child, there were those who knew what was coming."

"Did that really happen, Lorenzo?" Ian sounded startled.

I felt sick as I held Julian's knowing gaze. "Yes," I grated. "Some crazy woman kidnapped me and my brother when we were kids. That doesn't prove any of this is true. Like Julian said, the story was published in the paper. Anyone who read it could have come up with this story."

"But you know in your gut what I'm saying is true. I know you do." Julian's voice was urgent and he leaned toward me. "You know that Sableth is real. You've seen him with your own eyes."

"I'm not saying I don't believe that Sableth is real. I'm simply saying I can't be the one to stop him. I'm not The Vessel. I can't be."

"Why? Because you're scared?" Julian asked. "No one blames you for being scared. Buy you shouldn't lie to yourself because you're scared."

Sighing, Irene said, "Who could blame you for being terrified?"

I held Julian's unrelenting stare, gut churning. I didn't feel ready to fight anyone, let alone a malevolent evil entity. But the truth of Julian's words sank into me like bitter poison. His words woke something up inside of me that I'd tried my whole life to ignore. "I don't want this," I mumbled.

"I know." Julian nodded. "But it's happening all the same."

"You shouldn't put your faith in me," I said breathlessly. "I'm going to fail."

"No." Julian scowled. "You're going to train and then you're going to destroy Sableth. Have a little faith in yourself, Lorenzo."

"You expect me to destroy Sableth? Seriously?" I shook my head. "He's so strong. I'm nothing compared to him."

"You're everything." Julian moved closer. "Do you think I'd have put my faith in you if I didn't believe that with every part of my being? Do you think Thomas, Gordon, and Professor Buckler gave their lives because they didn't believe in you?"

Guilt washed over me. "I'm sorry they died, but there's no reason for more people to die."

"It's going to happen whether you fight or not." Irene sounded frustrated. "But there's no hope at all if you won't even try."

Clenching my jaw, I stood with my head down. I lifted the stone, almost glaring at it. It lit an almost florescent green as it vibrated against my palm. A flush of heat swept through my body, startling me with the intensity of it. Along with the buzzing sensation came a certainty that I had to fight Sableth. It was a terrifying inescapable truth that permeated my body and soul.

"Please, Lorenzo, you have to try." Julian's voice was hushed.

"No, he doesn't have to do anything unless he wants to." Ian's eyes glittered with anger.

"But we'll all die if he doesn't even try," wailed Irene.

"Yes," Julian said in a dull voice. "All of us will die, Lorenzo. Everyone you care about will die. Claire will die. Ian will die. *You'll die.*"

I lifted my gaze to his. "I'm telling you I really don't fucking *want* this."

"I know." Julian's eyes were pleading. "But you're our only hope. It's that simple."

I held his gaze as frustration and fear roared through me. I was angry and hopeless. There was no way I could do the things he wanted me to do. But the terror and pleading in Julian and Irene's eyes was too much to bear. With a groan, I relented. "Fine. I'll try. But I can't promise you anything. Not a damn thing."

Julian slumped with relief. "Thank you, Lorenzo. It'll be okay. You'll see."

"Yeah, right," I muttered.

Ian's expression was impossible to read. He didn't look happy, but he didn't say anything to discourage me either.

Julian blew out a shaky breath. "Right. We'll start with practicing the illusions."

I stared at him, trying to force myself to cooperate. Gritting my teeth, I rasped, "What do I do? If I just hold the stone, will it know what I want?"

Irene snorted a laugh but looked sheepish when Julian gave her a scolding glance.

"None of this is funny, Irene," Julian growled.

"Sorry." Irene looked cowed and she dropped her gaze.

I looked down at the stone again. "If it doesn't know what I want, how do I control it?"

"You'll have to connect psychically to the stone," Julian said. "Then it will know what you need."

"How?"

"It's like when you do psychic readings for people. You know how sometimes holding an item from a deceased person can help you connect to the spiritual world? That's basically what this is. You need to be in tune with the stone."

"Okay." I frowned.

"Hold the stone tight and concentrate on how it feels in your hand," Julian said. "If it's cold to the touch, it's listening to you. If it's tepid, it isn't connected to you, and if it's hot, it's angry and useless. It won't do anything you want if it's angry."

"What makes the stone angry?" Ian asked.

Julian shot me a wary look. "If Lorenzo is afraid, it won't like it. Or if he takes too long to master a technique, it might get annoyed."

"Unbelievable," I muttered. "Why would the stone judge me? I have no idea what I'm doing. It will take as long as it takes to master things."

Irene gritted her teeth. "You'll need to be more cooperative, Lorenzo. You can't fight the stone. You have to bend to it."

Julian grimaced. "No. It's more that they have to bend to each other. Think of your connection with the Mossfire Stone as a partnership."

I fingered the stone and mumbled, "A partnership where my partner is a prima donna."

Ian gave a gruff laugh.

Julian tensed his body. "Okay, try to make me see something, Lorenzo."

"How?" I frowned, nervous to even begin to try connecting to the stone.

"Rub the stone and picture something," Julian urged.

"Like what?"

Julian glanced up looking exasperated. "Anything you think might distract me. I won't be able to instruct you every moment when you're up against Sableth. You'll have to think for yourself."

"Julian," I groused, "It's the first time I've ever tried using the stone."

"True." He sighed, fiddling with his lip piercing. "Okay, just pretend I'm coming to attack you. What could you dream up that would make me stop advancing?"

"I have no idea."

"Let your imagination run wild, Lorenzo." Julian's voice was coaxing. "What sort of thing would make me stop in my tracks?"

I rubbed my thumb over the stone and focused on Julian. I tried to visualize something that might stop him, but struggled with what it could be. What would make him stop moving toward me if he were determined to kill me? I had no idea what sort of things Julian feared. Perhaps the vision didn't need to be personal or specific to Julian. It just needed to be something that would give anyone pause. Something scary.

Sweat broke out on my forehead as I pinpointed my energy at Julian. I tried to probe his mind and climb inside his thoughts. It was the opposite of what I usually did. I typically received information. This was the first time I'd ever attempted to put information inside another person's brain. It didn't come naturally to me. I felt guilty and sordid even trying to imprint thoughts onto his mind.

Gritting my teeth, I visualized the ground opening up in front of him, creating a wide, seemingly bottomless gorge. The stone chilled and throbbed in my palm, and I felt a bit lightheaded as I focused on the vision. Julian had taken a few steps toward me, but he suddenly stopped as the ground seemed to rumble and shake.

Narrowing my eyes, I said softly under my breath, "You can't begin to see the bottom. You'll be swallowed whole by waves of bottomless black water."

Julian widened his eyes. "Something is happening." He stumbled backward.

"Is it working?" Irene asked, perking up.

I continued to visualize broken ground and jagged deadly cliffs. The more I focused, the greater the details became. I could feel a chill and smelled rotting kelp wafting from the cavernous hole. Even though I knew I was the one who'd thought up the vision, my stomach swirled with uneasiness at how real it seemed. I could feel a frigid breeze sucking at me, pulling me toward the ravine.

"You did it," Julian said hoarsely. "I can't believe how real it seems."

Irene stood, eyes bugged. "Holy cow."

"Stay back," Julian said quickly, holding out a warning hand. "I don't know if it can actually hurt us or not." His Adam's apple bobbed. "It feels so real."

The strain of focusing so intently was too much. I let out a harsh breath, and my concentration broke. The gorge immediately disappeared, and I slumped to my knees, breathing hard. Perspiration now covered my entire face, and I felt queasy.

Julian appeared awestruck. "That . . . that was really good, Lorenzo. Especially for your first try."

"Was it?" I gave a weary smile.

"Definitely," Ian blinked at me. "I've only heard about the technique. Seeing in in person . . . wow."

Ian moved to me and he rubbed my back. "You okay?"

"Yeah." I blew out a shaky breath. "That was exhausting, but I'm fine." I forced myself to stand. My legs were wobbly, and my injured knee throbbed, but my strength was seeping back.

"It's worrisome that it took so much out of you," Ian murmured. "How would you use that on more than one person?"

Julian wrinkled his brow. "According to the lore, the stone will feed more energy to the user as it begins to trust. Right now, I suspect the stone is doing the bare minimum, which is why Lorenzo is so tired."

I stared down at the stone. It had gone dark, and it now felt lukewarm against my skin. "What if we don't have time for the stone to learn to trust me? I can't fight a group of people like this. I couldn't hold the illusion for very long, and even that drained me."

Julian said brusquely, "I think that will change with time. But even if you couldn't keep the illusion going for long, that gorge stopped me, and it would have halted anyone with me. If this had been a real situation, that illusion would have bought you time."

"Okay." I nodded, not completely sure I agreed.

"You should feel proud of yourself. The gorge was a smart choice, Lorenzo." Julian smiled at me, looking tired but pleased. "You have good instincts."

"Thank you. I . . . I think I could do even better if I knew what a certain person fears most. I had to just go for what would scare me."

"That works. Some things are universally scary." Ian gave me a reassuring smile.

"You should try again," Irene said.

Julian agreed, "Yes. Do something different this time. The more variety you have, the better."

I blew out a shaky breath. "Okay."

Julian once more advanced on me, and I focused on visualizing a wall of fire. I concentrated on Julian again, and tried to send thoughts of flesh-searing flames to his mind. When nothing seemed to happen, I gritted my teeth and tried harder. "Come on, stone," I whispered. "Help me."

The stone remained tepid as Julian came closer. "It's not working now," I said.

"No?" Julian frowned.

I squeezed the stone. "Why won't you work? I need more practice than that or you're going to get me killed," I muttered, rubbing the stone against the palm of my other hand. "Come on, rock, do something."

The Mossfire Stone vibrated against my palm, but still remained tepid.

I smacked the stone lightly. "Wake up." As the words had left my mouth the stone turned hot as fire, searing against my palm. "Ouch." I shifted it to my other hand. "What are you doing? Why are you so hot?"

"Uh, oh. It must be mad," Irene said.

"Mad? Why would it be mad?" I scowled.

Ian said softly, "Maybe try talking to it more gently, Lorenzo."

I glanced up. "You want me to sweet talk a rock?"

"Ian's right." Julian tone was chiding. "You have to be less bossy toward the stone. It has to want to work with you. You can't force it."

I groaned. "I really have to talk to the stone? I feel so silly doing that."

Julian said, "Like I mentioned, you're partners. Tell it what you want to accomplish together."

I let out a tired breath and caressed the smooth surface. All the different colors shimmering over the face of the rock really were beautiful. I tried to let go of my resentment. "Listen, stone, I…I want to work with you. If we're going to defeat Sableth, we have to respect each other. Don't fight me. Fight Sableth instead."

The stone cooled slightly, giving me some hope.

"I'm sure you'd rather be on the side of good, right? Sableth would be a horrible partner. He'd probably make you do all kinds of things you don't want to do. I suspect you'd rather do the right thing and make the world a beautiful place. Sableth wants to destroy everything. We can't let that happen, can we?"

The stone quivered and chilled some more. Feeling more optimistic, I said, "Okay. Let's try this. How about a wall of fire?" I concentrated on picturing red hot flames while stroking my thumb over the stone. It was difficult to focus so intently for an extended time, but I didn't give up. I kept picturing the color of the flames and the heat they'd throw off. I was thrilled when a wall of fire sprang up out of nowhere. "Yes," I said, feeling relieved. "Perfect."

Julian grunted and winced, lifting a hand as if shielding himself. He pulled his mouth tight across his teeth, shuddering. He stumbled backward, raw pain in his eyes.

"It's amazing," Irene called out, eyes wide.

"The heat is so intense," Julian hissed. "I feel like my skin is melting."

"Is it too hot?" Distracted by the idea I was hurting Julian, my concentration faltered. When that happened the flames instantly disappeared.

The stone that had been cool suddenly blazed hot against my hand. I yelped and dropped the stone, and it bounced across the floor, landing at Julian's feet.

Julian glanced up, frowning. "Why did you stop?"

"I was afraid I was hurting you." I studied the stone where it lay on the floor.

"It's not real, Lorenzo." Julian held out his arms. "See? Nothing is burned or singed."

"It sure seemed real. I thought you were really being burned."

Irene gave me a reproachful look. "You can't let things distract you, Lorenzo. You can't care that your opponent is injured. You want them injured so that they're incapacitated." She stood and pointed the sword straight ahead, then she lunged forward. "Then you go for the kill." She grinned. "See? This is war. You can't be afraid to hurt anyone you're fighting. You must only think of yourself."

"I know." I gave a wan smile. "But Julian isn't really my opponent."

"He is right now." Irene sat down again. "You gotta get your head in the game."

"Don't be discouraged, Lorenzo," Julian said. "Pick up the stone and try again. And don't let it bother you if I react."

I bent down to retrieve the stone, but it burned my fingers. Swearing under my breath, I dropped it again. The face of the green stone swirled and seemed to glower at me. Stuffing down my pride, I said gruffly, "Look, I'm sorry. I'm not weak. I simply don't like hurting people."

The stone continued to whirl and vibrate with displeasure. Irritation rose in me, but I pushed it down. Whether I felt like a fool or not, talking to the stone had worked before. I just had to swallow my pride and do what needed doing. I had to get the stone's sympathies.

I cleared my throat. "Be patient with me, okay? I'm not used to this sort of thing. I'm trying my best. I'm willing to fight Sableth. If I were a coward, I wouldn't even want to train with you, right?"

The stone's bright green color seemed to change into a softer, bluer green. The swirling calmed slightly, and the surface smoothed. I took a chance, reaching out to pick up the stone again. Thankfully, it felt cool, not hot. Relieved that it had listened to me, I stood and sought out Ian's gaze.

He gave me a small but encouraging smile, and I smiled back.

Julian shifted impatiently. "Are you going to create an illusion or not?"

Gritting my teeth at his peevish tone, I faced him. The stone heated against my hand, but it wasn't painful. I focused my energy on Julian, not worrying about hurting him this time. I put all of my thoughts into what the flames should be like instead.

The stone buzzed in my palm and a pulse of energy seemed to move through my body. A wall of flames whooshed into being, and this time when the fire materialized, it seemed easier to keep it steady. I was pleased that I didn't feel the strain as much this time. The first illusion had drained my energy swiftly, but this time holding the illusion in place felt less burdensome. It had to be because the stone was doing much of the work.

The flames leapt higher, and the heat increased. Sweat covered my face and body as I focused on Julian. The fire created a wind that ruffled Julian's hair and reddened his cheeks. Little dust devils appeared on the edge of the flames, spinning and blazing around the main fire.

Julian winced and stepped backward, shielding his face with his arm. "Jesus," he rasped. "It's too hot."

I didn't relent this time though. I kept focused on the flames, enjoying the way they built and licked at the ceiling of the room. I could feel the power of the stone coursing through my body and mind, and it was exhilarating. The experience was completely different once the stone was working with me. I felt powerful. Invincible. The idea of facing Sableth didn't feel nearly as terrifying as before. I knew that was because the stone was feeding me courage and energy.

"This is better," I whispered. "This isn't hard at all. I could keep this up for hours."

Julian gasped and fell to his knees. "Okay, enough, Lorenzo."

I felt a bit dazed as I watched him. Almost disconnected from his suffering. But I caught myself and purposely broke my concentration. The flames evaporated instantly, leaving a sooty scent in the room.

Irene ran to Julian. "Are you okay?"

He nodded, wiping at his flushed face. "That felt so real." Irene helped him to his feet. "Maybe we should move on to something else." He gave a wry smile. "I think you're getting the hang of that, and I'm not sure how much more of a thrashing, imaginary or not, my body can take."

Irene said, "You should have him try memory manipulation exercises, Julian. I'll bet he can do that easily."

"What's that?" I asked.

Julian used the bottom of his shirt to wipe his sweaty face. "It's where you alter the memories of another person. You can make them forget things like where they keep their weapons, or who they're loyal to."

"That sounds promising," Ian said.

"It can be." Julian went over and helped himself to a bottle of water from the case. "Going to battle for the cause is one thing, but when you suddenly can't remember why you're fighting, or who you're fighting for? It definitely takes the wind out of your sails."

Feeling more emboldened, I tightened my grip on the Mossfire Stone. I felt its energy coursing through my veins. We were bonding. I could truly feel it happening. The odds were probably still against us, but for the first time, I felt as if we had a ghost of a chance.

CHAPTER EIGHTEEN

I practiced the rest of the day and half of the night, creating terrifying illusions and confusing the other three by manipulating their memories. My body and mind were exhausted, but the hope I felt now that the stone was cooperating was exhilarating.

Once we'd finished the training for the day, Julian announced that he was sending Irene out to do some recon. He wanted her to touch base with some of the people in their network of allies.

"Isn't that dangerous?" I asked, feeling worried for Irene.

"Staying here is dangerous. Leaving is dangerous. Everything is dangerous right now," Julian said grimly. "But we need to see what's happening out there. When we found you at the Rosewood Motel, the city was in chaos. People were attacking each other, and there were some shootings."

"Really?" Alarm surged through me. "Was anyone hurt?"

"Probably." Julian sounded distracted. "I'm sure it's Sableth's doing. He's spreading chaos. I'm surprised he's waited this long to cause trouble."

I met Ian's worried gaze. "I hope Claire and your family are safe."

He winced. "Yeah. Me too."

Irene seemed fine with being sent on a mission. Almost eager in fact. I got the feeling she wanted to get away from Julian for a while. I understood that. He was controlling, although I also understood why. He was the one calling the shots, so he'd be the one blamed if everything went to hell.

Julian walked Irene to the door. "We've stayed here as long as we should. We're moving to the old church tomorrow. We'll meet you there. You remember where it is?"

"Of course." She lifted her chin. "You don't need to worry about me. I can take care of myself."

"I know how strong and clever you are. But *if* you're caught—" Julian swallowed hard. "Please, Irene, please don't give up our location. Even if they torture you."

She patted her broadsword. "Nobody is going to torture me."

Julian said softly, "I'm sure Gordon never thought he'd get caught either."

"I'm not Gordon or Thomas," she hissed.

"I know."

Her face was pinched. "I've told you a hundred times." She yanked open the door, scowling. "I'm *not* gonna go out the way Gordon and Thomas did." She slammed the door behind her.

Julian stood staring at the door for a while, then he turned looking embarrassed. He moved into the room, raking a hand through his hair. His light green eyes were dark with concern, and he looked heartbreakingly young. "I really wish the professor was here."

I felt pity looking at him. He was obviously under tremendous strain. "How long will I train before I face off against Sableth?" My stomach churned just thinking about it, but the waiting was also gut-wrenching. We could be discovered at any moment. I was scared, but I also wanted it over with, one way or another.

"I think we can spare a week to train, but not much more. It's best if we meet him on our own terms." He stood next to the door, shoulders bowed. "We'll train here all day tomorrow, and then we'll move on to the next hiding spot."

He yawned, but tried to stifle it. "You should rest. I'll keep watch tonight."

I frowned, taking in his obvious fatigue. "Julian, you're asleep on your feet."

"I'm fine."

"You're not fine." I met Ian's gaze. "Why don't we keep watch and let Julian get a few hours' sleep? I don't think he's had any since we got here."

"Fine by me," Ian said agreeably.

"I'm not letting you do that," Julian protested.

"Yes, you are. How much sleep have you had in the last week?"

Julian avoided my gaze. "There was a lot to do."

"What good are you if you're this tired?" I moved toward the door, and Ian followed. "Go sleep. I'm not taking no for an answer, Julian."

Julian sighed and seemed to relent. "Fine. But just a few hours, no more."

I wasn't bothering to argue, but I also wasn't going to wake Julian up unless we were attacked. The poor kid looked like he hadn't slept since the night the professor had died.

I slid down the wall next to the door, and Ian sat beside me. Julian walked slowly across the room to the far wall, head down and feet dragging. He laid down, and within minutes was snoring.

"I knew he was exhausted," I whispered.

"He's probably twice as stressed with Irene gone."

"True." I sighed. "Poor kid. What a shitty situation he's in."

Ian squinted at me. "You're not exactly having the time of your life."

"Well, no, but neither are you."

Ian laughed. "I guess we're all pretty screwed."

"That's a T-shirt if I ever heard one." I rested my head against the wall. "It's weird, a few days ago, my biggest worry was money. Now I'm not sure I'll live to see my next birthday."

"Don't say that. You will."

"At least when I die I'll be with Nico." I could feel his surprise that I'd brought up the subject of my brother. I wasn't really sure why I'd mentioned him. Probably because I'd been thinking about death a lot the last few days.

"You don't talk about him much."

"No." I stared across the empty room. I was sick of being cooped up breathing nothing but stale air and sweat. I longed to go outside and suck in the scent of pine trees. I wanted to feel the cool night air on my skin and listen to the sound of living creatures rustling through the undergrowth. Anything to remind myself that there was a whole world out there still.

A world I apparently have to save.

"Do you mind telling me how Nico died?" Ian asked softly.

His question caught me by surprise. He was generally so careful not to pry. "Does it matter?"

"No." He clasped his knee, interlocking his fingers. "But I'd like to know you better. I'd like to know your life story."

"In case it ends here?"

He frowned. "No. God, no. That isn't what I meant."

I laughed gruffly. "I wouldn't blame you for thinking that way. The odds of us surviving this—they're probably very slim."

He let out a shaky breath. "I hope you're wrong."

"Me too."

We were quiet for a moment, and then he said, "So will you talk to me about Nico?"

A few days ago, I'd probably have been irritated that he was pushing me to talk. But for whatever reason, I wasn't mad. I felt connected to Ian. I trusted him. I had no idea why he affected me that way when others didn't. "I don't talk about him much because remembering is painful. Nico was the sweetest, gentlest, most beautiful soul that ever lived."

He didn't say anything. He just nodded.

"He looked up to me, which is funny because I'm not anyone worth looking up to."

"Bullshit."

I frowned. "You barely know me."

"What I do know says that's bullshit."

"Well, either way, he didn't know any better." I picked at a thread on my shirt because it was easier than meeting Ian's searching gaze.

He asked, "How is it you and Nico are here, but your parents are in Texas?"

I forced myself to meet his gaze. "The year I graduated high school, they decided they wanted to live in Texas because they have no income tax."

"That was their reason?"

"Yeah." I grimaced at his disbelieving tone. "They were selfish and only cared about their needs. Nico was terrified at the idea of switching schools. He had horrible anxiety and was scared to start all over. He had his childhood friends here, and he felt safe. I decided since I was legally an adult that I'd petition for custody of Nico."

"Your parents didn't fight it?"

"Hell no. They weren't good people or good parents. They were drunks. Honestly, I think they were relieved to get the burden of us off their backs."

"Jesus."

I shrugged. "That's how they were."

"So you didn't move to Texas."

"No. I got a job at an autobody shop instead of going to college, and I started doing the psychic gig part-time too. Then I petitioned the court for custody of Nico, and I got it."

Ian grunted as if he sympathized. "And you were only eighteen?"

"Yeah."

"That's a big responsibility for a kid to take on."

I lifted one shoulder dismissively, uncomfortable with the respect in his voice. "I felt like I had to do that for Nico."

"Wow." Ian took my hand. "I don't know what to say."

"I loved him, and I thought it was the best thing for him." I frowned. "But then two years later—" My throat closed up and I couldn't talk.

He squeezed my hand. "Take your time."

The lump in my throat burned, and my eyes stung. But Ian's hand felt warm and comforting, and slowly my throat relaxed and the tears abated. When I felt calmer, I said, "He took a fatal dose of sleeping pills."

"I'm sorry," Ian said quietly. "God, how awful."

"I . . . I didn't even know anything was wrong. I didn't see the signs," I whispered. "I'm a fucking psychic and I didn't see any signs."

Ian pulled me closer, putting his arms around me. I buried my face in his shirt, somehow holding back the tears. He rubbed my back, kissing the side of my head, but he didn't speak. I was glad he didn't. There wasn't really anything to say. Nico had died and that was that. No words of comfort could make that hurt any less. Telling me it was okay, when it most definitely wasn't, did no good. His gentle touch was enough to let me know he cared that I was hurting.

After a while, he asked quietly, "Did he leave a note? Anything to help you understand?"

I winced, not wanting to relive the moment. "He did leave a note, but all it said was 'It's too painful.' I don't know if that meant life was too painful, or being my brother was too painful. To this day, I don't know why he did it. I thought he was happy. I thought we were doing fine. Was life perfect? No. But when is life ever gonna be perfect?"

Ian sighed. "Never. But his suicide probably had nothing to do with how perfect or imperfect things were. The sad truth was he just didn't want to live anymore."

"I think you're right. He was so sensitive. He was almost too empathetic. Maybe that's what he meant?"

"Maybe."

I gritted my teeth, hating that the old familiar doubt and pain returned no matter how many years passed. "It's the not knowing why that drives me crazy. I know I have to let it go and just accept that he's gone. And for the most part, I do that. But now and then, it just eats at me that I don't know what I did wrong. I don't know why he left me alone to face life all by myself."

Ian made a sound low in his throat as if he was in pain, and he tugged me closer. "You're not alone, okay?"

"I hate that I wasn't enough to keep him here."

"You can't think like that. His suicide doesn't have anything to do with you. Not really. I have no doubt he adored you. But he was hurting, and he wanted a way to make that stop."

I blew out a shaky breath. While reliving Nico's death was agony, in one respect it also felt good to finally tell someone all the things that had eaten at me over the last five years. "It's frustrating that of all the spirits I can talk to, Nico isn't one of them."

"You can't talk to him?" There was obvious surprise in his voice.

"No." I said softly, "I'm afraid he's mad at me."

Ian scowled. "For what? For loving him? For protecting him?"

"For not seeing he was hurting."

Ian shook his head. "You only see what people want you to see."

I shrugged. "I'm supposed to see what people don't see. I'm supposed to see beyond the physical. Especially when it comes to someone so close to me. I should have been able to sense something was very wrong."

"You're still only human. I'm sure it was no easy thing raising your younger brother. You were just a kid yourself."

"Maybe he'd have been better off in Texas with my loser parents," I said hoarsely, admitting one of my worst fears.

Ian turned to face me, his gaze serious. "Do you really believe that? With all your heart, do you truly believe he'd have been better off with them?"

"No," I said immediately. "But it's hard not to feel like somehow I failed him."

"You didn't. You need to stop even letting that thought in your head. You did your best for Nico. You loved him, and you protected him. But you're not magical. If someone really wants to die, they're gonna find a way."

Ian wasn't saying anything new. I'd heard most of what he'd said many times before. But for some reason, hearing Ian say it got through to me. I didn't think Nico would have been better off in Texas with my parents. I knew that Nico had been mostly happy living with me. Something had hurt him so deeply, he'd been unable to move past it. I'd never know what that was. I had to accept that.

I leaned into Ian, and he tightened his hold. "Claire is the only person I've ever talked to about Nico's death."

"Yeah?" He rubbed my back. "I'm glad you trusted me enough to tell me too."

"You have a good bedside manner."

He said quietly, "I don't give this special treatment to just anyone, Lorenzo."

"I guess I'm special."

He rested his chin on my hair. "I assume you already know that. I've been chasing you since the day we met."

"Sometimes the chase is the best part."

"Not even remotely true."

I smiled, happy he'd rejected my jaded theory.

Julian suddenly jerked awake, yelling, "Watch out, Irene. Behind you." He sat up, looking dazed. His blond hair was plastered to his head with sweat. He shook his head, mumbling, "God, I just had the worst dream."

"What was it about?" Ian asked.

Julian shuddered, avoiding our gaze. "Never mind."

"You should try to sleep more," I said.

"No. I won't be able to." He got up and went to grab a bottle of water. He drank it down quickly, and then approached. "You two can go sleep now."

"You sure?" Ian asked. "You weren't out very long."

"It was enough." He waved off my concern. "Go on. Sleep. Tomorrow will be another long, tiring day of training before we move locations."

"Isn't it more dangerous to move?" I asked, getting to my feet. Ian held out his hand to me, and I pulled him up. "Can't we just stay where we are? So far we've been safe here."

"It's best to move around." Julian's tone said it wasn't up for debate.

"Well, you're the expert." I walked across the room to the corner.

Ian followed, dragging his feet. "I miss my bed."

"Same," I agreed, lowering myself to the hard ground. "I'll never take central heating, beds, or hot meals for granted again."

"Amen," Julian said from across the room. "Or showers."

Ian and I laid down, backs pressed together. Exhaustion immediately claimed me, and I fell into a deep peaceful sleep. I dreamt of Ian and Nico. My dreams were warm and hazy, but comforting. When I woke, it was still dark, and Ian was beside me, snoring softly.

I was about to drift off to sleep again, when I heard the scrape of a shoe on the cement floor. The hairs on my nape prickled as I froze. The most obvious reason for the noise was simply Julian moving around. But every instinct in me screamed it wasn't. My heart began to race and goosebumps rose on my flesh as I caught a hint of star anise and nutmeg.

I'm imagining this. Julian is keeping watch. This is all in my head.

Then Weston Bartholmew's snide voice rasped, "Rise and shine, Lorenzo."

CHAPTER NINETEEN

Panic rushed through me and instinctively I slipped my hand into my pocket and clutched the Mossfire Stone. Ian's breathing had changed at the sound of Weston's voice, and I knew he was awake. Without really thinking I squeezed the stone tight and visualized the first thing that came to mind: wasps.

Instantly, the room was filled with the loud buzzing of winged insects and Weston let out a panicked scream. I jumped to my feet, as did Ian, and we turned to face Weston. Weston stood a few feet away, his long red hair covered his face as he violently swiped at the air while thousands of insects swarmed him. Behind him were three other men, also flailing at the wasps, and near the wide-open door stood Julian, hands bound and mouth gagged. His panicked cries were muffled by the cloth in his mouth, and his eyes were bugged.

I grabbed Ian's arm and we bolted toward Julian. Nobody tried to stop us—they were too preoccupied with swatting wasps away. Thankfully, Julian's legs weren't tied, so he'd be able to run. I yanked the gag out of his mouth, and it flopped loosely around his neck.

"I don't know how they got the drop on me," he rasped, face flushed. "I didn't fall asleep, I swear."

"It doesn't matter. Just run." I pulled him after me, and the three of us ran out into the main area of the warehouse. I'd fully expected more people to be waiting outside the office door, but there didn't appear to be anyone else.

We got to the main door and escaped into the cold dark night. With every step I expected someone to stop us. I had no idea how long my illusion would hold if I wasn't there to keep it going. As he ran, Julian managed to struggle out of the ropes that bound his wrists. There was nothing but the sound of our feet hitting the pavement, and our ragged breaths.

"Where should we go?" I hissed, searching the darkness for somewhere safe to hide. "We can't run forever."

"This way," Julian said, pointing to the left.

We made a sharp turn, following him down a slope. I half-walked, half-fell down the hill, cursing as branches scratched my face. Once at the bottom, Julian led us down another hill. We ran for an eternity, down winding streets and through cul-de-sacs. Eventually we wound up in an alley behind some stores in a part of town I didn't recognize.

Julian ran up to the back of a tattoo parlor that had rune symbols etched into the building, and he banged on the door. Glancing around, his eyes wild, he truly looked terrified. "They must have used a spell on me. I didn't see them coming into the room until it was too late." He pounded on the door again. "Cecil, open the damn door!"

After a moment, the door rattled and opened. A slight man with silver hair tied up in a manbun and half his face covered in tattoos stood there. He wore fitted black pants tucked into knee-high leather boots and a black T-shirt. A diamond piercing glimmered in one nostril, and he looked startled as he blurted, "What in the hell, Julian. What are you doing here at this hour?"

"I have The Vessel with me. We need shelter. They found our hiding spot."

Cecil blinked at me, and his face twitched with a look of awe. "Oh."

"Where's Irene?" Julian asked.

Cecil's expression was blank. "I haven't seen her in days. I thought she was with you."

"I sent her here. She didn't arrive?" Obvious concern fluttered through Julian's voice.

"No." Cecil glanced around and then stepped aside. "Come in. Quickly."

Julian pushed me through the doorway first. I stumbled into the dark shop, tripping over my own feet. I felt my way along a long wall, noticing a red emergency exit sign lit at the front of the shop. The pungent scent of rubbing alcohol filled my nose as I moved through the small store. Behind me, a light was flicked on, and the room was doused in light. There were three tattooing work stations with tattoo machines, ink cups, needles. There was a reception area near the front windows and a narrow counter. Posters on the wall showcased some of the designs offered, and there was also a shelf with what looked like flash sheets and portfolios of the artist's work.

"How did you escape?" Cecil asked. "If Sableth found you, how did you get away?"

"It wasn't Sableth himself. It was his followers." Julian slumped down into one of the tattoo chairs, breathing jaggedly. "If it had been Sableth, we'd probably all be dead."

"Weston Bartholomew was one of them." I met Cecil's gaze. "Do you know him?"

Cecil nodded. "He's a psychic."

"He's a fake," I snapped.

Curling his lip in disgust, Cecil said, "Yes."

"I should have known he'd be on the side of evil," I muttered. "He came to my shop the other day and wanted me to merge my store with his. His offer made no sense." I pulled the stone out of my pocket, and it shimmered against my pale skin. "If Weston is working for Sableth, I'll bet he was looking for the stone. That's why he offered to help clean up the mess."

Ian grunted. "Whoever or whatever ransacked your shop must have been searching for the stone too."

"It must have been Sableth that night. I remember feeling his evil presence," I murmured. "The stone was in my pocket, but I didn't know it. That's why he couldn't find it."

"Then you accidentally activated the Mossfire Stone in the library." Julian gave a wry smile. "And my cover was blown because I had to save your ass."

"Thank goodness you came in time." Memories of my first horrific meeting with Sableth shuddered through me. "And we've been running ever since."

Cecil scratched his stubbled jaw. "You never said how you got away from Weston."

Julian shot me an admiring glance. "Lorenzo used illusion. It worked beautifully."

Julian was making it sound as if I'd planned the illusion that had helped our escape. Nothing could have been farther from the truth. "I didn't even know what I was doing. It just kind of happened."

"Lucky for us." Ian frowned and shifted uneasily.

"All the drills paid off. Lorenzo was amazing." Julian seemed proud of me. Almost like I was his prize hog.

"That's good." Cecil nodded. "That means it was instinctive."

"It was probably the first time the stone didn't fight me at all. It just worked flawlessly. I thought of wasps, and they were suddenly there."

Julian smiled wearily. "Maybe the stone is finally accepting you, Lorenzo."

Ian moved to sit in one of the other tattoo chairs. There were lines of strain around his eyes, and he looked grim. "So what now? Do we just keep running from place to place, praying they don't get their hands on the stone? How long can we conceivably stay ahead of them? Tonight was too close, don't you think?"

"I agree. What do we do next?" I instinctively looked to Cecil, perhaps because he was older than Julian. But he simply glanced questioningly to Julian.

Julian let out a fatigued sigh. "As much as I'd like to keep training Lorenzo, I think we've run out of time. We managed to escape today, but that was mostly luck and surprise on our side. Next time, Weston and the others won't be caught off guard."

"Yes." Cecil's expression was grim.

"I wish I knew where Irene was," Julian rumbled. "She loves a fight. I hesitate going up against Sableth and his followers without her."

Cecil's expression tensed. "You don't suppose she's been grabbed, do you?"

"God, I hope not." Julian's voice was strained.

"They got the drop on Gordon and Thomas," Cecil said. "It's not inconceivable they could grab her too."

Julian's smile was tight. "I know what you're saying, but Irene is a wily little thing."

Ian seemed unusually ill-tempered as he said, "Hopefully Irene is safe wherever she is, but for now, I'm worried about Lorenzo's safety. If we're not going to keep hiding, and running is impossible, what's the best plan of action?"

A pained expression swept Julian's young face. "Unfortunately, I think it's time we faced Sableth."

Ian scowled. "Just like that?"

Julian narrowed his eyes. "If you think I like the idea of going head-to-head so soon with Sableth, you're mistaken. But we've reached the point of no return. There's nowhere we can really hide. Not forever. By not playing offence, we run the risk of being caught with our pants down again."

"Do you seriously think Lorenzo is ready for that?" Ian shook his head. "He's had one full day of training."

"I know," Julian snapped. "Don't you think I know that?"

Cecil studied me, his dark eyes curious. "Yet when Weston got the drop on you guys, Lorenzo instinctively did the right thing."

"Yes," Ian said softly, "Thankfully, he did."

Cecil pursed his lips. "You know, the lore doesn't talk about years of training. In fact, it barely mentions that. What it mostly addresses is the importance of bonding between The Vessel and the Mossfire Stone. It speaks a lot of the protection provided by The Guardians and The Companion. It goes on and on about the wisdom and vision of The Teacher, who we now know was Professor Buckler. Training isn't a priority, it would seem."

"True," Julian nodded.

I frowned. "The Companion? Who is The Companion?"

Julian's face hardened. "We're not sure if that is actually a true part of the lore."

Cecil shot a surprised look at Julian. "Since when?"

Julian avoided his gaze. "Professor Buckler wasn't sure if he was interpreting that title correctly. The protection of The Vessel is the responsibility of The Guardians alone."

Cecil laughed gruffly. "Julian, that just isn't true. I studied alongside the professor for many, many years. He absolutely believed The Companion was real."

Julian's jaw had a stubborn jut to it. "I don't agree."

Cecil's gaze was shrewd as he watched Julian squirming. "Hmmm."

"Anyway," Julian said brusquely, "the time has come to face down Sableth. Fox Harbor is in chaos, and soon that will spread. He needs to be stopped now."

While my stomach churned with anxiety at his words, I realized he was right. Sableth had to be stopped now, if possible. "And the theory is I'm supposed to somehow enter Sableth's spiritual body and destroy him?"

"That's what the lore describes." Cecil rubbed his chin, studying me with a thoughtful expression. "It's not merely a physical invasion. It's also a psychic one."

"Right. Julian explained that to me." I shuddered at the thought of what was coming. "I also know if I'm not strong enough, I could die."

Julian said softly, "We all will."

"Yes." Naturally, I was worried for myself. But it was unbearable to think that my failure would mean the destruction of those I'd never met as well as those I cared about. I could barely breathe thinking of Ian or Claire dead.

I literally couldn't conceive of that. The bitter knowledge that my failure would be the obliteration of Fox Harbor and possibly the world was still beyond comprehension. It wasn't fair that all of that would fall on my shoulders. It wasn't right. Yet I knew in my soul it was true.

I sat down quickly, my legs giving out. Ian rose and moved to my side, his hand resting on my shoulder. He didn't speak, he just kept his hand there. A sense of calm descended over me, and I looked up to meet his honey-brown eyes. Once more that feeling that I'd always known him washed through me. I needed to remember this feeling when I faced Sableth. I needed to remember that failure wasn't an option. I had to defeat Sableth. I had to. I had to protect the people I loved.

The thought that I loved Ian probably should have terrified me. It would have in the past. But knowing what I had to face with Sableth, it suddenly felt like a gift. I could feel he felt the same toward me, and instead of being scared, I felt honored. Grateful that someone like him would want me. Care about me. Protect me, if possible. How could that ever have seemed like a bad thing?

"When?" I asked hoarsely. "When should I fight Sableth?"

"In the morning." Julian's face was drawn. "It's probably useless to tell you to rest, but obviously if you're at your best tomorrow, that would be optimum."

"I have living quarters upstairs," Cecil said. "You and Ian can rest up there." Julian scowled, but Cecil ignored him. "There's a shower, food, and a warm bed. Take advantage of that."

"What am I, chopped liver?" Julian groused, appearing slighted.

Cecil sent him a reproachful look. "You should know better, Julian. They need time together. You can pretend you don't know the lore, but we both know you do."

Guilt rippled through Julian's light green eyes, but he didn't respond.

Ian and I followed Cecil to the back of the shop where there was a narrow staircase. We went up the steep steps, and at the top there was a door. Inside was a small apartment. There was a tiny kitchenette with dated olive green appliances and a bedroom just off the cramped living room.

Once we were alone, Ian asked, "Shower?" He smiled. "I smell like a buffalo."

I laughed. "No, you don't. But I won't say no to getting clean."

"I'm starving, but I'll feel better if I shower first. How about you?"

"Whatever you want," I said quietly. "I feel numb."

His expression gentled. "Come on. Let's take a nice hot shower together, okay?"

"Okay."

The bathroom was, as expected, also small. But the shower itself was fairly roomy. Especially compared to my tiny shower back home at the shop. We stripped in silence, and Ian got in first and turned on the water. He gave a little yelp when the water first hit him, and I laughed. He grinned at me, and for one moment, I let myself forget about the impending terror.

As I joined Ian under the water, I relished the feel of his hands and the clean water on my naked flesh. This could easily be my last shower. My last meal. My last fuck. I was going to enjoy each of those things with all my heart.

He soaped me up with cucumber and green tea shower gel. I sighed as he stroked me and kissed the nape of my neck. As I stood there I regretted the last five years I'd spent like a zombie. I'd turned my back on life because of what had happened with Nico. Now my life could very well end for real tomorrow, and I'd have given anything to get those five years back. Maybe if I'd met Ian sooner, we could have been happy those five years. Instead, I'd lived as if I'd died along with Nico. I'd wasted what was left of my life, grieving.

My heart ached as Ian kissed me, and I clung to him like I wanted to cling to life. His tongue explored my mouth, and I explored his muscular, soapy body, so happy I had one more chance to touch and taste him. We took our time, enjoying each other. By the time he entered me, I was trembling with need. He looked into my eyes as he thrust deep and slow, and it was so fucking intimate I could have cried.

I dug my nails into his back, moaning with pleasure and despair that I'd wasted so much of my life. I wanted more moments like these with Ian. I wanted a full life with Ian. I wanted dinners, arguments, movie nights, and all the things normal people who weren't going to die the next day got to experience.

But that wouldn't be my fate.

I cried out as I came against his stomach, and he groaned as his warm release filled me. Mouths joined, we shuddered and moaned, giving and receiving pure pleasure. My body shook and quivered as my climax slowly ebbed and flowed through me. He finished inside me, and after planting one sweet kiss on my lips, gently pulled out.

We rinsed off and then dried off, opting to walk around with towels around our waists rather than redressing in our dirty clothes. We'd have to put them back on tomorrow, but for now I enjoyed the feeling of being clean.

When we went into the kitchen, Ian opened the fridge. "Eggs? Sandwich? Steak? What are you in the mood for?"

"Remember the first time we slept together? I promised you a grilled cheese that you never got to have."

"That's true." He met my gaze, and regret flickered there. "I wish I hadn't left you that night."

I shrugged. "I wish I'd asked you to stay."

"Yeah." He grabbed butter, bread, and cheese. "Okay, grilled cheese is easy. Let's do that."

I helped by buttering the bread, and Ian fried the sandwiches. Then we sat at the bar and gobbled them down. We stuck to water, forgoing the beer and wine available to us. I couldn't afford to kill off any brain cells. I'd need them all to be firing tomorrow.

Once we'd eaten, we got in the bed and moved together. Again regret ached through me, but I pushed it away and tried to enjoy the feel of Ian's arms. I rested my head on his bare chest, inhaling his clean skin. If I died tomorrow what awaited me? I wasn't sure I believed in Heaven or Hell. I hoped I ended up with Nico, and Ian if he died too. And Claire. My eyes stung, but I blinked the tears away. I didn't want to spend possibly my last day with Ian bawling.

"Was Cecil implying I'm The Companion?" Ian suddenly asked.

I hesitated. "I think so. Maybe. Much to Julian's chagrin."

"Yeah, Julian didn't look happy about the idea. Cecil kept giving me strange looks. And then he insisted I come up here with you." He rubbed his hand up my back. "I'm not complaining, mind you."

"I'd have hated to spend tonight alone." While the clean cotton sheets felt like heaven against my bare skin, I'd have happily slept on a bed of nails if that was the only way to spend my last night on Earth with Ian. "I'm grateful Cecil had you come upstairs with me."

He kissed my hair. "I'd have snuck up here probably anyway."

I smiled. "Yeah?"

"Sure. Why not?" He shifted closer to me. "Nothing could have kept me away."

I smirked. "Is that because you wanted to sleep on a real mattress?"

He laughed. "No. Because I wanted to be near you."

I nuzzled his smooth chest. "Maybe you really are The Companion. That's a very companionable thing to say."

"It makes sense I'd be The Companion. That would explain why the minute I met you, I wanted to protect you. I wanted to be near you. Needed to be near you."

"Well, not the minute you met me. When you first met me, you were a dick. Remember?"

"Oh, yeah." He grimaced and glanced down at me. "But you've forgiven me, right?"

"Definitely."

"Okay, good." His voice was a bit drowsy as he added, "This bed is amazing."

"It is." I smiled at how sleepy he sounded.

His breathing slowed and deepened, and a soft snore escaped him. I closed my eyes. I hoped to sleep too, but wasn't sure I could. I focused on Ian's sounds and the feel of his warm skin. If I died tomorrow, and there was an afterlife, I hoped I could bring the memories of Ian with me.

I didn't ever want to forget how Ian had made me feel while I was alive.

CHAPTER TWENTY

It was decided that we'd have the showdown with Sableth in the old abandoned Catholic church where we'd planned to shelter next. When we arrived at the church, there was still no sign of Irene, which had Julian worried. I suspected he'd hoped she'd be waiting at the church.

Inside, time had not been particularly kind, and the once-vibrant sanctuary now lay in eerie silence, forgotten and forlorn. The heavy wooden doors groaned in protest as they opened, revealing a dark and bleak interior. The high-vaulted ceilings, once adorned with intricate frescoes and elaborate paintings, now bore the weight of cobwebs and dust. Cracks marred the once-immaculate stonework, and sections of the ceiling had crumbled away, leaving an impression of decaying splendor.

Stained glass windows that had once bathed the church in a kaleidoscope of vibrant colors were now dull and lifeless. The light that filtered through the grimy panes cast ghostly shadows on the worn and weathered stone floors. Rows of empty pews, once polished wood, were now worn and weathered. The air carried a musty smell, tinged with the scent of decay and dampness. The altar stood in shambles. The ornate crucifix had fallen from its perch, its broken form lying pitifully on the floor.

The Mossfire Stone was cool in my hand. It had been warm all night, as if it too was preparing for battle. Julian, Ian, Cecil, and a large group of supporters from our side were there too. Their job was to keep Sableth's human followers from attacking me while I was fighting Sableth. I'd tried telling Ian to stay out of harm's way, but he'd had a very stubborn look on his face. I suspected he hadn't heard a word I'd said.

Julian cleared his throat. "Ready, Lorenzo?" His voice echoed in the big hall.

"Probably not how I'd put it, but I'm here." My heart thumped as I took the Mossfire Stone from my pocket. I felt breathless as the jewel rippled and swirled, changing from light green to almost black, and then back again.

"You sure this is a good idea?" Ian asked, his voice threaded with stress.

I met his uneasy gaze. "Sableth is coming for us anyway. At least this way we know when and where it will happen."

Ian grimaced but didn't speak.

Julian tugged his knife from the sheath on his hip. The green jewel shimmered brightly. "Might as well get the ball rolling, Lorenzo." His bravado was slightly marred by the wobble in his voice.

Nodding, I rubbed my thumb over the stone, and it instantly chilled and throbbed. It felt almost eager in my hand, and a strange exhilaration washed through me. I knew that feeling of elation was coming from the stone, but I didn't mind. It helped to chase away my fears.

Not sure what to expect, I held my breath, waiting for Sableth and his minions' arrival. His followers arrived first. Within minutes the doors to the church slammed open, and a group of raggedy-looking people swarmed in. I wasn't surprised to see Weston with them, but I was hugely shocked to see Irene beside him.

Weston wore his usual paisley vest and boots, but his long red hair spilled loose over his slender shoulders today. Irene looked like his twin in fitted pants, knee high black boots and a leather vest. Although her blonde hair was pulled back in a tight ponytail.

Irene's face was pink as Julian stared her down, but she lifted her chin and said, "I told you I wouldn't end up like Gordon and Thomas. You should have listened, Julian."

"I guess I should have. But it never occurred to me you'd be a cowardly *traitor*," Julian growled.

The flush on her face deepened. "Better a traitor than a dead fool."

"You deserve to die for this. You betrayed your duty to The Vessel," Julian hissed, advancing on her. "You betrayed all of us."

Ian grabbed his arm. "Hold up, Julian."

Julian tried to shake off Ian's grip, but he held tight. Julian asked Irene harshly, "Did you tell Weston and the others where we were? Is that how they found us the other night?"

Irene's face twitched. "You're on the losing side, Julian." Her sheepish gaze flicked to me, but she looked away quickly. "I can't help it if you're too dumb to know it."

"You bitch," Julian yelled, veins bulging in his face and throat. "How could you turn on Lorenzo? Me? How could you do that? They killed the professor. They killed Gordon and Thomas."

"Exactly," she hissed. "You're never gonna win against Sableth. Don't you get that yet? Wake up. You should join me, Julian. Before it's too late."

"Never," snapped Julian, looking pale and shaken. "I'll happily die beside The Vessel before I'll ever join you."

"Then you're a bigger fool than I thought," she said.

He shook his head, looking anguished. "I trusted you, Irene. I fully trusted you." Julian's voice broke.

Irene's face flinched, but she didn't speak.

I moved to put my arm around Julian's shoulders. "It's okay. We don't need her."

"It's not okay," he muttered. "We were born to protect you, Lorenzo. She turned her back on her destiny."

Irene rasped, "It's nothing personal, Lorenzo. I just prefer being on the winning side."

"Then you picked wrong," I said, giving her a cold look.

Her bottom lip quivered, and she turned away.

"Oh, come on, give her a break. It's not her fault she doesn't like hanging out with losers." Weston snickered. The look of glee on his face made my stomach churn. It was obvious from his delighted expression that he hadn't even considered the possibility that his side might fail.

"Nobody asked you, Weston," I snapped.

"Oh, my, my. Are we a little on edge, Lorenzo?" Weston guffawed.

I shot him a look of disdain but held my tongue.

"Nice trick with the wasps the other day, Lorenzo. But you won't slip away this time." Weston's voice shook with excitement. "You should have taken me up on my offer. Now it's too late."

"I don't regret a thing." I forced a smile, hoping I looked confident. I mostly felt agitated as more people piled into the church. We were definitely outnumbered. I hoped that wouldn't matter once I used some illusions on them.

Weston scowled. "You'll regret it when Sableth obliterates you."

"You know, I always knew you were a fake and a crook, Weston, but I didn't realize you were also such a fool. Do you actually think life will be better with Sableth in control? Haven't you seen what he's capable of? How cruel he can be?"

Weston shrugged one shoulder. "Life will be much better for me. Maybe not for you."

"You don't care that he's chopping people's heads off? Causing chaos in town? That's all just fine with you?" I asked incredulously.

He smirked. "So long as it's not my head being chopped, I don't give a flying fuck."

"Wow." I shook my head. "You're a disgrace of a human."

"Not to mention a complete asshole," Ian muttered.

The stone suddenly jiggled in my hand, emitting the same screeching sound it had made the night Sableth came for us at the Rosewood Motel. I winced at the bloodcurdling shriek, stroking my thumb over the smooth surface. "It's okay. We want him to come this time," I whispered.

The crowd of Sableth's people pushed forward, but our group held them back. They started screaming and yelling at each other, and people started swinging swords and chopping at one another. The shrieking and bloody violence made my stomach turn. I needed to do something to drive back Sableth's people—and protect my followers.

Gritting my teeth, I envisioned swarms of bats. The stone pulsed like ice in the palm of my hand as the imaginary bats appeared. Sweat broke out on my face as I directed the make-believe bats to divebomb Sableth's group. Many of them screamed and fled, but most of them stayed, swiping at the air as they battled the fantasy creatures I'd created.

When the bats seemed to lose their effectiveness, I switched visions quickly, trying to think of something scarier. Snakes came to mind, so I focused on creating piles of slithering rattlesnakes. The slithering reptiles definitely helped clear more of Sableth's people from the church. They ran in terror as fantasy snakes hung from the rafters and squirmed on the ground.

When the snakes seemed to lose their effectiveness, I then moved onto flesh-searing flames. The screaming and gnashing of teeth from Sableth's people was horrifying to witness, but I knew it needed to be done. Sableth's followers seemed far more violent and bloodthirsty than those on our side. I had to at least try to protect my followers.

I was forced to abandon my focus on Sableth's minions when the pressure in the chapel suddenly changed. I knew immediately that signaled the arrival of Sableth. Fear roared through me, and the blood rushed through my ears as the air crackled with energy. The scent of ozone filled the room as Sableth's malevolent presence seeped into the room like sewer gas. I shuddered as the chill of him surrounded me.

Whether I was The Vessel or not, it took all of my willpower not to turn and run as a swirling spiral of smoke and flame formed a few feet from me. Pure evil seemed to wash over me, and I choked on the rotten scent of it. Naturally, when faced with such wickedness, my instinct was to retreat, but I knew that wasn't an option. Everyone was counting on me.

I stepped forward, my senses immediately assaulted by heat and putrid odors. The world around me seemed to morph into a distorted dreamscape, an ever-shifting labyrinth of horrors. The ground felt like writhing serpents beneath my feet, and the walls seemed to breathe with a sinister life of their own.

Sableth's malicious presence pressed against my mind, trying to force its way in. I gritted my teeth, resisting the intrusion. Instead, I tried pushing back, probing the swirling heat and smoke in front of me with chilled determination. The heat was so intense, I knew the only reason my skin wasn't blistering was the frozen Mossfire Stone in my hand. I clutched it even tighter, well aware that if I dropped it, I'd be finished.

A chorus of voices echoed through in my head, whispering and hissing threats. The air grew thick with the stench of decay and sulfur, making it even harder to breathe. I couldn't see Ian or Julian anymore. The air around me was too thick and acrid. I felt panicked that I couldn't get enough oxygen, but I told myself to calm down. I had the Mossfire stone. I needed to keep moving forward. That was the only path for me. Coughing and hacking, I took another step.

Sableth's form seemed to shudder with anger at my impudence. I could feel its rage and fury that I dared to advance. It gave me an almost twisted sense of pleasure though—knowing Sableth was furious with me. After running from him for so long, it felt perfect to now come at him instead. I could feel a sort of icy shield around my body, almost as if I was wrapped in the Mossfire Stone's frigid arms.

The sound roared around me, the volume of wind and heat almost lifting me off my feet. I cried out when debris smacked against me. It was difficult to hold my concentration, but I somehow managed. I had to get inside Sableth's swirling vortex. That was the only way I could explode him into oblivion. While it seemed like an impossible task, especially since I'd only traveled mere inches in all this time, I knew I had to do it.

Up to that point, I'd really only been advancing on him with my body. Now I tried pushing forward with my mind as well. I dipped my thoughts into the nightmarish realm swirling around me. The darkness seemed to solidify into a towering demonic figure. Its eyes burned with malevolence, and its twisted form radiated an aura of dread.

When it reached for me, terror jolted through me. Sableth clawed at me, as if trying to gouge my heart from my chest. I evaded the attack with a swift backstep, the force of the creature's assault leaving trails of black energy in the air. The chamber shook with the intensity of our clash, and instead of waiting for him to reach out to me again, I moved toward him instead.

Adrenaline pumped through my body with the knowledge that one misstep could be fatal. But now was not the time to weaken my attack. I needed to psychically crawl inside Sableth and eradicate his very soul. With every inch closer to Sableth, the stone pulsed and vibrated like ice in my hand, as if rejoicing.

I stiffened when I thought I heard my brother Nico's voice. When he suddenly materialized in front of me, I was stunned. I gaped at him, my heart throbbing with shock.

I wanted to hug him. Hold him. Beg his forgiveness. His smile was just as I remembered, warm and shy. His eyes, the same chocolate brown. Even his scent was the same, and his voice—that husky, plaintive voice—almost brought me to my knees.

It's not real. Nico isn't here.

I didn't want to believe that. I wanted Nico to be real. I desperately wanted him back. When the stone seared my palm, I cursed and glanced down at it. It was so bright, I winced at the brilliant green. It looked angry, a glaring expression spinning over the face of the stone. It looked as if it was mouthing threats at me. Uneasiness moved through me because as the heat increased from the stone, the more powerfully I felt Sableth's evil seeping into me.

If the stone gave up on me right now, I'd die for sure. That meant Ian and Claire would die. Julian would die. Cecil would die. All the brave souls who had come to fight against Sableh would die. All because I was allowing Sableth inside my head. He knew my weakest spots, and Nico was definitely one of them.

Gritting my teeth, I ignored the vision of Nico. It hurt to pretend I didn't see or hear him, but I knew he wasn't really in front of me. No matter how real he seemed, I had to focus on destroying Sableth. My body trembled with fatigue, but I kept inching forward. I probed Sableth's energy, trying to find a crack I could slip into.

I could no longer hear or see anyone in the room. It was just Sableth and me now, wrestling with each other's minds. I prayed Ian and the others were okay, but I couldn't think about them right now. I gasped when something slammed against me, knocking me almost to the ground. The stone slipped in my sweaty hand, but I held on to it. I couldn't see what had struck me, so it was impossible to avoid it happening again.

As the flames attempted to sear my flesh, the Mossfire Stone vibrated against my skin, freezingly cold. As I clutched the frozen stone, the screeching noises began to make sense to my brain. I realized with a jolt that the Mossfire Stone was speaking to me in a language I didn't recognize, but was able to comprehend.

Pull him in. Let Sableth inside.

Shock resonated through me as I began to understand the words swirling through my mind. Ice crystals seemed to splinter through my brain as the stone's message became clear. I wasn't meant to enter Sableth; I was *The Vessel*. I was meant to pull Sableth into *my* body and soul. The professor and Julian had misinterpreted my reason for existing. But that purpose was clear to me now: As The Vessel I was born to literally *contain* Sableth's evil presence.

I now realized I had the ability to hold Sableth inside my body. So long as I played my hand correctly, the world would be safe. I had to entice Sableth into possessing my body. If I psychically overpowered Sableth, he'd be destroyed. But if Sableth overpowered me, he'd still be contained inside my spirit. Even if I failed to obliterate Sableth, he'd go with me into the afterlife. He'd be forever removed from the mortal realm, never to return.

Everyone will be safe whether I live or die.

Acceptance washed through me, and a strange calm descended. I had no choice but to push forward. I had hope I could win against Sableth. He was so overly confident, I was certain he didn't suspect my true reason for existing. I could feel his hubris vibrating around me. It wouldn't take much to lure him in because he'd underestimated me from the start.

A harsh laugh broke from my tight throat as I stepped closer to the swirling black vortex in front of me. Voices roared around me, but the chilled stone in my palm comforted me. The stench of sulfur filled my nostrils, and the heat increased. But I didn't cower. I held the stone out, confident the chilled rock would keep me safe.

"Enter me, Sableth," I whispered. "I'm far too weak to keep you out."

A growling laugh swept around me like a tornado, mocking me. Needling me. The heat increased, and black smoke puffed in my face as if taunting me.

I gave a choking cough and rasped, "Come on. Don't be shy, asshole."

I grunted as molten heat seemed to seep through the pores of my skin. Sableth also tried to enter my brain, clawing and hissing, but that I couldn't allow. I poured all my energy into my psychic shield, allowing Sableth to inch into my body but not my mind. Sableth rammed my psychic shield, but it held. He roared and slithered, but he didn't make any headway.

Sweat covered my entire body as I strained to bring Sableth inside without losing my mind in the process. The heat of him ached through me, and the hot wind whistled in my ears. Panting, I tried to pull Sableth deeper inside my core. I cried out in agony as he entered me, burning like an ulcer.

In the distance, I heard Ian's voice. Then he was beside me, slipping his hand into mine. His blond hair whipped around his head, and his eyes glittered with determination. Even though I was scared for him to be so close to Sableth, instinctively I drank in some of his energy. It flowed through me like sweet honey, and I felt a surge of excitement and power.

I tried to speak to Ian, but the wind was so violent, my words were ripped away. Instead, I laced my fingers with his, drawing fresh strength from him. My skin felt tight and my ribs ached as Sableth's presence expanded, trying to claim his spot inside of me. I shuddered as the pain increased, and for one terrifying moment, I feared I didn't have the strength to continue.

Then I heard Nico's voice.

The husky sound threaded through the harsh wind, and he materialized in front of me. Unlike when Sableth had used the memory of Nico to confuse me, this vision comforted me immediately. I tangibly felt his warmth and goodness wrapping around me like a cocoon. Tears filled my eyes as I inhaled his familiar scent. Words of encouragement spun around me, reassuring me that I could defeat Sableth.

Ian squeezed my fingers as I met Nico's brown eyes. Nico's smile was sweet. Inspiring. I could feel his love and knew without a doubt he'd never blamed me for anything. I'd tortured myself with guilt, but Nico had never wanted that.

Nico whispered, "Say the words that need saying, brother, and let this be finished."

Without even giving it thought, words imprinted on my mind from another time and place spilled from my numb lips. "Cleanse this malevolent spirit from our world, and send Sableth to the bowels of the earth, never to return."

The Mossfire Stone blazed like a supernova, and there was a hot white flash that momentarily blinded me. I expected intense heat, but what I felt was extreme cold. Teeth chattering, I shivered as everything around me seemed to contract. The universe appeared to heave and shudder, and Sableth let out a roar that made the ground rattle. In an instant, Sableth's malevolent presence was ripped from my body, and I seemed to float and spin like a deflating balloon.

A deafening silence filled my ears, and I realized I was lying on the ground. I couldn't move, my body so weak even breathing was difficult. There were voices around me, and hands grabbed hold of me.

"Don't touch him. Don't move him." Ian's voice was urgent.

I felt his familiar touch skirting over my head, neck, spine. I groaned, feeling dazed. I wanted to ask if it was safe. I wanted to know if I'd succeeded in destroying Sableth, but my lips wouldn't move. The sound of sirens came to me, and hard as I tried I couldn't keep my eyes open. I stopped fighting so hard to stay awake, and drifted into oblivion.

EPILOGUE

My eyelids felt glued shut, but when I finally managed to open them, I found a nurse fiddling with an IV bag next to my hospital bed. I recognized Nurse Brown from my previous stay after my appendectomy.

She glanced over, pinning me with her piercing blue gaze. "Oh, you're awake. We need to stop meeting like this. People will talk."

I gave a weak smile and whispered, "Can I have some water?" The room I was in was almost identical to the room I'd stayed in the last time. There was another patient sleeping in a bed across the room, but so far, no ghosts were hovering.

"Of course." She filled a small pink plastic cup with water from a matching pitcher. She pushed a button, and the back of my bed raised, lifting me into a more upright position. She handed me the cup. "Don't drink it too fast. I don't need you puking it all back up again."

"I wish you'd stop being so charming, Nurse Brown. People really will talk."

She gave a gruff laugh and went to adjust the blinds. I winced as the afternoon sun peeked through. "I guess you're feeling better if you can sass me." Her silver hair seemed even shorter than the last time I'd seen her, but her warden-like demeanor remained unchanged.

I glanced down at the bruises that covered my arms. "I feel like I've been run over by a train."

"I've said it before and I'll say it again, you're one lucky guy." She studied me. "No broken bones. Just a whole heck of a lot of bruising."

"That's good, I guess." I sipped the water, embarrassed when some dribbled down my chin. I wiped at it and sighed. "I'm so tired I can barely drink water."

"I'll bet." She sighed and began straightening my sheets. "People are saying you're a hero."

My face warmed. "I'm no hero."

"That's not the scuttlebutt." She patted my leg. "Rest. You probably won't be released until tomorrow."

Before I could respond, Ian walked into the room wearing his white coat. My heart flip-flopped at the sight of him. He looked handsome but concerned as he approached my bed. While we'd faced down Sableth together, oddly enough it was memories of our night together in Cecil's room that occupied my thoughts. We'd been so open with each other that night, and I felt shy as he stopped beside my bed. He had scratches on his face and hands, but he looked otherwise unharmed.

"You're finally awake," he said. While he was smiling, there were lines of strain beneath his eyes. "I was worried sick about you, Lorenzo."

"I'm happy to see you seem unscathed," I said, wishing I could touch him. But it seemed too awkward to initiate that with Nurse Brown in the vicinity.

"Physically, yes. Emotionally, I was a wreck." He laughed sheepishly. "I fear I did a lot of hovering."

"That he did." Nurse Brown nodded. "He about wore a rut in the tiles going back and forth from your bed to his other patients."

"Guilty as charged." Ian took my hand finally, sending tingles along my skin.

Nurse Brown gave a knowing smile. "I'll leave you two alone." She winked and left the room.

Leaning down, Ian pressed his mouth to mine. Then he whispered, "You've been asleep for three days. You scared the shit out of me, Lorenzo."

"I was asleep for *three* days?"

He straightened, nodding. "Yes."

"Was I in a coma?"

He grimaced. "No. Not technically. You just didn't want to wake up."

Panic surged inside me as I remembered why I was in the hospital. "Is Claire okay?"

He nodded. "Yes, she's safe. She's fine. She was here the last three days sitting with you. I forced her to go home and rest. She'll be back later. Julian and Cecil are also fine. We're all a little banged up, but we're alive."

"Thank God." My stomach churned as I met his gaze. "I'm afraid to ask, but, did I succeed? Did I get rid of Sableth?"

"You did." He winced. "I'm sorry, I assumed you knew. I should have told you that right away." He squeezed my hand. "Everything seems back to normal. You did it, Lorenzo."

I slumped. "Oh, thank God. I was so afraid you'd say I'd failed."

"You didn't fail." His eyes gleamed with pride. "You were . . . amazing. Brave."

I smiled weakly. "You left out scared shitless."

"Scared or not, you did what you needed to do."

"Thank goodness. I can barely believe this is real." I closed my eyes, relief flooding through me, and then opened them again. "Did I imagine that Irene changed sides?"

He gritted his teeth. "Unfortunately, no. She betrayed you. She betrayed Julian. He was devastated."

"What happened to her and the others who followed Sableth?"

"There was a lot of bloodshed. A lot of innocent people died." He gritted his teeth. "While you were fighting Sableth, our people and theirs clashed. It was brutal." He studied the scratches covering his hands. "I'm afraid to say, even I had to join in the fight to keep them away from you, and I'm no warrior."

"But you're safe, and that's what matters to me."

He smiled. "Back at you."

"What happened to Weston?" I asked gruffly.

Ian's face hardened. "He was arrested."

"That's the best news of all." I felt enormous satisfaction picturing him in handcuffs in the back of a police car. "What did they arrest Weston for?"

"Detective Monroe found a connection between him and Professor Buckler. Apparently, Professor Buckler visited Weston's shop. He drank some special tea Weston prepared for him. Funny how he ended up dead after drinking that concoction."

"Weston poisoned Professor Buckler?" I asked, eyes wide.

"That's what Detective Monroe believes because he's arrested him for murder. I believe he's also narrowing in on who killed Gordon and Thomas. Apparently Sableth's followers weren't hugely worried about leaving behind DNA evidence. They wrongly thought Sableth would be running things when it was all said and done."

"You don't think it was Irene who killed Gordon and Thomas, right?" While in the end she'd been a traitor, I couldn't accept the thought she'd have murdered her own people. She'd seemed genuinely fond of Julian and the others at first.

Ian's eyes softened, although he also looked conflicted. "No, I don't think she'd have hurt any of them. While you were fighting Sableth, she couldn't even bring herself to go after Julian. I think she regretted her decision to betray him, but it was too late. He'll never forgive her."

"Nor will I," I growled. Because of Irene we'd almost been caught at the warehouse. "She could have gotten us all killed. I'll never forget what she did just to save her own skin."

"No. I believe she'll live to regret her choice." Ian sat on the edge of my bed, and his gaze warmed. "Anyway, enough about Irene. It looks like with Weston in jail, you'll be the only psychic in town."

"I guess that's good news?" I wasn't sure how I'd just go back to finding lost pets after all I'd experienced. My eyes had been opened to a much bigger understanding of the psychic world. My thoughts went to my brother. "I . . . I saw Nico. When I was battling Sableth, Nico came to me. He encouraged me."

"I know."

Surprised, I leaned toward him. "How do you know?"

He let out a shaky breath and admitted, "I saw him too."

Shocked, I blinked at him, not sure what to say. Finally, I said, "How is that possible?"

"I don't know. I think perhaps it's because I was holding your hand? You were the conduit."

"Oh, I hadn't thought of that. Yeah, maybe that's why." Remembering the warmth and forgiveness I'd experienced from Nico, I smiled. "Nico wasn't mad at me. I was punishing myself for nothing. I could feel he still loved me."

"I had a feeling that would be the case." He smiled gently. "I'm glad you got closure, Lorenzo. I know how much you needed that."

"Yeah." I shrugged, holding his gaze. "I really did need that. I'll never really know why Nico took his own life, but at least I know he loved me and didn't resent me."

"Yes. Even I could see that. His love for you was so obvious. He came to protect you." He swept his thumb over my skin, looking thoughtful. "I've been forced to recognize I was too closed-minded." He glanced up. "That's all changed, thanks to you, Lorenzo."

"Has it?" My pulse sped up at the look in his eyes.

"Definitely. Just because I can't see something doesn't mean it isn't real. I finally understand that."

I turned my hand over and grabbed his fingers. "I was closed-minded too," I said quietly. "About love. About being open to love. You helped me see I was wrong."

"I'm glad it was me."

"Are you?" The warmth in his eyes helped chase away any doubts I might have had that his feelings for me were just physical. There was real emotion there, and even more telling, he'd stood beside me to fight Sableth. His energy had helped me defeat Sableth.

"Of course, I'm glad it was me." His smile was teasing. "After all, what's a companion without someone to companion *with*?"

I laughed, feeling lighthearted. "I don't know if that's a thing, but I like the sound of it."

"Yeah?" He leaned closer, his brown eyes heated. "I hope you don't mind, but I told the nursing staff here that we're dating."

My face warmed. "Did you?"

"Yep. It felt good too. The surprise on their faces was priceless."

"Is that why you told them?"

He frowned. "No. I told them because I couldn't keep it to myself. After what we just went through, I've realized life is too short."

"Yeah," I said softly, "I've realized that too."

"Oh." He straightened and reached into his white coat. "I have something for you." He tugged out the Mossfire Stone, and he put it in the palm of my hand. "You were clutching so tight to this after you passed out, I was worried we'd have to break your fingers to get it out of your grasp."

I took the stone, shivering as it quivered against my skin. I smiled at the stone, eyes stinging. "We did it. Together." The stone pulsed and turned a brilliant green.

"What will you do with it now?"

I smiled up at him. "It wouldn't make a very good ring. It's far too clunky."

"It would make an excellent paperweight."

The stone rattled and heated against my hand, turning a dark, swirling green color. "Uh, oh. I don't think it likes that idea at all."

"No?" Ian lifted his brows. "Such a temperamental little stone."

I turned the stone over with my fingers. "How about a necklace?" The stone vibrated, the swirling surface almost appearing to smile. "I know another green stone I'd like to introduce you to."

Ian laughed. "Are you matchmaking?"

I glanced up, grinning. "Why should Nico's stone be all alone?"

Ian's smile faded, and he leaned down to kiss me. His warm lips were soft and teasing, and he whispered, "Nothing and no one should ever be alone."

"I agree, darling companion." I put my arms around his neck. "I'm gonna need a ride home from the hospital tomorrow. Are you available, Doc?"

"Absolutely."

My chest squeezed at the emotions swirling in his eyes. "I'm ready to start living again, Ian. I don't want to hide anymore."

"You can hide if you want. You can live if you want. You can be whoever you need to be. Either way, I'll be by your side, Lorenzo."

Eyes stinging, I pulled his head down to kiss him, and the stone hummed happily in my hand.

ABOUT THE AUTHOR

S.C. Wynne is a Lambda Award winning author and has been writing MM Romance and Gay mystery since 2013. She lives in California with her wonderful husband, two quirky kids, and a loony rescue pup named Ditto. www.scwynne.com

Other Books by S.C. Wynne

Crashing Upwards—Lambda Literary Award winning Stand-alone Gay Romance

Strange Medicine—Book One Dr. Thornton Mysteries

Last Gasp—Book One Kip O'Connor Cozy MM Mysteries

Shadow's Edge—Book One Psychic Mysteries

And many more.